NO CRIME FORGOTTEN

THE DUBLIN MURDER MYSTERIES

VALERIE KEOGH

Print ISBN 978-1-913419-94-3

ALSO BY VALERIE KEOGH

THE DUBLIN MURDER MYSTERIES

No Simple Death

No Obvious Cause

No Past Forgiven

No Memory Lost

PSYCHOLOGICAL THRILLERS

The Three Women

The Perfect Life

The Deadly Truth

For Ursula, who wanted a fifth.

An Garda Síochána: the police service of the Republic of
Ireland.

Garda, or gardaí in the plural.

Commonly referred to as *the guards* or *the gardaí*.

Direct translation: "the Guardian of the Peace."

1

The detective unit in Foxrock Garda station was Monday morning quiet. There were a few minor cases ongoing but nothing to take Detective Garda Sergeant Mike West from his desk where he was staring at the latest of the unending audits devised by Inspector Morrison for no other reason, West thought, than to drive him crazy. The murmur of voices drifted in from the main office. It would be either Baxter, who'd recently moved in with his girlfriend, extolling the joys of cohabitation, or Edwards telling yet another of his risqué stories. Sudden raucous laughter made West smile. *Risqué wins.*

There was no sound from Peter Andrews. West guessed he was hunched over the rota, checking and double-checking. Andrews would look up from it after a while and send the team scurrying to work without having to say a word.

West wasn't in a hurry to start work and joined his hands behind his head thinking about the nice weekend he'd spent. The day before, he and Edel had made the most of the unseasonably warm March weather and gone for a walk around Marlay Park, stopping in the café for lunch. It had been a perfect day. *Edel Johnson*. She was never far from his thoughts, hadn't been since they'd first met almost a year earlier.

So much had happened in that year. Remembering the catalogue of disasters made him shake his head. Edel was trying to shrug off the most recent one... the loss of her publishing contract. The woman who'd been responsible, Fiona Wilson, wouldn't bother either of them again, West had made sure of that. Last he'd heard she was in Chicago – it wasn't far enough away. It was the best he could do but it was frustrating that he couldn't do more.

The ring of his desk phone interrupted his thoughts. He glared at it, then with a sigh reached for it and picked it up.

'West.'

'I've had the oddest call from Joe Ryan, the sacristan of St Monica's Church,' the desk sergeant Tom Blunt said without bothering with preliminaries. 'If I didn't know the man, I'd have said he was drunk.'

West heard an indrawn breath and waited.

'I'd normally dispatch uniformed Gardaí to do a preliminary investigation, as you know, Mike, but Ryan is a solid man, not easily given to dramatics and all I could get from him was *you have to come*. Whatever has happened, it sounds bad.'

Blunt commanded a lot of respect in Foxrock Garda station. He was also normally concise to the point of being brusque. West couldn't remember the last time he'd heard him string so many words together. Joe Ryan hadn't said much, but an experienced man like Blunt could read as much in tone of voice as the words. Maybe something bad had indeed happened.

'No harm in us being first to a scene for a change,' West said. It might be nothing for the detective unit to be involved in, but if he had a choice between doing audits or heading out on what might be a wild goose chase, he'd choose geese any day.

He dragged a reluctant Andrews away from his perusal of

the rota and they headed off on the short drive to St Monica's Church.

'Is that the sacristan, Peter?' West asked as he turned into the car park and pulled up near the front of the church.

Broad, shallow steps led up to the wide double doors, one side of which stood open. A man leaned against the shut door. His unnatural stillness and pallor were striking and told West clearly that Blunt had been right, it was going to be a bad one. He should have known. Blunt had an uncanny ability to sense when something was wrong.

'Yes, that's Joe Ryan,' Andrews said. 'I know him to see, that's all. Joyce and I come to mass here now and then because Joyce likes the choir. Ryan is known to be very efficient. The sacristan's role has grown over the years and nowadays they run everything. It's him you have to meet to organise christenings... and weddings.' Andrews waited a beat to let that sink in before continuing. 'Basically, he runs the church. If you want to know anything about St Monica's, he's the man to ask.'

West pulled disposable shoe covers from a box behind his seat and handed a pair to Andrews. 'I suppose we'd better go and have a word with him.'

As they climbed the steps towards the door, they heard a hum that made both stop and look around. 'What is that?' West said, eyes scanning the surroundings.

It was Andrews who identified the cause. 'It's coming from the sacristan. I think he's praying.'

The sound grew louder as they reached the top step. Andrews, of course, was right. West couldn't hear the words, but he recognised the cadence. The sacristan was indeed praying, his lips moving incessantly, the rest of his face and body rigid.

West felt the muscles in his belly clench. The sacristan looked to be in shock. It seemed Blunt had underestimated the situation. This was going to be much worse than "bad".

'Mr Ryan?' West addressed the sacristan quietly.

It was a few seconds before Ryan's eyes focused, and a few more before the recitation stopped.

'Can you tell us what happened?' West said into the heavy, uncomfortable silence. He was used to dealing with members of the public who accidentally became involved with crime, but it never got easier and he wasn't surprised when the sacristan's lips twisted in horror, one of his bony hands creeping up to cover them as if afraid of what they might say. His other hand, trembling uncontrollably, pointed through the open door behind him.

West looked at Andrews and shook his head. They'd get a statement from the man when the shock had worn off.

'I can't see past the entrance hall.' Andrews peered into the church.

'Vestibule,' West corrected him automatically. Not that it made any difference what it was called. It was a dull, grey day and the little light that managed to slide through the outside doors dispersed the darkness within but not the shadows. The inner double doors on the far side of the vestibule were shut. Whatever had shocked the sacristan so badly, lay beyond.

West and Andrews slipped on shoe covers and headed through the open door. They moved slowly, checking the darker corners of the small vestibule, their hands resting lightly on their holstered weapons. When they reached the inner doors, they stopped and listened for any sound from within.

West slipped on a pair of vinyl gloves, met Andrews' eyes in silent agreement and reached for the brass handle. It opened outward and immediately there was the recognisable smell of every church West had ever been in, a mix of furniture polish and incense that brought him back to childhood years of compulsory churchgoing. Nowadays, his á la carte Catholicism rarely brought him inside a church but the scent continued to invoke old memories. Good ones mostly. He brushed them aside and stepped into the body of the church with Andrews close behind.

St Monica's Church was designed in the way of most traditional churches. A wide central aisle ran from the entrance doors through rows of wooden pews to the altar. On each side, between the pews and the walls of the church there was a narrow side aisle. High stone pillars, six to each side, supported the high concave ceiling over the central aisle while what looked like oak beams stretched across the ceiling over the side aisles.

It was all very traditional.

But what wasn't, and what drew a gasp of shock from both men, was the body suspended over the central aisle in front of the altar.

'Jesus,' Andrews said softly.

West was going to make a smart remark about it definitely not being him. It was a reactionary remark, humour in the face of horror. But it wasn't the place for it. He wasn't a churchgoer, but Andrews was, and this was his church.

Despite the shock, both men knew the drill and went into automatic mode. There was no point in rushing to assist the victim. Even from where they stood, they could tell it was too late for him. First rule in this case, secure the premises: the perpetrator of this macabre act could still be in the building. Drawing their weapons, they did a quick search of the main church, moving down the central aisle, checking each pew as they passed.

Although regular firearms training was compulsory and West considered himself a good shot, he'd never fired his weapon outside the shooting range. Every time he unholstered his regulation SIG Sauer, he knew that situation could change.

But there was nobody lurking in the pews and seconds later they were a few feet from where the dead body was suspended.

'Not crucified,' Andrews said quietly and West heard the relief in his voice.

Up close, they could see how the arms were extended and tied to a long piece of wood, ankles tied together with rope, the body naked apart from a pair of stained white boxer shorts.

'Not crucified,' West agreed, 'but close enough.' He pointed to the beam that crossed the roof of the side aisle. 'It looks as if they threw a rope over that and fixed it with a slip knot. The victim was already tied to the wood, they threaded the loose end around it, then–' he pointed to the aisle on the far side '–threw the end of the rope over that beam and used it like a pulley system to raise the body.'

Nodding, Andrews moved closer until he was almost underneath the body.

The victim's head hung down, chin resting on his bare chest, the skin dark and mottled. Andrews pointed towards the body as West joined him. 'See there on the left side of his chest? Looks like a wound.' His voice had regained its usual composure.

West agreed. 'There's no blood.' He scanned the floor. To the naked eye, it looked clean. 'Nor any other bodily fluids. He was killed elsewhere.'

'And the body was brought here.'

'Let's finish our search.' West dragged his eyes from the victim and jerked his chin towards the confession boxes on the left side of the church. 'We'd better check out the confessionals.'

They were obvious hiding places and the two men approached them cautiously. The only sound in the quiet church was their breathing, their footsteps, but they kept alert.

The sacristan had switched on the main lights but the side aisles were dimly lit. West stopped at the first of the two confession boxes. With his gloved hand he grasped the door handle of the first penitent's box and at Andrews' nod, wrenched it open. There was little light within, but enough to show it was empty.

They quickly moved to the central priest's boxes and the penitent's box on either side and followed the same process with the second confessional. Each box was empty.

'Smells strange,' Andrews said, stepping away from the final door.

'I don't think they're used much anymore: they're probably musty.' West looked back towards the altar. 'Let's move on.'

The working, behind-the-scenes part of the church – the robing rooms, sacristan's office, and offices used by the priests – were accessed from the church through a door behind the altar. The two Gardaí covered one another with practised efficiency, checking the rooms thoroughly in their search for potential hiding places. The rooms were empty but at the end of a short corridor a single exit door to the outside hung open. It swayed in a breeze too gentle to slam it shut.

'The sacristan must have come in this way, but he'd hardly have left it open, would he?' Andrews said, going through the door and looking around. He stepped back inside, slipped a disposable glove on and shut the door. 'It opens into a courtyard, but there's a gate leading into the car park.'

West frowned. 'Maybe whoever did this escaped this way when the sacristan went to open the church door?' He shook his head. Supposition. There'd be a lot of that in the hours ahead. The important thing was to keep an open mind and not jump to conclusions.

Andrews flicked the catch that secured the door and they returned to the body of the church, holstering their weapons as they went.

Circling around the suspended victim, they stopped and looked up. West took a few steps backward, then frowned and took a few more. 'This isn't good.'

Andrews took a few steps backward to join him. 'Someone wanted to make a point.'

From where they stood now, the victim was posed directly in front of the life-sized crucifix that hung on the wall behind the altar.

'Yes,' West agreed. 'And look at the spear wound on the corpus.'

Andrews looked at him. 'Now you're pulling my leg. There isn't a spear wound on the corpse.'

West heard the tension in his partner's voice despite his attempt at levity. 'Corpus, not corpse. It's the correct term for a three-dimensional portrayal of a body on a cross.'

'If you say so.' Andrews took a step closer and squinted upward. 'Yes, I see what you mean, the wound on our vic correlates with the spear wound on the... corpus.'

West almost smiled at Andrews' acquisition of the new word. Instead, he stepped closer and joined him staring up. This was going to be a tough one. Someone had gone to a great deal of trouble to make a point. He hoped they wouldn't need to go to an equal amount of trouble to find out who had done this terrible thing, and why. 'We haven't seen any sign of a break-in. Don't they have an alarm?'

'We'd better get the sacristan to talk to us, I'll go and see if he's up to it.' Andrews turned for the exit as he spoke.

'You'd better give the station a buzz: we're going to need more manpower as well as the Garda Technical Bureau and the state pathologist.' West watched Andrews raise a hand in acknowledgement and knew that whatever needed to be done would be done.

West moved closer to the victim again. Identification from this angle was impossible. The musculature and tautness of the victim's skin indicated a younger rather than older white man, maybe early thirties. He wouldn't have been easily overpowered.

With no sign of a break-in, they had to have been hiding somewhere inside when the church shut for the night. West looked around the cavernous church. *They.* His eyes narrowed. Instinct told him this was the case. One clever man might have overpowered the victim, brain succeeding where brawn couldn't, but to hoist him up like this... Even using the beams as a pulley system, that took a lot of strength and more than one pair of hands.

The powers-that-be would want this case solved quickly. Despite recent scandals, the church was still a powerful force to be reckoned with. West would have bishops and archbishops breathing down his neck along with Inspector Morrison. It was all he needed. He sat on one of the pews near the exit and let his mind relax. But if he hoped for divine intervention it hadn't come fifteen minutes later when the quiet of the church was broken by the sounds of voices coming from the vestibule. Loud voices, and lots of them.

Andrews would have given Blunt the details and the desk sergeant would have pulled in all the favours he was owed to get the manpower he knew they'd need for this case. West heard one voice raised in laughter. That would stop when they opened the door. Even the hardiest, the toughest of them couldn't fail to be shaken by this. Many, like him, would be lapsed Catholics, but the teachings of their childhood ran deep and few had managed to completely erase it. They'd be silent when they came through. But they'd work together and they'd get this son-of-a-bitch. West turned away from the body and headed towards them.

2

———

West was right. The loud voices faded to a shocked silence when he opened the door and the assembled uniformed Gardaí had their first glimpse of the macabre sight. Their voices were more subdued as they gathered around him. He gave directions for some to canvass the housing estates that circled the church and others to guard the pedestrian and vehicular entrances. They dispersed without further ado and West joined Andrews who was standing beside the sacristan speaking in low tones that didn't carry across the short distance.

Whatever Andrews was saying to the shocked man was having a positive effect: he looked less frail, and some colour had returned to his grey cheeks.

'Mr Ryan is positive he closed the door to the courtyard after him this morning,' Andrews said as West joined them.

'Closed and locked.' Ryan emphasised the two words. 'There's a problem with that door, if you don't press the catch down to lock it, it swings open.'

West met Andrews' eyes. They knew how their killer got out; now they needed to figure out how he got in. 'Is there an alarm?'

'On the doors but not the windows.'

'No internal motion detectors? No CCTV inside or out?'

The sacristan frowned. 'No, they went for the simplest system they could to keep the cost down. Anyway, it was people breaking in to steal we were worried about, not...' His voice broke and he lifted a trembling hand and waved toward the church.

'Can you talk us through what happened from the time you arrived?' West asked.

'Yes, of course. Whatever I can do to help.' Ryan gave them a quick rundown of his arrival, the unlocking of the door, disarming of the alarm. 'I made coffee and drank it while I checked the diary for today's events.' He stopped abruptly and looked at West, wide-eyed. 'There's a funeral at ten.'

West shook his head. 'I'm afraid we're going to need to keep the church shut for a few days.'

The sacristan sighed as if it had been what he expected. 'I'll contact the undertakers, see what they can do. They can speak to the family.' He returned to his description of the morning's events. 'When I finished my coffee, I came into the church and switched on the main lights. My mind was occupied with the details that needed to be organised so it wasn't until I was at the bottom of the altar steps that I saw him.' The colour leached from his face again and he staggered slightly with the force of the memory.

His voice was frail and reedy when he spoke again. 'I remember backing away, then I ran and opened the front door. There isn't a good phone signal inside, you see. My mobile was in my pocket. I have Foxrock station on speed dial so I rang them and spoke to Sergeant Blunt. I'm not sure I made much sense but he said he'd send someone. Then I rang Father Jeffreys. He's the parish priest,' he explained.

'You didn't go back inside?' West asked.

The sacristan shook his head.

A car pulling into the car park drew their eyes and a sigh of relief from the sacristan. 'That's Father Jeffreys now.'

The man who rushed from the car wore the traditional garb of a priest, the black suit, worn and shiny in places, the white collar looking too tight in the fold of his neck. A thick shock of grey hair flopped forward over a forehead creased with lines of anxiety. He strode past the detectives and enfolded the sacristan in his arms. 'Father Dillon is on his way,' he said, pulling away slightly to look at him. 'He'll take you home and stay with you until your wife gets there.' He gave West and Andrews a nod of acknowledgement and, in a tone of voice that said he wasn't willing to enter into debate, he said, 'If you have any further questions, you can speak to Mr Ryan tomorrow.'

'One final question for now,' West said. 'What time was the church shut last night?'

'At ten,' Ryan said. 'I shut it myself.'

Another car turned into the car park. It was stopped briefly by the uniformed Gardaí before being waved on, coming to a halt beside the parish priest's car. The man who got out and hurried forward was dressed in jeans and T-shirt.

'It's Father Dillon,' Andrews said quickly, recognising him despite the casual clothes.

The younger priest's eyes swept over the detectives and the open church door, a puzzled line appearing on his smooth forehead as he took in the picture of the sacristan still held tightly in the parish priest's arms. 'What's going on?'

'Take Joe home,' Father Jeffreys said, ignoring the question. 'He'll be able to fill you in on the way. Stay with him until Millie gets home from work.' Loosening his grip on the sacristan, he pushed him gently towards Fr Dillon.

'What about the funeral... at ten,' Ryan said. 'I need–'

'You need to go home,' Jeffreys insisted. 'Tell Father Dillon the name of the undertaker. He can sort it out.'

'Of course I will.' Father Dillon took the sacristan's arm and led him to his car, opening the door and settling him inside as if he were a child.

Jeffreys turned to West and Andrews. 'I assume from Mr Ryan's shocked expression that he wasn't exaggerating the seriousness of the situation, gentlemen?'

West shook his head. 'I'm Detective Garda Sergeant West, and this is my partner, Detective Garda Andrews.'

'Joe mentioned a dead body. I want to know the details.' The parish priest's tone indicated he was used to having his questions answered without delay. The likeness to the manner of Inspector Morrison was uncanny... and unwelcome.

West was saved from having to answer by the arrival of two white vans. 'That's a forensic team from the Garda Technical Bureau,' he explained. 'I'll need to go and speak to them for a moment. I promise I'll come back and fill you in.'

With Andrews at his side he went to greet the team manager, relieved to see the man who stepped from the first van was someone he knew, and with whom he had a cordial working relationship. It always made it easier.

Detective Sergeant Maddison, a tall, thin man with a ready smile, stretched his hand out as the two detectives approached. 'I'd like to say it was good to see you both,' he said and jerked his head towards the church. 'So, tell me.'

'It's a bad one,' West said. Leaving Andrews to fill in the rest of the team on the little they knew, he walked with Maddison to the church door. He slipped another disposable glove on and pulled the interior door open.

Maddison said nothing for a few seconds. 'Someone wanted to make a point, didn't they?'

'They did a pretty good job.' West released the door and it

swung shut. 'Dr Kennedy is on his way,' he explained as they made their way down the steps.

'Always good to arrive before the state pathologist. I'll send the photographer in before he descends upon us.' Maddison left to organise his team. Within minutes, the two vans were backed up to the church door for convenience, a photographer was at work and other technicians had begun a survey of the outside of the church and the surrounding car park.

Reluctantly, West returned to where the parish priest and Andrews were standing, silently observing the scene. 'The technical team are starting on the outside while they're waiting for the state pathologist to arrive,' West explained.

Father Jeffreys inclined his head in acknowledgement. 'So Garda Andrews said. But he wouldn't give me any details of what has happened. As the senior officer, perhaps you would tell me what is going on.' He held a hand up. 'Before you give me any runaround, let me remind you that like you I have superiors to answer to. I need to know the facts.'

West searched for words to explain. Whoever had done this awful deed was sending a message to someone. Maybe to the parish priest himself, or to one of the other priests. West had no idea what that message was... maybe Father Jeffreys would know... or maybe interpret in some way for them. It was worth a shot. 'It is difficult to explain, easier to show. But prepare yourself: it's shocking.'

Father Jeffreys raised an eyebrow but inclined his head in acceptance and followed West and Andrews without a word. They stopped in front of the inner door. Once more, West slipped on a glove and grasped the handle before taking a deep breath and pulling the door open.

The priest's gasp was loud and prolonged, his fingers reaching to touch forehead, breast and each shoulder in the sign of the cross. A talisman to ward off evil spirits. West almost smiled.

'Who is he?'

'We don't know yet,' West replied. 'The state pathologist will be here soon. When he arrives, the Garda technical team will lower the body. Then we'll start the process of identification.'

The priest narrowed his eyes. 'He's not crucified, is he?'

'No, he's attached by ropes. We think he was killed elsewhere. We're not yet sure how.'

'And hung up there, like that.' The priest dragged his eyes from the body and looked at West. 'Why? Some type of anti-religious protest?'

'Possibly. It's one of the avenues we'll explore over the coming days. Anti-religious, anti-priest, anti-man, anti-human. We'll keep our minds open until we find the reason.' West gave a slight smile. 'But don't be surprised if there isn't one.' He waited a beat and the smile faded. 'There's also a chance that the perpetrator is sending a message.'

Jeffreys looked at him and raised an eyebrow again. 'And you thought I might know what that message is, did you?'

'Do you?'

A heavy sigh followed the question. Jeffreys, reluctantly, looked back to the man suspended in front of him. 'Someone took a lot of care to position the body like that,' he said. He pointed to the crucifix on the wall behind the altar. 'Jesus died for our sins. At a guess, I'd say your perpetrator is telling us that this poor man, whoever he is, was killed for his.'

West looked back to the body. Killed for his sins? A revenge killing, perhaps? Revenge was a good motive. Identifying the body might give them a direction to follow and help point a finger at one perpetrator. With luck they might solve this quickly.

West tightened his lips. He knew he was kidding himself.

The complicated pulley system, the iconoclastic staging of the body. Somebody had spent time on the planning and execution of this. More than one person.

Something told West this was only the start of the nightmare.

3

'Man's inhumanity to man.' Father Jeffreys sighed. 'I'll go and inform the bishop. He's not going to like it.' On that understatement, the priest turned to leave the church. 'Keep me informed,' he said and pushed open the door before they could stop him.

West shook his head. 'Tell Maddison he'll need to do elimination fingerprints for the door, Peter.'

'Will do.' Andrews headed off to speak to the manager.

Left alone in the silence of the church, West took a deep breath. This was going to be a tough one. He didn't mind the work, and normally enjoyed unravelling the puzzle of a crime, but he took in the juxtaposition of the dead man and the crucifix and a shiver ran through him at the unholy nature of it. Father Jeffreys would tell the bishop, the bishop would tell the archbishop who would, no doubt, be in touch with the chief superintendent. By the time the weight of all that filtered down to Inspector Morrison it would have grown ten heads, all with wide mouths, and loud voices. And West was next in line.

He heard the door open behind him and turned to see the familiar figure of the state pathologist coming through. He could usually depend on Dr Niall Kennedy to lighten even the most sombre mood with a quip, but this time even he was reduced to silence by what he saw.

'Bloody hell,' Kennedy muttered as he approached, his eyes fixed on the suspended victim. His boyishly handsome face was unusually serious. 'You have the rottenest luck, Mike. Only a month ago, you had a tiny body in a suitcase.' He waved a hand toward the body. 'Now this.'

The child in the suitcase. *Abasiama.* It had been a tough case, but they'd given the child back her name, and with a lot of hard work and some unbelievably good luck, they'd solved the mystery of her death. West hoped they'd be as lucky this time.

As Kennedy headed out to consult with Maddison, Andrews returned from doing the same.

'Maddison made some comment about getting our sticky paws on his crime scene but apart from that he was okay,' he said. 'They're getting on with it. Maddison says there is definitely no evidence of a break-in. No damage to any of the windows or doors.'

'Just as we concluded.'

'Yes, it looks like they must have been inside when the church was locked up for the night. Hiding somewhere.'

West looked around the church. Plenty of places to hide if you wanted to do so. The sacristan wouldn't have searched every pew or each confession box before he locked up. 'I could imagine the perpetrator wanting to hide, but the victim? It doesn't make sense.'

'Maybe he was already dead.'

'Maybe.'

They stood to one side when two technicians came through with a roll of plastic they laid along the central aisle to protect any evidence that might be there. Once that was done, Dr Kennedy and Maddison entered with several of the technical team trailing behind and for several minutes they discussed the best way to proceed.

They didn't need help or advice from the detectives who stood back to await their next move. West watched silently, but Andrews gave a running commentary under his breath on how he would proceed. Since, invariably, this was the most logical way it was exactly what the team did. Andrews never refrained from muttering an *I told you so.*

West let the words drift around him as he watched the men untie the rope and lower the body slowly to the ground. His eyes narrowed as he watched. It took four men. Granted, they were under instructions from both Maddison and Kennedy not to damage the pulley system as they worked or the body as it reached the ground. But still, wasn't it proof that it had needed more than one to execute the plan?

He moved restlessly, pushing one hand through his hair. Recognising it as a gesture of impatience, he shoved both hands into his jacket pockets.

Finally, he saw Kennedy look towards them and raise a hand. 'Right, come and see what we've got.'

The victim lay on plastic sheeting at the base of the altar steps. Despite the removal of the wooden beam and ropes, his arms were still outstretched and his chin pressed to his chest.

'He's in full rigor mortis,' Kennedy said. 'I know you'll be hoping for a time of death but best I can give you at this stage, taking into account the ambient temperature, is that he met his maker between twelve and fourteen hours ago.'

West checked his watch and did a quick calculation. Between 7.30 and 9.30 the night before. It was the first piece of information they needed.

'Thanks, that'll help,' he said. He crouched down to peer closer. With the victim's features contorted as they were, it was impossible to identify him. But he guessed he was younger than he'd previously thought, maybe mid-twenties.

'I'm not sure about the wound,' Kennedy commented, pointing to the round hole in the man's upper abdomen. He turned to look at the crucifix on the wall. 'I'd almost say you're looking at a bizarre form of copycat killing, although I seriously doubt that the perpetrator used a spear.' Turning back to the body, he lifted his hands in a *your guess is probably as good as mine* gesture. 'I'll be able to get the shape and length of it from the post-mortem. That should give us somewhere to go. At this moment, I can't even give you cause of death. Even if the puncture wound hadn't been the cause of death, it would have bled copiously and, as you can see, there is no blood underneath the body, nor is there any other of the bodily fluids we'd expect to find.'

It was a conclusion he and Andrews had already come to but West acknowledged the information. 'He didn't die here.'

4

Kennedy inclined his head. 'That's it exactly.'

'The sacristan locked up at ten,' Andrews said, checking his watch. 'Eleven and a half hours ago.'

The pathologist shrugged. 'I can fix the time more precisely when I get him back but I'd say he was dead before that.' He turned away to organise the transport of the body. With the arms outstretched as they were it took several minutes of manoeuvring and many muttered imprecations before it was loaded onto a gurney to his satisfaction.

Outside, there was a minimum of fuss as the body was loaded into the waiting ambulance and within minutes it was heading toward the mortuary in Connolly Hospital where the post-mortem would take place.

'As soon as I can,' Kennedy said, holding up a hand. 'I can't promise today; it might be the morning.'

'The parish priest has gone to contact the bishop and probably the archbishop.'

Kennedy raised an eyebrow. 'Should I be trembling in my boots?'

'You don't have to deal with them,' West said with a grimace.

The first smile of the day appeared on the pathologist's lips. 'No, thank the Lord, I don't. Okay, listen, I'll do the best I can. I might–' he held both hands up '–only *might* – be able to squeeze it in this afternoon. I'll check when I get back and let you know. Can I assume you'll want to attend?'

'I'd like to,' West said. It wasn't obligatory and he wouldn't learn anything he didn't read later in the report, but he found post-mortems fascinating and sat to watch them with a feeling of anticipation. Sometimes, as with Abasiama, he felt he owed it to the deceased to be there.

Waving the pathologist off, West turned to Andrews. 'If he's right with that time frame, it means our victim was dead before the church was shut for the night.'

'Killed inside or elsewhere and brought here afterwards.'

West shook his head. 'He was a well-built guy and we know how heavy dead bodies are. How would someone have managed to get the body inside and hidden away without anyone noticing? Wouldn't there have been someone in the church?'

'There's mass at six on a Sunday evening,' Andrews said. 'Generally, that would finish around seven, then you'll get some folk who want to stay to say the Stations of the Cross or a novena or something.'

'I can't imagine even the most devout would be able to ignore a dead body being dragged in.'

'Or carried in, if we're thinking about more than one perpetrator.'

'You saw them taking him down, Pete: it took four of them. I can't imagine one person would have managed to get him up.'

They turned together as Maddison came down the church steps with an animated expression they both recognised. He'd found something interesting. 'You'll want to see this.' With a jerk of his head towards the church, Maddison retraced his steps, leaving them to follow.

Inside, two of the technical team were standing outside one of the two confession boxes, the three doors of which stood open. West and Andrews had checked behind all of them earlier. But they'd been looking for a killer, nothing else.

'Have a look inside,' Maddison said. 'But don't take a deep breath.'

'I said there was a strange smell, remember,' Andrews said as they moved closer.

The central door, behind which the priest sat to hear the confessions of his parishioners was small, the space filled with a wide wooden chair, the only nod towards comfort being the red cushion on the seat. A fine mesh grill, with an ornate design of a cross in the centre, covered a two-foot by two-foot aperture in the wall between the priest's box and that of the penitent's box on each side. A red curtain covered the grill on one side. On the other it had been pulled back.

As a child, West had attended confession regularly. He couldn't remember the last time he'd gone, but he could still remember the irrational fear of being shut in that dark box waiting for the rattle of the curtain being pulled back to expose the pixelated head of the priest. Even now, all these years later, the words he'd have said by rote were ready on his tongue; *Bless me father for I have sinned.*

He looked away from the box to where Maddison was standing behind him. 'There's an odd smell.'

'It's mostly dissipated, but it looks as if some form of aerosol sedative spray might have been used.' He pointed to the mesh on the right-hand side of the priest's box, where the curtain had been pulled back. 'If you look closely here, see there's a shiny film. It's my guess that whoever sat here, waited until the victim knelt in the penitent's box and sprayed him full in the face.' He pointed to the penitent's box. 'Some of the odd smell is the remnant of the aerosol spray but most of it is from in there.'

Their earlier search of the confessional in the search for an intruder hadn't exposed the bloody mess on the floor.

'The lights weren't on in the side aisles when we did our original sweep,' Andrews said, embarrassed at missing it.

'We were looking for a perpetrator, not a crime scene,' West said. He peered into the box. Blood and bodily fluids were soaked into the carpet of the small space. 'The victim was making his confession?' West leaned forward and looked through the mesh into the priest's space.

'They don't have confessions on a Sunday night,' Andrews said.

West stepped back. 'Yes, but did our victim know that?'

'I'll leave the why and wherefore to you,' Maddison said. 'At least we've found your murder site.'

'Yea, that's the case almost solved,' Andrews said.

Maddison raised an eyebrow but ignored the sarcasm. 'We've taken swabs from the mesh and forensics should be able to identify what was used. Unfortunately,' he added, 'there were no fingerprints to be found either in the priest's box or on the door handles. Everyone's an expert these days.'

'You might be lucky elsewhere,' West said philosophically. 'We'll leave you to get on with it.'

Back outside, the grey day had decided to add to their misery and a gentle rain was falling. West stood in the vestibule looking out before turning to stare at Andrews. 'Sergeant Maddison was simply trying to be helpful, Mr Sarcastic.'

'I swear he thinks he solves the case and we sit in the office drinking coffee.'

Andrews, West knew, was still annoyed and embarrassed that he hadn't spotted the blood and gore earlier. There was no point reassuring him that securing the area had been their priority at the time. West headed out into the rain, smothering a groan when he saw Father Jeffreys getting out of his car and hurrying towards them. West wasn't sure what the parish priest expected at this stage but he was damned if he was going to get wet while he had a conversation that was destined to go around in circles. He stepped back inside the vestibule and waited for the priest to join him.

'Well?' Father Jeffreys said before he'd finished ascending the five steps to the front door, the one word laded with impatience and tinged with hope.

It was tempting to say *well what* but West resisted the temptation to copy Andrews' sarcasm. 'As I'm sure you've noticed, the body has been removed. Dr Kennedy will perform the post-mortem and give us whatever information he can. Meanwhile, we'll see if his fingerprints are on our database–'

'How soon can we reopen the church?' Father Jeffreys asked.

'It's up to the Garda Technical Bureau,' West explained. 'Have a word with the manager, Detective Sergeant Maddison. He'll have an idea. They have,' he added, 'found where he was killed. It was in one of the confession boxes.'

The priest, already pale, turned a sickly shade of grey. 'In a confessional? How?'

West hesitated. At this stage in an investigation, everyone was under suspicion. That included the parish priest.

'Tell me,' Father Jeffreys insisted, his expression tightening.

West's lips narrowed in response. The power of the Catholic Church had waned over the years but it was still a force to be reckoned with. He had no doubt that the parish priest would get whatever information he wanted by getting the bishop or archbishop to make a phone call. He was going to have to deal with this man until the case was solved. There was no point in making life difficult for himself or the team.

'They think someone sat in the priest's box and sprayed a sedative through the mesh, rendering the victim unconscious. There is sufficient blood in the penitent's box to indicate he was subsequently killed there. As yet, we don't know the cause of death.'

On a morning of shocks this was another. Father Jeffreys clutched his chest before reaching into his pocket for a small bottle and handing it to West who took one look, unscrewed the bottle and tilted one tablet into his hand. He slipped it into the priest's mouth, led the man to his car and made him sit in the passenger seat.

It was a few minutes before the priest's colour returned to normal. 'Angina,' he said, 'I'll be okay now.'

'You sure you don't need to go to hospital?'

Jeffreys shook his head. 'No, that won't be necessary. I've lived with it for a long time. It's the stress of the morning.'

The stress of the morning? West almost smiled at the understatement. 'Is there someone we can call to be with you?'

'Father Maher is on his way.' As if by magic, a car pulled into the car park and an older man got out and hurried over to them.

'He's had an angina attack,' West explained. He waited until Father Maher sat into the driver's seat before bending to speak to the parish priest. 'We're going to need to ask some questions to help with our enquiries. Perhaps, if you're feeling up to it, we could call around later?'

'Whatever you need to get this sorted, Detective Sergeant,' Jeffreys said, his voice frailer than it had been earlier. 'There are four of us. You have yet to meet Father McComb. We live together at 225A Westminster Road. If it suits, I can make sure we're all available to assist, maybe later this afternoon, around four?'

'That would be extremely helpful,' West said.

Father Maher started the engine and seconds later the car slowly exited the car park.

5

'Has Father Jeffreys been parish priest for long?' West asked as he watched the car join the line of rush-hour traffic.

'For as long as I've been here, and that's fifteen years,' Andrews said. 'They don't tend to leave once they're appointed. He's probably a year or two off retirement. Maher and Dillon have been here a few years. McComb is the newest: he only joined about a year or so ago.'

They'd be looking at them all. There might be a reason why the perpetrator targeted this particular church. Maybe a message for one of the four priests.

'This isn't going to be an easy one, Pete,' West said, his eyes scanning the area around the church. It was set near a busy junction and its huge car park separated it from houses on the roads behind.

'I doubt if a canvass of the neighbourhood is going to turn up anything.' Andrews pointed to the traffic cameras set high above the junction. 'I'll have the traffic cameras checked. We might be lucky and they might take in the entrance to the car park.'

West looked from the junction to the entrance. 'Unlikely, but worth a go.' This was the boring part of police work, the checking of every conceivable detail in case it might be the crucial link they were looking for. He was lucky with Andrews who was happy to investigate every lead, no matter how remote, without complaining.

There was no point in either of them hanging around the church. The uniforms would work through the canvass and report back to the station. The Gardaí assigned to the entrances would keep the curious and the reporters away. For the moment. No doubt the reporters would park on the residential roads behind and make a nuisance of themselves.

Maddison, he guessed, would shut the church door and ignore them.

Sergeant Blunt was at the front desk when they arrived back to Foxrock Station. He looked up from his computer screen when they pushed through the creaking front door. 'I was right to send you,' Blunt said, reading their grim expressions.

Since the reception was unusually empty, West leaned on the desk and gave Blunt the details.

'Grim,' was his only comment. As was his way, he said no more and the two men headed into the detective unit.

The main office was relatively quiet. Detective Garda Mark Edwards was tapping without much speed or enthusiasm on a keyboard and Detective Garda Mick Allen was staring into space. They and the members of the team who were out of the office would be dealing with the few ongoing investigations: small-time drug peddling outside a local secondary school, a domestic violence case that was proving more complex as more agencies became involved and some dodgy dealings in a local garage. The usual bread and butter of the detective unit.

Andrews grabbed two mugs of coffee and joined West in his

office, handing him one and taking the seat opposite. 'A nasty one this,' he said, taking a sip.

'It's a day for understatements,' West said, picking up his mug and shaking his head when Andrews threw him a puzzled look. 'Forget it,' he said. 'We'll need to talk to everyone who had access to the church, the sacristan when he feels up to it, the various priests, the cleaning staff and… who else?'

'Flower arrangers, organist, altar boys.'

'Yes.' West sipped his coffee. 'And not just for yesterday. The perp needed to know the layout of the church so he'll have been in it before. Hopefully someone will have noticed a nefarious individual hanging around.'

Andrews looked dubious. 'If "nefarious" means "evil bugger", I doubt it. They never do look as rotten on the outside as they are on the inside.' He ran a hand over his short brown hair. 'It would be nice if we had a name for our victim before we visit the priests. They might recognise it.'

West agreed. 'Maddison said he'd check the fingerprints as priority. He usually goes back before the team are finished to start processing the data. I'll give him a couple of hours before I start to nag.'

'Right, since it doesn't look as though Allen is doing anything useful, I'll get him to check missing persons. We might get lucky.'

Luck. There was that word again. If the general public knew how much they depended on it, he guessed they wouldn't be impressed. Someone else who wouldn't be impressed was Mother Morrison. Rather than going to his office, West reached for the phone. He had to speak to the inspector. There was no point in putting off the inevitable and doing it by phone would be easier, Morrison wouldn't be able to see his expression.

To say that Morrison was unhappy would have been yet another understatement. 'In the church?' he almost squeaked when West had finished filling him in. 'We'll have the parish priest down on us.'

'The sacristan called him so he arrived shortly after us. He mentioned the bishop,' West said, trying not to let a smile show in his voice. 'And the archbishop.'

'The parish priest, bishop and archbishop.' Morrison's voice left West in no doubt as to how he felt about the clergy.

'I'm sure they'll have little to do with us, Inspector.'

'Make sure of it.' Morrison hung up without another word.

West put the phone down and shook his head. It sounded as though the inspector had a fear of priests... there was a name for it, he remembered it coming up in a case back when he was a solicitor... hierophobia, that was it. He'd have to tell Andrews: it would be another new word for him. West's amusement quickly faded as he wondered how he was supposed to stop the parish priest, the bishop, or the archbishop for that matter, from sticking their oar in where it wasn't wanted. He'd no idea.

He guessed Morrison didn't either.

West's computer powered up with its usual reluctance. Every month since he'd transferred to Foxrock, he'd requested a new one, and every month he'd been promised it would come. It had become a standing joke between him and the requisition manager, only sometimes, like this morning, it didn't seem so funny.

He spent the next hour answering emails, filling in documentation, alerting anyone who needed to be alerted to the morning's murder. Paperwork, the bane of his existence. Sergeant Clark, who was supposedly in charge of the robbery side of the detective division in Foxrock, ignored it all but that wasn't in West's nature. Besides, he'd trained and practised as a solicitor, compared to the paperwork he had there, this was basic. It was also boring but he plodded through.

When he was done, he checked to see if, by the remotest

possibility, another similar murder had occurred anywhere in the twenty-six counties of the Republic of Ireland. He didn't know whether to be pleased or annoyed that it appeared to be unique. Unique was harder to solve.

Finally, he stretched, looked at the clock and picked up the phone to ring Maddison's office in the Phoenix Park. It would be days before they finished processing the scene, but he knew Maddison often headed back to the Park to deliver samples to the forensic department which was located nearby and to start the slow process of collating the information they'd already gathered.

'I'd have rung if I'd anything to give you,' Maddison said when he finally came to the phone.

'We're going to be under huge pressure with this, David,' West said easily. He waited a beat and added, 'If we had his identification to work with it would make a huge difference.'

There was a noisy exhale of breath before Maddison replied, 'I'm sure it would.'

West heard the crackle of paper and held his breath. Maybe they'd got something for him.

'You are in luck: your victim was in the system. Ian Moore, a twenty-seven-year-old from Dublin. He was a guest of the state, released two months ago.'

That was all Maddison had for him, but it was enough to satisfy West. He pulled his keyboard forward. And within seconds the screen filled with a photograph of the victim.

Getting to his feet, he headed to the general office to find Andrews who was leaning over Allen's shoulder as the younger man searched the missing person's file.

'You can call a halt to your search,' West said. 'Maddison came through for us.'

Andrews followed him back to his office, Allen close behind.

West sat and turned the screen toward them. 'Ian Moore,

twenty-seven years old, released from Mountjoy two months ago after serving eight months for the rape of nineteen-year-old Laetitia Summers.'

'Eight months?'

'Yes, he was sentenced to five years but he'd no priors and no history, so with time served and good behaviour he was given an early release.' Remembering the grisly scene in the church, he said, 'He'd have been safer serving a longer sentence.'

Allen enlarged the photo and stared intently at it before looking back to West. 'You think maybe Laetitia Summers was involved in some way?'

'He was released two months ago. Now he's dead. Maybe someone didn't think he'd been punished enough.' West turned the screen back around. 'We'll keep an open mind but we'll need to interview Ms Summers and her family, boyfriends et cetera. So far, they're the only obvious motive.'

'So far,' Andrews said, standing. 'We'll start looking into his background, check out family and friends. You going to inform his next of kin?'

West sighed. Breaking bad news was a job he'd never learned to be comfortable with. It was tempting to wait for the cause of death before he went, but that ran the risk of them finding out from another source. This kind of news, the worst kind, always leaked out. He checked his watch. 'They live in Dun Laoghaire. I'll go to them after the meeting with the priests.' He shot Andrews a quick look. 'And don't think you're getting out of that, by the way. I'll need support from a churchgoer to deal with the clergy.'

Andrews smiled. 'You might need the services of a priest someday.'

A bark of laugher from Allen was quickly smothered when West shot him a quelling glance. 'Start looking into Moore. Find out everything there is to know about him, family, friends, girl-friends.'

Allen beat a hasty retreat.

Deciding it was better to ignore Andrews' less than subtle hint that he should be thinking about getting married, West reached for his jacket and pulled it on. 'Let's go see what these priests have to tell us.'

6

———————

It wasn't a long drive from the station to Westminster Road but it was a busy area and it was stop-start most of the journey. West never minded sitting in traffic: it gave him time to think. Priests; the victim, Ian Moore; and his victim, Laetitia Summers. Already, he could feel the stress mounting. He slipped the car into second gear, moved a few yards and came to a halt again. 'We need to tread very carefully on this one, Peter.'

'Discretion, that's my middle name.'

'Well, make sure it's everybody else's middle name too. This is going to be a messy one.'

Foxrock was an upmarket area and the houses on Westminster Road tended to be big and detached. Halfway along the road, West's satnav told them they'd arrived at their destination on the left. A wooden gateway stood open and he pulled the car onto the gravel driveway in front of a rather dilapidated two-storey building. The church may have owned it but it looked as if they weren't willing to spend money maintaining it.

'A lot of these older houses were knocked down and replaced years ago,' Andrews said, getting from the car and leaning on the roof of it to look around the extensive gardens. 'A developer would love this; there's room for two, maybe three houses here.'

The house might have shown signs of neglect but the same couldn't be said for the gardens. Daffodils had popped up in neat rows in the flower beds that edged the driveway and there were no weeds or moss marring the expanse of velvety green grass.

'Nice gardens.' West made a mental note to get out into his much smaller one to tackle the weeds before they started taking over.

The doorbell was answered almost immediately by a solemn Father Dillon, who waved them in with a murmured greeting.

Inside, the house was even more neglected than it appeared on the outside. The narrow hallway was decorated in a loud floral paper that might have been popular in the sixties. The parquet flooring needed sanding and polishing, the paintwork was flaking and chipped and there was a distinct odour that screamed rising damp.

'Father Jeffreys isn't as strong as he'd like to think he is,' Father Dillon said. There was an element of warning in the tone.

'I'm aware Father Jeffreys has angina,' West said, refusing to take umbrage. 'I assure you we're not here to cause him distress but this is a murder enquiry: investigations need to proceed.'

Dillon's mouth tightened and it looked as if he were going to argue. Maybe he would have done but Father Jeffreys came through a doorway at the end of the hall claiming their attention, and when West looked back at Dillon, he'd resumed his solemn mask.

Mask. West filed away the word that had automatically popped into his head for consideration later. Everyone, at this stage, was under suspicion – especially someone who could hide his feelings as easily as Dillon appeared to be able to do.

Father Jeffreys waved them into a large airy room at the back of the house where some effort had been made at redecorating. The walls were a pale cream and the floor a sea of beige carpet. A typical three-piece suite of furniture was arranged in front of a fireplace, the three-seater sofa directly in front of it, a single seater to each side. A fire was set in the grate but not lit.

'Come in, Detective Sergeant West, Detective Garda Andrews. You've met us all apart from Father McComb.' Jeffreys indicated the slight man who hovered in front of an armchair. 'We're all eager to be of assistance in the hope you can get this terrible business sorted as quickly as possible.' Jeffreys sank onto the central seat of the three-seater sofa and patted the space beside him. 'Sit, ask whatever you need to ask.'

West had no choice but to take the seat offered. Dillon stayed standing, an elbow propped on the mantlepiece, and insisted that a reluctant Andrews took the seat on the other side.

'May we offer you tea or coffee?' Father Jeffreys asked, turning awkwardly to West.

'No, thank you,' West said quickly. He wasn't going to stay in this uncomfortably cramped situation longer than he could help.

'Detective Sergeant Maddison informed me that it could be at least a week before they'll be finished their investigation.'

'It's a slow, painstaking process,' West said, resorting to cliché.

'And your investigation?'

West glanced around the room, at the intent faces looking at him, at Andrews who was staring at his clasped hands waiting for West to tell these clergymen that he hadn't a clue how long it would take. He resisted the temptation to resort to cliché again, to say it would take as long as it took, and with more difficulty resisted the temptation to say he'd not yet had divine inspiration. 'It's only begun.' The truth was often the easiest way to go. 'We have identified the victim which is the first step.'

There was a rustle, as each of the seated priests sat forward expectantly.

'His name is Ian Moore,' West said. 'Does the name ring a bell?'

Every head shook in the negative. He felt in his jacket pocket for his mobile, brought up a screenshot he'd taken of the man's photo and handed his mobile around. 'Anyone recognise him?'

It was a slim chance. There was one other question he had to ask. 'If he'd come to you for confession, would you have recognised him through the mesh in the confession box?'

'Unlikely,' Jeffreys said. 'There isn't a light in the penitent's box and the mesh blurs the features of the people on the other side.'

'This man, Ian Moore, he'd been in prison. In fact, he was only out a few months. He might have been attempting to start again by going to confession. Would you remember someone who came to confess to a brutal crime?'

He wasn't surprised at their quickly shuttered expressions. The sanctity of the confessional was absolute. If Ian Moore had gone to seek forgiveness for raping Laetitia Summers, they wouldn't be able to tell him.

It was Father Jeffreys who eventually answered in a reproving tone. 'I know something of your history, Detective Garda Sergeant West. You were a practising solicitor before you joined the Gardaí, you should know better.'

'As a solicitor, I was taught to ask even the most difficult questions,' West said unapologetically. 'I owe it to the victim.'

Jeffreys laid a hand gently on his knee. 'We both have challenging roles at times. Now,' he said, shuffling to his feet, 'if there is nothing else.'

There was a lot more to ask but sitting there hemmed in on all sides, this wasn't the place to ask awkward questions. Anyway, West decided, getting to his feet, the other priests might feel freer to speak without the beady eye of the parish priest staring at them. 'I will need to speak to each of you individually,' he said, looking from one to the other. 'Perhaps it would be easier if you came to the station in the morning.'

Jeffreys frowned. 'Is this necessary?'

'It's standard procedure to get a statement from everyone involved. During the course of such statements we often uncover information that people don't realise they have.' It was a fishing expedition and would be the first of many in the case. He smiled gently at the parish priest. 'It's in all our interests to get this case solved as quickly as possible.'

Father Jeffreys couldn't argue against that. 'Fine, we'll be in tomorrow morning.'

With a promise that all four would arrive sometime in the morning between nine and eleven, West and Andrews bid the priests goodbye and left. It wasn't until they were sitting back in their car that Andrews let his breath out in a long, loud, 'Whew!'

'My sentiments exactly.' West smiled. 'I felt like I was back in school.'

'Do you really think Moore might have gone to get absolution for his crime?'

'Stranger things have happened. Maybe he found God in his eight months in prison.' He felt Andrews' eyes boring into the side of his head and turned to look at him.

'Why do I have a strange feeling I'll be speaking to the Mountjoy prison chaplain tomorrow?'

'Brilliant idea,' West said, starting the engine. 'Now why didn't I think of that.'

Andrews grunted but said nothing until they were once more waiting in traffic. 'Do you want me to come to Dun Laoghaire with you?'

West shook his head. 'No, thanks. I'd prefer if you checked in with the uniforms to see if by the remotest possibility anyone saw anything suspicious. Baxter and Jarvis should be back too. Fill them in and get them to start looking into the various connections.'

'Will do. If Allen has turned up anything exciting on Ian Moore, I'll give you a buzz.'

West dropped Andrews off outside the station. He left the engine running and took out his mobile to ring the pathologist's office.

'Niall, it's Mike West. Any luck in organising the post-mortem?'

Dr Kennedy's reply was unusually acerbic. 'Luck has absolutely nothing to do with it.'

There wasn't any point in answering that, so West didn't bother. He waited patiently. He'd known the pathologist long enough to realise Kennedy was simply venting the frustrations of the job.

'It's been one of those days,' Kennedy said in a calmer tone. 'And tomorrow is equally bad. Best I can do, is eight o'clock Wednesday morning.'

Not as soon as he'd hoped but there was no point in railing about it. He knew Kennedy: if he'd been able to do it earlier, he would have done. 'Okay,' West said. 'I'll see you then.'

The drive to Dun Laoghaire was slow. West turned the radio to classical music and thought of the ordeal ahead. The Moore family would have already been rocked by Ian's imprisonment for rape and he was about to bring them yet more suffering. There were no words to make the telling any easier and there would be no way to stay outside their pain and sorrow. It would become part of him and leave its mark. It always did.

The Moores lived in a two-storey Victorian house on Patrick Street. There was parking on the street immediately outside and West pulled in and stared at the neat, well-maintained house. It looked well-loved and taken care of. Double-fronted, its glossy black door was set with a brass doorknob and letter box, both gleaming in the glow of a lamp set to one side.

West checked the time. Almost six. He took out his mobile and hit a speed-dial button. 'Hi,' he said when it was answered. 'I'll be another hour and a half, at least.'

'No problem.' Edel's voice sounded preoccupied.

'Have I interrupted your muse?'

Her laugh was immediate, her voice more relaxed when she replied, 'No, I think my muse has gone on holiday. I'll see you when you get home.'

West put the mobile away and smiled. A happy home life was the anchor that kept him from drifting. He looked at the house again and with a sigh, opened the car door and climbed out. He shut the door and stretched before straightening his jacket, checking his tie, and crossing the wide pavement to the front gate. It opened into a small, pretty, gravelled garden.

A shallow step led up to the front door. He could hear the faint sound of a radio, or maybe a television. There wasn't a doorbell, just the brass knocker. He picked it up and let it fall once. Almost immediately the faint sound from inside stopped, and a moment later he heard a key turning in a lock and the door was pulled open.

The tiny woman who stood with one hand on the door, and the other on the collar of a large and mean-looking dog of indeterminate breed that seemed too big for her to control, gave an inquisitive tilt of her head. 'Can I help you?'

7

West held his identification forward. She looked at it first with a puzzled frown, then took it from him and read the details.

'Detective Garda Sergeant West,' she read, and handed it back to him. 'What can I do for you?'

'Are you Eve Moore?'

The woman's pleasantly puzzled expression changed, taking on a more worried look. 'Yes, that's right.'

'May I come in, Mrs Moore?' he said. He hoped there was someone else inside, someone to hold this delicate-looking woman together when he told her the news.

Her eyes filled as she took in the implications. Without letting the dog go, she turned her head and called out, 'Ben!'

One word but filled with anxiousness. It brought the owner of the name hurrying to her side. 'What's going on?' he said, putting an arm around her shoulder. The dog, alert to the change in emotions around him started to growl, a low sound that made the hairs on the back of West's neck stand on end.

'Sinbad!' The man took the dog's collar and opening a door beside him, pushed the dog gently inside. 'Lie down, Sinbad,' he said and shut the door. He put his arm back around his wife's shoulder and addressed West. 'He's very protective,' he explained. 'Now, what's this all about?'

'It would be better to discuss this inside,' West said, holding his identification forward again.

The man peered at it. 'A guard,' he said, eyes flicking from it to West.

'Detective Garda Sergeant West.'

The man's anxious expression was instinctive. West could almost see the cogs whirling in his brain as he tried to make sense of a member of the Garda Síochána appearing on his doorstep. It was never likely to be good news.

'I'm Ben Moore.' With a sigh, as if at the necessity, he looked down at his wife and they both stepped back. 'We can go into the sitting room.'

This large cosy room was at the back of the house. Curtains were closed against the night and a fire glowed in the fireplace. It was warm and inviting.

Ben Moore settled his wife into a small sofa near the fire and with a final caress of her shoulder, turned to West. 'Please take a seat.' He indicated a chair the other side of the room and took the one beside his wife, reaching over to take her hand.

West felt the two sets of eyes boring into him. 'This is never easy,' he said. It was a cop-out, he knew, looking for sympathy for his role as bringer of bad news. He lifted his chin. He never had been one to search for the easier option. 'I'm afraid to tell you I have come with bad news about your son.' He watched the truth register on their faces, the woman's collapsing in on itself as if the heart of her had been dragged out, the man, more stoic, biting a lower lip that continued to tremble despite this anchor.

'I am so sorry.' Pathetically useless words were all he had. 'He was found dead this morning in St Monica's Church.' That was all he was going to offer at the moment, he'd spare them the details and hoped they wouldn't ask.

It was always impossible to anticipate people's reactions. He'd seen calm stoic acceptance of death, he'd also seen the loud wailing refusal. What he hadn't anticipated was puzzlement as Ben and Eve exchanged glances and a brief smile.

'That's impossible.'

West had heard denial before, but never quite so calmly or with such emphasis. 'It's never easy–'

'No,' Moore said holding up a hand. 'I'm sorry. I don't know who you think you found in St Monica's, but it wasn't our son. We spoke to him about three hours ago.' He pointed to where a laptop sat on a small side table. 'Via Skype. Ian is an engineer, he works in Dubai.'

'Dubai,' West parroted. It was tempting to ask were they sure, but that would have been making a farcical situation only worse. 'It's not often I'm lost for words,' he said. 'I am, of course, relieved for your sake that your son is safe.'

Moore's relief gave way to anger. 'You come here and give us this terrible news, nearly frightening us to death! Surely, you should have had your facts straight.'

West thought he had. 'My apologies. Fingerprints were checked, the information they gave us was that the young man was Ian Moore and that his parents lived at this address. I have absolutely no idea how such a glitch occurred.'

'A glitch!' Eve Moore's voice was scathing.

It was a poor choice of word, one West regretted as soon as it was said. He ran a hand over his head. 'All I can do is apologise. It is very unusual for such a mistake to occur. To be honest, I have no idea how it did.' He waited a beat. 'I hate to cause further offence but would there be any reason for your son's fingerprints to be in our system?'

Moore shook his head and replied calmly. 'Ian was never in

trouble a day in his life. After university he got a job with a big US conglomerate in Dubai and he's been there ever since. Almost ten years now.'

So, no reason for his fingerprints to be on their system. 'It's not much, but all I can do is apologise again and promise that I will find out how this–' he sought for an appropriate word '– terrible mistake occurred.'

'It's very strange,' Moore said. 'I would like to be kept informed.'

Promising to do so, West stood and with a final apology, escaped.

Back in his car, he thought about ringing Andrews. Instead, he sat and thought about the body suspended in the church. A difficult case had become a lot worse.

Who was the man? And why did his fingerprints lie?'

8

____

West puzzled over the fingerprints on the drive to Greystones. He pulled up behind Edel's car, switched off the engine and looked at the light shining from the windows of his home. Tension left him in one long sigh. Home... it was so much better now.

He and Edel Johnson. They'd been through a lot in the months they'd been together. From an inauspicious start where she was the prime suspect in a case he was investigating, through a series of crazy escapades involving kidnap, poisoning, a near-death experience in a cave and the targeting of her by a crazed woman, they had managed to survive. *No,* he amended, *not merely survived, grown stronger.*

As he pushed open the front door, he heard music drifting from the kitchen and the smell of something cooking wafting from the same direction. It used to be that he'd need a whiskey to relieve the stress of such a difficult day, now simply coming home was enough.

'Sorry I'm late,' he said, opening the kitchen door.

Edel turned to him and smiled. 'It's grand, don't worry, I got more writing done.' She stepped closer and raised a hand to caress his cheek. 'Bad day?'

West bent to kiss her lips. 'Good now.'

He took off his jacket and hung it on the back of a chair, undid his tie and shoved it into a pocket. With his top button undone and his shirt sleeves rolled up, he was in full relaxation mode. He sat and watched as Edel fussed about and a few minutes later sniffed the plate of food that was put in front of him.

'Very nice.'

'A chicken casserole is an easy one to keep for a while. It doesn't mind being a little overdone.'

West ate quietly for a while. When he looked up, Edel was watching him. He smiled. 'Sorry, it's been a strange day.'

'You want to talk about it?'

'Maybe later, first, tell me about your day. How are sales?'

Thanks to a smear campaign by a forensic technician that West had met in the course of his job, Edel had lost the publishing contract she had with FinalEdit Publishing for her debut novel, *A Family Affair*. Instead, she'd decided to self-publish. He guessed by her expression that it wasn't going too well. 'I had two sales yesterday,' she said. 'Better than none.'

And obviously none today. West wished there were something he could do. 'Have you heard from your agent?'

She shook her head. 'He's emailed but I haven't answered. What's the point?'

Edel didn't like to tell him that she'd virtually given up. She'd lied about writing, she'd not written a word in days. The news about her sales too was a lie, there hadn't been two yesterday, there'd been two in the last month. Self-publishing, getting the book available for readers to buy, was the easy bit – it was the marketing that she was finding impossible.

Owen Grady, her agent, wanted to approach other publishers but only if she'd agree to write under a pseudonym. The compromising photos of her that had been sent to all and sundry had, he said, tarnished the name *Edel Johnson*. It didn't matter: she'd promised to use the name *Johnson* as a tribute to the man who'd died as a result of dealings with her late husband, Simon, and she wasn't going back on her word. Her agent had emailed her a few times in the last week, but she hadn't read them. There was no point.

She tried not to show West how despondent she was. He'd done so much for her. She knew he'd pulled strings to have that horrible woman, Fiona Wilson, given her marching orders. He said she'd gone to work in the US. It wasn't far enough away for her liking.

'Do you want to have a cup of coffee while we watch the news?'

A glass of wine would have been her preference but they'd agreed not to drink during the week. She couldn't remember whose idea that had been, hers she thought vaguely, with an eye to the calories she'd be saving rather than any health aspect. 'Actually, I fancy a glass of wine,' she said, deciding she deserved it.

'That sounds good, I'll join you.' West stood and cleared the plates away, stacking them into the dishwasher while Edel opened the wine and poured two glasses.

She carried them through while he switched on the lights and TV and they settled down on the sofa with Tyler, the chihuahua, curled up between them. She sipped her wine, trying to put her failure behind her. It was only when West sat forward that she focused on the television screen. She recognised the church straight away. 'That's St Monica's, isn't it?'

West didn't reply. Within a few minutes she knew why. A dead body. Almost on the station's doorstep. He'd be involved. 'Do you know who he is?' she asked when the news report was over. It hadn't given much information.

'I thought we did.' West took a gulp of his wine. 'That was my last call tonight, to go and inform the next of kin.'

'Never an easy task.'

He gave a short laugh. 'Especially when they weren't.'

Edel thought she might have misheard. She shuffled forward in the seat and turned to look at him. 'What did you say?'

'I went to tell the parents that their son had been killed.' He took another mouthful of wine. 'They were shocked, obviously, but it quickly became clear that I'd made a mistake. Their only son is in Dubai. They'd spoken to him a couple of hours before I'd arrived via Skype.'

Edel reached a hand out to squeeze his arm. 'A little embarrassing.'

'To say the least.' He frowned, then drained his glass. 'It's a new one for me. They said he'd never been in trouble so there was no reason for his fingerprints to be on record so it can't have been something as simple as a mix-up. Two men with the same name scenario. It's all very bizarre and it throws us back a step. Now we've no idea who our victim is.'

There was a long uncomfortable silence. Did he realise what he'd said? Two men with the same name... a year ago, her late husband had been in much the same situation. 'Identity theft,' she said softly.

He turned to look at her then and she saw his expression change. 'Oh Lord, I'm sorry,' he said, reaching for her hand. 'I didn't think.'

'But you think it could be?'

'My first thought was there had been some kind of cock-up but the Moores insist their son has never been in trouble, so his fingerprints couldn't be in the system. The only other rational explanation is that our victim was using their son's name.' He raised the glass to his mouth, smiled to find it empty and put it down on the table in front of him. 'It's more complicated. Our victim had been in prison. His identification had to be good enough to get him through the courts.'

Edel squeezed the hand that still held hers. 'It's going to make it a more complicated case, isn't it?'

'A bit.'

Edel watched as his attention went back to the news. *A bit?* It sounded like this was going to be a very complicated case indeed.

9

As was his way, West was in the station before the rest of the team arrived. He could already feel a band of tension tightening around his head at the thought of telling Mother Morrison about the previous day's fiasco. Before West faced that, he needed some information but 7.30 was probably too early to expect answers.

In the main detective's office, he emptied the dregs of the overbrewed coffee down the sink and made a fresh pot. Someday he'd buy some decent coffee, a promise he made regularly but never got around to fulfilling. He poured a mugful and, since there was no milk, drank it black while he perused The Wall. The previous year, during the complicated investigation into the death of Gerard Roberts, West had discovered that the large empty wall on one side of the office was a far more effective place to present their information than the too-small display boards provided. It had worked so well that it stayed in use. There wasn't much on it now, but over the next few days, information would be added.

At this stage, there was a photo of Ian Moore – or whoever he was – sitting square in the centre. The only other piece of information was the fingerprint analysis. West had intended on bringing the report up on his computer. Instead, he pulled the hardcopy down and perched on the side on a nearby desk, sipping the bitter coffee and reading the short report.

It was straightforwardly informative. The victim's fingerprints were in their system. According to it, he was Ian Moore, whose parents, Eve and Ben Moore, lived in Dun Laoghaire. Straightforwardly informative, apart from the fact that it wasn't true. There was also a home address. West would have it checked out that morning. Maybe they would learn something that would clear up this mess.

Andrews was the first of the team to arrive. He filled his mug with coffee, looked around for the milk, shaking his head to see none, and emptied three packets of sugar in. 'How did it go last night?'

Instead of replying, West pointed towards The Wall. He'd found a black marker pen, drawn a large question mark on a sheet of paper and stuck it under the picture of their victim.

'A bit dramatic for this early in the morning,' Andrews said, stirring his coffee with the end of a pen. 'You hardly expect us to know who killed him yet, this isn't–'

'CSI, wherever,' West said, interrupting one of Andrews' favourite expressions. 'Who killed him isn't my question. No,' he said, waving a hand towards the photo, 'it's who is he? Because he certainly isn't Ian Moore.'

Andrews stood silently while West filled him in on the previous evening's disaster. 'It was one of the most embarrassing and awkward situations I've ever been in. They went from being distressed to apoplectic in the space of a few seconds. And I didn't blame them.'

'Embarrassing all right.' Andrews took the report from The Wall and read it. 'And very odd, fingerprints don't normally lie.'

The rest of the team arrived. West left Andrews to fill them in while he went to ring Maddison who, West hoped, would have a rational explanation for the mix-up.

Unfortunately, Maddison didn't. 'Everything is as it should be,' he assured West. 'Ian Moore, or whoever he was, had his fingerprints taken when he was arrested and charged with the rape of Laetitia Summers. There was DNA evidence. Your victim, Mike, was the man charged with the rape. His name according to everything I have, is Ian Moore.'

'Okay,' West said.

'Sounds like this one is going to be a bit of a headache.'

More understatements. *Headache*. This one was going to be a nightmare.

Pulling his keyboard towards him, he brought up Ian Moore's arrest sheet and read through every word twice. Nothing was out of the ordinary. It was all straightforward. Believable. It had fooled everyone.

He read the transcript from the interview with Laetitia Summers. She'd known her attacker, their victim, to see for some time. He worked at a garage near where she worked and she had to pass it on her way home in the evening. They'd gone, she told the interviewer, from a smile to a wave, then one day he'd asked her if she'd like to go for a drink.

They had both drunk too much and were noted by witnesses to be staggering when they left the pub. But she was quite clear, she'd never planned to have sex with him and had told him *no* when he had tried it on as they made their way home. She was still saying *no* when he dragged her into a laneway and raped her.

West glossed over the medical report and the impact statement. They never made pleasant reading. Instead, he scrolled through to a character reference given by Ian Moore's employer. Ronan Tedford. Moore had worked for him for several years, was a diligent worker, honest, a good timekeeper and never got into trouble.

West tapped the desk with his fingers. To work for Tedford, to have paid tax, Moore had to have had a personal public services number. If it had been his first job, he'd have had to apply for one. Either way, the man had to be known by the Revenue. Maybe this wouldn't be so hard to sort out after all.

Getting to his feet, he headed to the main office. Andrews had already handed out assignments and both Seamus Baxter and Mark Edwards were frowning at their computer screens, tapping on the keyboard, Baxter with speed, Edwards with his middle-finger stretching from key to key.

'They're getting background information on our current list of characters,' Andrews said as West perched on the side of his desk.

'When they've finished, get one of them to check with Revenue. He has to have a PPS number to work: find out when it was issued. A child born and registered in Ireland is automatically assigned one at that point. If our victim was using Ian Moore's, how did he get hold of it?'

'You said the real Ian Moore went abroad immediately following university. Maybe he'd never had to work in Ireland so never actually used it.'

West, remembering the well-to-do couple, agreed. 'Yes, they didn't look to be short of money and he is their only son.' He checked his watch and swore softly. 'I need to go and see Morrison and tell him of this complication plus to warn him that those priests will be coming in shortly. I think the inspector may suffer from hierophobia.' He expected Andrews to latch onto this new word but instead his partner nodded.

'A fear of priests, yes, that wouldn't surprise me.' Andrews smiled. 'Thought you'd catch me out, didn't you? Fact is, I had a friend, years ago, who had a bad case of it, used to break out into a sweat if he as much as saw a priest in the distance.' Andrews checked his watch. 'Okay, I'd better go and lay claim to the Big One before Sergeant Clark decides he needs it for something or other.'

The two interview rooms were identical and joined by a single observation room. Officially, they were designated Interview Room One and Two, but for a reason that West was never able to discover, they were always known as the Big One and the Other One. When he'd arrived in Foxrock almost two years before, he'd called them by their official names but within a few months, he'd given in. Despite it being identical to the other, the Big One was seen as the more important of the two rooms. As such, it was the room his robbery counterpart, Detective Garda Sergeant Clark, liked to use. West didn't care, but he knew Andrews did so left him to lay claim to it while he went off to update Mother Morrison.

When West found himself wondering, yet again, how the very unmotherly Morrison had ended up with such a nickname, he knew he was trying to put off the inevitable. Rather than phoning, he decided to head up to his office on the first floor.

He was in luck and Morrison was alone, his door slightly open to show him hunched over his desk, a deep furrow between his hairy eyebrows.

West sucked in a deep breath and rapped his knuckles smartly against the wood.

'Come in,' Morrison said immediately, looking up from the papers in his hand.

West shut the door behind him. 'Morning, Inspector, I wanted to update you on our progress in the murder investigation.' There was no chair this side of Morrison's desk. West refused to stand before him like a penitent child so had taken to leaning one shoulder against the wall. Sometimes, like this morning, with Morrison's rather small eyes pinning him to the wall, it was an effort to appear relaxed. He resisted the temptation to shuffle nervously. 'We ran into an unexpected problem,' he said, trying to sound casual.

'Yes?'

'We identified the victim by fingerprints. According to the information we were given, his parents lived in Dun Laoghaire so I went yesterday evening to break the bad news.' He did shuffle a little when he remembered the Moores' reaction. 'Unfortunately, our information was incorrect.'

'Incorrect?' Morrison's hairy eyebrows met. 'Fingerprints don't lie.'

'Our victim was in Mountjoy. His fingerprints are in the system. And Ben and Eve Moore, who live at the address he gave, do have a son called Ian. But he is very much alive.' West shook his head, remembering their reaction. 'Their son lives in Dubai. They'd been speaking to him on Skype a few hours before I called.'

'A bit of a mess.' Morrison drummed his fingers on the desk but his voice was even, he wasn't assigning fault.

West, although he knew he wasn't to blame, relaxed. 'Our victim worked in a garage in Marino. We're following his employment record. We should be able to unscramble it soon.'

'How long has he been working there?'

'Several years. He's obviously been using the fake identification all these years and it was good enough to fool the courts when he was arrested. We're looking into how he got hold of Ian Moore's PPS number.'

'Sounds like we have another case of identity theft on our hands.' The inspector sat back and folded his arms. 'Is that why he was killed?'

'We've a long way to go before we decide that, Inspector. It might be something to do with it, but it might also be totally unrelated.'

'A red herring.'

'Exactly. It's one of any number of avenues we'll be exploring over the next few days.' It was time to break the other bad news. 'The priests from St Monica's are coming in to give statements this morning.'

Morrison went rigid. 'Is that really necessary?'

'The positioning and staging of the body... that was done to make a point, almost to make a mockery of the church. It may have been directed at one of the priests.' West shrugged. 'Or maybe all of them.'

'It might simply be someone who hates the clergy.' Morrison's voice was decidedly tetchy.

'Or the Catholic Church.' West pushed away from the wall and held his hands up. 'The best way forward, as I see it, is to speak to anyone even remotely involved with St Monica's and go from there.'

'Yes, reluctantly, I agree.' Morrison's shoulders slumped in resigned acceptance. 'It doesn't sound like this is going to be a quick solve.'

'We've had difficult cases before, Inspector.' West hoped he sounded more confident than he felt.

It was always the same at the start of a case, he decided, making his way slowly down the quiet, strikingly-cold stairwell. The central crime with its tentacles of possibilities, suspects, red herrings, dead-ends and tantalising unknowns. A smile hovered at the corner of his mouth. It was exactly why he'd wanted to become a detective.

10

———————

Over the course of the morning, one at a time, the priests from St Monica's came into the station. They seemed perfectly relaxed in the interview room while West and Andrews sat opposite and tried to tease information from them. It was a frustrating exercise. The priests saw the world through God-tinged, rose-coloured glasses. That and their adherence to the sanctity of the confessional meant they'd little to share that might have given the detectives a road to travel along.

The parish priest, Father Jeffreys, was the last to come in, looking healthier than he had done the day before.

'We appreciate you coming in,' West said, trying to keep the note of frustration from his voice. The morning was almost gone and, so far, they'd learned nothing they didn't already know.

'We want to do all we can to help.' The words were correct but there was a light in the old priest's eye that said, as clearly as if he'd spoken aloud, it would be on his terms only.

West understood, but it was time the parish priest did too. 'We appreciate the constraints you're under, Father Jeffreys, but you must understand we will do everything necessary to bring the perpetrator of this murder to justice.' Having made his position clear, he spent the next several minutes leading the priest through the same questions he'd asked the others, but as he'd expected Father Jeffreys' answers were all in the negative. He'd seen nothing suspicious and couldn't think of anyone who would have a grievance against the church or him.

The next question was more difficult, but it was one West knew he had to ask. 'I'd be remiss if I didn't ask if you, or any of the priests in your parish, were involved in any way... directly or indirectly... with any case of child abuse.'

Colour drained from the parish priest's face and the hands that had been resting relaxed on the table between them clutched one another. West expected an angry outburst; instead, tears filled the priest's eyes. 'Such sadness that you have to ask, Detective Garda Sergeant West. Such sadness that this abhorrent behaviour has become so associated with the clergy.' Jeffreys reached one trembling hand into his pocket, retrieved the bottle of tablets that West had opened for him the previous day, opened it, knocked one tablet into his hand and tossed it into his mouth.

He held a hand up as both West and Andrews rose to their feet. 'Sit, sit,' he said testily. 'Angina is more dramatic than serious.' As colour returned to his cheeks, he reached for a glass of water and took a sip. 'Let me make it very, very clear,' he said. 'Each of the priests who works with me has been thoroughly vetted and there is nothing in their past to indicate any problems in that regard.' His shoulders slumped as his hands continued to twist. 'The church has a lot to answer for, but I can assure you, not this time.'

~

'It had to be asked,' West said later. He and Andrews were in his office drinking coffee and working their way through a packet of fig rolls.

'As Father Jeffreys said, sad that it needed to be,' Andrews said with a shake of his head. 'I feel sorry for the man. When I was a child, priests automatically got respect from everyone; nowadays things are different and there are many people who look at them askance.' He drained his mug, threw the empty biscuit packet into the bin and got to his feet. 'I'll go and see if the lads have come up with anything.'

West, left alone, sat back with his hands clasped behind his head. Jeffreys, he guessed, believed what he'd said, that each of the priests was innocent of any form of abuse. That didn't, however, mean it was true. The church had been guilty of cover-ups over the years. Who's to say it wasn't continuing? They'd need to look deeper into each man, dig into previous parishes, see if there was any gossip.

Gossip. Digging through it was an unsavoury part of detective work. It was an evil necessity, especially if they had nowhere else to go because sometimes there was a kernel of truth in even the most ridiculous gossip and rumours.

When Andrews didn't return, West decided to go out to the main office to see what was happening. The day was half over and so far, they had diddly-squat.

Andrews was leaning over Baxter's shoulder, peering at his computer screen. Seeing a level of intense interest, West joined them and leaned over Baxter's other shoulder. 'What've you found?'

'Ian Moore's Revenue paperwork,' Baxter said, tapping on the keyboard, then stopping to point at the screen. 'According to them, he is Ian Moore whose parents live in Dun Laoghaire. His PPS number is correct. He's been working and paying tax for the last nine years.'

West peered at the screen. 'It all looks official and correct except we know he isn't Ian Moore.'

Andrews straightened and stretched. 'Somehow, he got hold of the right paperwork and PPS number.'

West took a final glance at Baxter's screen. 'It looks like I'm going to have to speak to the Moores again.'

'I'm waiting to hear from our vic's landlord regarding getting access to his flat.' Andrews glanced at his watch. 'I'd expect to hear from him soon. I can take Baxter or Edwards if you'd prefer.'

West considered what needed to be done. He liked to have a hand in every part of the investigation but he knew it wasn't possible and was unfair to his experienced team. Still, he shook his head. 'No, I'd like to put some flesh on our victim's bones by seeing where he lived, I'll come with you.' He turned for his office, turning back on another thought. 'Who's talking to Laetitia Summers?'

Andrews smiled. 'I saw Garda Foley with nothing to do so sent him off with Jarvis to talk to her.'

West raised his eyes to the ceiling. Garda Foley was officially assigned to Sergeant Clark in robbery who wouldn't be happy to lose him even if they were quiet. 'Did you ask Clark?' he said, knowing the answer would be *no*.

'I put a requisition slip in his in-tray.' Andrews could do innocent like nobody else West knew. Clark ignored his in-tray, everyone knew it. Andrews proceeded to justify his actions. 'Foley was a good choice to go. Jarvis is too inexperienced.'

West had to admit he was right. Foley was the solid, dependable type who instantly made people feel at ease. He and Jarvis would make a good team to speak to the rape victim.

'Right, if Clark comes looking for him, tell him to take it up with Morrison.' Clark, he knew, avoided Morrison almost as much as he did everything else.

Sat back at his desk, he considered phoning the Moores. It would have been faster and easier but after yesterday's fiasco he decided he owed them the courtesy of a visit. Anyway, in his experience, people were more inclined to talk more in a one-on-one setting.

He dealt with a few emails before grabbing his jacket from the back of his chair and heading back to the main office. Andrews was on the phone; he hung up and scribbled something on the notepad in front of him as West approached. 'That was the landlord's secretary. She says he'll meet us at four at the apartment block.'

West glanced at his watch. It was twelve thirty. He had enough time. 'Okay, I'll meet you there. I want to visit the Moores, see if they can throw some light on how someone had access to their son's data.'

'I've an appointment to see the administrator in Mountjoy in an hour.' Andrews stood and took his jacket. 'I'd better get going. Hopefully, I'll learn something there.'

'We need to learn something, somewhere,' West said caustically. They headed out to the car park together, Andrews grumbling about Clark's laziness yet again, West with his thoughts firmly on the Moores.

Outside, it was a blue-sky day. It was a day for walking along Dun Laoghaire pier. For having an ice cream in Teddy's. Instead, he returned to the Moores' rather lovely home and once again knocked on their door.

This time it was Ben Moore who opened the door, his pleasant, amiable features hardening into a scowl when he saw who it was. 'What is it this time?'

West held his hands up, a conciliatory gesture that had no effect on Moore's expression until his wife appeared by his side. 'Oh, let him in, Ben. It wasn't his fault, after all.'

West followed the couple into a large cosy kitchen. A big

pine table sat to one side, surrounded by matching chairs. At one end of the table was a teapot, half-filled mugs and a couple of open packets of biscuits.

'Have a seat,' Eve Moore said, pointing to a chair near the other end. 'We were having a cuppa, will you join us?'

It was easier to accept and moments later, West, shaking his head to the offer of biscuits, clasped his hands around a large mug of tea. Behind the table was a large window overlooking a well-maintained garden. 'It looks pretty out there,' he commented and saw a sardonic lift of Moore's eyebrow reminding him that this wasn't a social visit.

He gave a half-smile and took a sip of his tea before putting the mug down and pushing it away. 'I'm sorry to intrude again but something came up that made a visit necessary.' He saw the couple exchange worried glances. 'Did your son ever work here before he went to Dubai? While he was in university, maybe?'

Moore thought for a moment and shook his head. 'He did talk about taking on a part-time job at one stage but nothing ever came of it.' He gave a dismissive shrug. 'He's our only child and we wanted him to enjoy himself so there was never any pressure on him to find work. He studied hard, though, and came top of his year and, even before he qualified, he was offered that position in Dubai. Initially it was to be for a year, then he was going to look for something here, but it didn't work out that way.'

West saw the sadness in their eyes. Their only son, a long way from home.

Moore seemed to brush aside the sadness as his expression turned belligerent. 'Why are you asking?'

Time to get to the crunch. 'The man who was murdered was using your son's name. He was also using his personal public services number.'

'His what?'

'His PPS,' West clarified. So many people used the initials without knowing what it stood for. 'According to Revenue, our victim *is* your son, Ian.'

'That's bloody ridiculous!'

'PPS numbers are assigned when a birth is registered. You say your son has never worked in this country, so he never needed it. All someone had to do was prove they were Ian Moore and they'd be free to use it.' He waited until this sank in. 'He'd have needed certain documents to get it though. A birth certificate, for instance. Is there any way someone would have been able to get hold of that?'

Ben Moore wiped a hand over his mouth, his eyes sliding to meet his wife's. 'We were burgled.'

'When?' West leaned forward. This was it.

Moore shook his head. 'Nine, maybe ten years ago.'

'Ten,' Eve said emphatically. 'Do you remember? It was the month before Ian went to Dubai. It was he who insisted we got our first dog. Not Sinbad,' she said with a smile to West. 'Our first dog, Whiskey. He was a brilliant guard dog.'

Moore nodded. 'Yes, that's right.'

'Can you tell me about it?'

'We were out for dinner, the three of us, when we got back the front door was open and the alarm blaring. Your lot,' Moore said with a sniff, 'arrived about ten minutes later.'

Eve Moore put a hand on her husband's arm. 'The burglars made a right mess. The guards thought there had to have been more than one person because they went through every room, methodically taking anything of value. They emptied drawers, boxes, files.'

'Paperwork,' West said. He wondered if that had been the reason for the break-in. Someone who knew Ian was going away, that he'd never worked and his PPS would be going a-begging.

'Do you know if Ian's birth certificate was one of the things that went missing?'

Moore stared at him blankly before turning to look at his wife. 'Was it?'

'I don't know,' she said. 'It's not something we've needed to look for. Ian already had his passport.' She got to her feet. 'After the burglary, we tidied up as quickly as we could, trying to put it behind us, you know. I remember picking up the box where I kept all that sort of stuff and putting everything back inside neatly. There was nothing of monetary value so I never thought to check that everything was there.' She headed from the room as she spoke and moments later, West heard doors opening and closing.

'I'm sorry about all of this,' he said to the quiet man sitting opposite.

'Eve is putting on a brave face. That burglary really shook her. It didn't help that Ian was leaving shortly afterward. Whiskey helped, of course–' a smile flickered '–the dog, not the alcohol.'

'Here we go,' Eve said, returning to the room with a box in her hand that West immediately recognised. His mother had a similar one. An old Black Magic chocolates casket with a red tassel on the lid, probably thirty years old, maybe more. Eve opened it and began to take out the same sort of memorabilia that his mother kept in hers: old school reports, an old library card, a First Communion rosette, other bits and pieces that meant nothing to West but obviously did to her. She handled each item reverently.

'It's not here,' she said, when the box was empty. She looked at West with a stricken expression.

'And you're sure it wouldn't be anywhere else.'

Her headshake was emphatic. He didn't doubt her for a

moment, his mother too would know exactly where she'd put something so precious.

'I haven't needed to look for it,' Eve said, as if trying to explain away her lapse.

'You wouldn't have,' West agreed, his mind elsewhere. So that solved the puzzle of where their victim got the paperwork but it gave him a further puzzle. Who was the victim? And why had he needed to change his identity?

11

———

While West was coming up against more puzzles in Dun Laoghaire, Edel Johnson had taken a look at the miserable sales of her book on Amazon and in a fit of frustration deleted all the pages she'd written of what she'd hoped to be a sequel. What was the point if nobody was going to read it? And anyway, she couldn't seem to get into the characters anymore and hadn't written anything in days. When she'd started writing her first, a family saga stretching over generations, she'd been happily married and her world was innocent. Now she knew better and the words didn't seem to want to come.

Maybe she should change genres. She sat in front of her computer and thought of what she'd been through in the last year. She'd told Mike that she wasn't interested in writing about her experiences, and she meant it. She wasn't interested in writing the facts of what had happened to her but perhaps she could use what she had learned and write a crime novel.

'Or maybe give up and get a job,' she muttered, closing the lid of her laptop with too much force but she was too fed up to care.

She had all day to fill. A quick search of the kitchen

cupboards for biscuits brought no luck so she pulled on her coat, grabbed her keys and headed out to the local shops. Twenty minutes later, she was heading back with a plastic carrier bag full of biscuits and chocolate to help get her through the doldrums.

Her head was down, her mind elsewhere when she turned the corner onto the street where she lived. She was within a few yards of the house before she looked up and when she did, when she saw the man standing on the doorstep peering in through the glass panels of the front door, she didn't stop to think. Instead, she automatically turned tail and hurried back around the corner. There, sheltering behind a high garden wall, she caught her breath before peering around.

He was still there on her doorstep. She'd recognised him immediately. How could she forget the tall, elegantly-dressed editor who had treated her so badly? Aidan Power. What the hell was he doing on her doorstep? As far as she was concerned, he was partially to blame for her losing her contract with Final-Edit Publishing. He could have fought her corner with the owner of the company, Hugh Todd, and hadn't done so.

What did he want with her now? Hadn't he done enough?

It was a few minutes before she watched him retreat down their short front garden path, open the gate and leave. A red Volvo parked on the roadside flashed its lights as he remotely unlocked the doors and with a final look back at the house, he shook his head, climbed into it and drove away.

Edel waited until the car disappeared around the far corner before hurrying down the street, anxious in case the car returned. With a last look around, she pushed open the front door and shut it quickly after her, slipping the catch down on the Yale lock, and sliding the safety chain into place.

Her mobile phone was on the counter where she'd left it. She dropped her bag of shopping beside it and picked it up.

She'd ring Mike, he'd sort it out for her. Tell Power to leave her alone. Ride to her rescue. The way he'd done so often. And she'd be a victim. All over again.

For the last year it had been one thing after the other.

She looked at the phone, feeling her throat thicken. It wasn't fair. She put the phone down, took a packet of biscuits from the bag and sat at the table, tearing the packet open with her teeth. Within a few minutes, the biscuits were gone. They didn't make her feel any better but the tears that threatened were gone.

Maybe it was the sugar jolt from the biscuits, maybe the memory of dealing with that conniving Fiona Wilson who'd thought Edel would be easy to destroy. She wasn't sure, but whichever it was, she felt a new sense of purpose. No, she wouldn't take the easy option of ringing Mike and asking for his help. She drummed her fingers on the table. This time, she'd sort things out for herself.

According to Mike, Aidan Power and her agent Owen Grady were in a relationship. She'd been ignoring Grady's emails: maybe Power's visit was something to do with that. Maybe it was simply that he was coming to apologise for treating her so badly.

There was one way to find out. She had no intention of darkening the doors of FinalEdit Publishing but she could visit Grady's office in the city. Suddenly it seemed the right thing to do and within minutes, she was heading out to her car.

Roadworks in the city had made driving there a nightmare. Instead, Edel drove to the car park next to the DART station in Greystones. The electrified trains of the Dublin area rapid transport were popular and as a result their car parks were always busy, and frequently full. Edel wasn't feeling lucky and drove around it listlessly wondering, after all, if this was such a good idea. It was on her second drive around, when she'd almost decided to give up, that she saw a car pulling out a short distance ahead. She quickly drove towards it and indicated to stake her claim.

Her luck held and only seconds after stepping onto the platform, a DART pulled up. It was a lovely day but the view out to sea as she travelled along the coast was wasted on her, lost as she was in thoughts of what she was going to say to Owen Grady. Trying to put him and Power out of her head, she let her mind drift to the other decision she'd made that morning. Crime novels... an idea was brewing in her head, she concentrated on it and by the time the DART stopped in Tara Street station, she'd a rough idea for a storyline.

She was still thinking about it when she walked into her agent's office. The receptionist, Tina, surprised to see her, asked if she had an appointment.

'No, but I really need to see Owen,' Edel said, hoping her tone of voice conveyed the importance of the matter. The last time she'd been into the office she'd made a similar demand so she wasn't surprised to see a faint uplift of an eyebrow in response.

'You might be in luck,' Tina said, turning in her chair to stand. 'His last appointment was shorter than expected. Hang on and I'll check with him.'

Edel hovered around the desk until the click-click of stilettos told her the receptionist was returning.

'He's on a call, he'll see you in five minutes. For a minute,' she added quickly, then, more kindly, 'Why don't you have a coffee while you wait.'

With a murmured thank you, Edel headed for the vending machine partially hidden behind the artificial plant in the corner and poured a cup, sipping it while she waited. She felt surprisingly calm.

It was ten minutes before a frowning Owen Grady appeared

through a door to her right. 'This is unexpected,' he said, holding out a hand.

Edel found her hand grasped tightly and held while Grady's eyes assessed her. 'You look well,' he said. 'Better than the last time I saw you.'

That had been a little over a month before. The scandal of the pornographic photos that had ended her publishing contract. 'That was a difficult time,' Edel said simply.

With a nod, he dropped her hand and led the way to his office. 'Have a seat,' he said, taking his own behind the desk.

Edel sat on the edge of the chair. Now that she was there, she wasn't sure what to say. It seemed the best thing to come straight out with it. 'For the last year, my life has been in a bit of a turmoil. I'm not willing to allow that to continue.' There, it was out. She raised her chin and looked at him. 'I don't know what he's up to, but Aidan Power was on my doorstep only a few hours ago. I want to know what he was doing there.'

'You never read my emails, did you?' Grady asked, folding his arms across his chest, and tilting his head slightly.

'There didn't seem much point. You wanted me to change my name in order to get another publishing contract and that was never going to happen. As it happens, I've self-published, so I don't need a publisher, or, for that matter, you.' She knew she sounded rude and didn't care.

'And how's that going for you?'

She wanted to lie, to say she'd sold hundreds, thousands even, but she couldn't bring herself to. Anyway, it would have been an easy lie for him to have discovered. A quick glance on Amazon would have told him how terrible her ranking was, and a terrible ranking equalled terrible sales. 'It's early days,' she said.

'That bad?' His voice was sympathetic. 'It's a shame, it was a good story. Have you started the next?'

Edel sighed. She rarely got the chance to speak about her writing. Mike was supportive but it was an alien world to him. 'My life has changed since I first wrote it so I've decided to switch direction.' A smile wavered on her lips. 'Actually, I've decided to try my hand at writing a crime series.'

'Well, well! As it happens, I'm writing one myself. I had a great experience when I was taken into Foxrock station.'

Mike had told Edel how delighted Grady had been to have been brought to Foxrock station for questioning. It had, he'd said, added veracity to his writing. 'I suppose your friend, Aidan will be able to put a word in with FinalEdit Publishing.' She heard the bitter twist to her words and shook her head. 'Anyway, I'm not here to discuss my writing career, that's no longer any of your business–'

'Actually, it is.' Grady held a hand up to stop her. 'You signed a contract, remember. I still represent you.'

Edel sat with her mouth slightly open.

Grady leaned forward. 'Listen, I know you went through a rough time, but you obviously haven't read any of the emails I sent you. If you had, you'd know two things... why I am still interested in representing you, and what Aide was doing on your doorstep.'

12

West drove into the car park of the apartment block where their victim had lived and saw Andrews standing by his car, leaning on the open door. Pulling into a designated visitor's parking space alongside, he climbed out and stretched. 'I wasn't sure I was going to make it on time.'

Andrews straightened and shut his car door. 'How did it go?'

'As we'd suspected. The Moores were burgled ten years ago. Mrs Moore hadn't had any reason to look for his birth certificate since and hadn't been aware it was missing. No doubt, whoever our vic is, he took it and enough additional paperwork to enable him to steal Ian Moore's identity.'

Andrews frowned. 'He had to have targeted that house in particular. Maybe someone their son knew?'

Exactly what West had been thinking on his drive over. 'It's a possibility. He'd finished university shortly before: perhaps it was someone he'd met there. We'll pull up the paperwork on the burglary when we get back to the station, see if anything leaps out.'

They were leaning against West's car mulling over the case

when a bright yellow sports car pulled in at ten minutes past the hour.

A dark-haired, attractive woman jumped out, extending a hand as she hurried to their side. 'Laura Bonini, so sorry for being late,' she said with a charming smile that elicited a similar response from both men.

It was an effective tool and West guessed she used it a lot. 'You're the landlord?'

Her smile grew. 'I prefer the term *property manager* but according to the Property Register Association, yes, I'm the land-lord.' She lifted a hand as if to bat away a fly. 'I don't let these outdated notions worry me.'

West had seen the steely look in the woman's eyes despite her friendly smile. She was a woman who used every trick in the trade. He'd met her type before. Fiona Wilson immediately popped into his head, making his mouth twist in distaste.

Andrews was frowning. 'Your secretary referred to you as *he*.'

'People make assumptions based on sex, I try to invalidate them,' Bonini said, pulling a large bunch of keys from her shoulder bag.

Andrews wasn't impressed, the frown staying in place as he shot West a glance.

West shrugged. She was a slippery customer, but so far, not a criminal.

The apartment block was old. Despite freshly-painted doors and windows, it looked defeated and tired. Inside the front door, a bicycle with punctured tyres propped against one wall drew a *tut-tut* from Bonini, but it was obvious her heart wasn't in it. 'They're told time and time again that they're not allowed to keep stuff here,' she complained, 'I may as well be talking to the wall.' She jangled the keys in her hand. 'It's on the second floor.'

When they got to apartment six, she removed a labelled key from the bunch, slid it into the lock and pushed the door open.

'I'll wait in the car,' she said, standing back. 'I have some calls to make, so take your time.'

'Before you go,' West said, stopping her, 'Were you aware your tenant was recently in prison?'

Bonini looked at him with the same disarming smile. 'What's that expression they used to use in the US army? *Don't ask, don't tell?* As long as the rent is paid, and the tenants obey the simple rules we have, what they do is their concern.'

'And Ian Moore always paid on time?'

'Sure, even while he was in prison. Eight months, direct debit. Never an issue.'

'And you never had any indication he wasn't who he appeared to be?'

Bonini shook her head. 'He gave a reference from his job and one from his previous address. Both were adequate so I had no reason to refuse him.'

'His previous address: can you let us have that? And the address of the person who gave the reference.'

'Of course. I'll look that up and give them to you before you leave.' Her phone chirped. 'Okay, I have to take this,' she said, her brow furrowing. She walked off without another word.

'Pay your rent, we don't care what you do,' Andrews said derisively, turning to peer through the door into the apartment.

West was more pragmatic. 'It's a business. She wasn't his mother.'

The apartment was small. A single bedroom, tiny combined lounge and kitchen and a bathroom. There was little storage: a small built-in wardrobe in the bedroom and two compact cupboards in the kitchen. The tenant had improvised; two suitcases under the bed held extra clothes, a rack in the bathroom stored towels. A small sofa sat about two feet from an over-large TV screen mounted on the wall. Everything was designed to make the maximum use of minimal space.

It was under the sofa that West found what they'd been hoping for. A slim attaché case filled with paperwork. 'Eureka,' he said, pulling it out. Inside, he saw it was crammed with a mishmash of papers. 'We'll take it with us,' he said, zipping it shut.

Andrews shut a kitchen cupboard. 'Nothing else here.'

'Let's go.' West took the apartment key from his pocket and locked the door after them. 'This place has seen better days,' he said, noting the worn carpets in the common areas, the overall air of neglect.

'I'd say Ms Smiley-Face only does enough to stop the tenants complaining and nothing more.'

'Cynical but probably correct,' West agreed.

Outside, Bonini was leaning against her car, her phone pressed to her ear. She raised her head at the sound of their approach and by the time they'd reached her she'd finished her call. 'Got what you were looking for?'

West lifted the attaché case. 'We might be lucky. Did you manage to get that address for us?'

'Of course.' This time her smile was only for him. She took a slip of paper from her bag and held it out.

'Thank you.' West's eyes flicked over the address. He folded it and put it in his pocket.

'A pleasure.' She looked towards the apartment block. 'So, what's the story? Can I remove all his stuff?'

Andrews coughed, drawing her attention to him. 'I assume rent is paid to the end of the month.'

Her smile faded a little and her eyes narrowed. 'That's correct.'

'Hopefully by then,' Andrews said in a voice that clearly stated *don't hold your breath*, 'we'll have managed to contact a next of kin. I'm sure they would like to pack his belongings themselves.'

Deciding it would be a good idea to leave, West handed her back the key, thanked her again for her time and crossed the car park to his car.

'Thinks she's the bee's knees, that one,' Andrews said scathingly.

West threw the case onto the passenger seat and straightened to look at him. 'It's a tough business being a property manager. It looks to me as if she's learned how to handle it.'

'Remember the last woman who was making sheep's eyes at you, and how that ended.' Always liking to have the last word, Andrews climbed into his car and seconds later was pulling out of the car park.

As Bonini had already reminded West of Fiona Wilson, he hadn't needed Andrews' dig. It would be a long time before he would be able to forget the woman who had almost destroyed his relationship with Edel. He felt in his inside pocket for his mobile and pressed the speed-dial key for her, wanting suddenly to hear her voice.

'Hi,' he said when it was answered. 'I might be a bit late. Would you like to go out for something to eat when I get home?'

'No, I've it all organised. I'm doing your favourite.'

There was a moment's panic as West tried to remember what that was. He was about to say lasagne, but there was an air of excitement in her voice that didn't seem to sit with a minced meat and pasta dish. He decided to temporise. 'Excellent, I'll be looking forward to it.'

He hung up and tapped the phone against his chin. Things had been good between them recently but, despite what she'd told him, he knew sales of her book weren't going well. He wondered what had happened to improve her mood. After what was proving to be a long, difficult day, he hoped that whatever she had to tell him was going to be something he could respond to with a simple nod and smile.

Andrews was already sitting at his desk by the time West got back to the station, the rest of the team standing beside the percolator, sipping the coffee that by this time of the day had taken on a greyish tinge.

'Right,' he said, dropping the attaché case on Andrews' desk before turning to look at them. 'It's getting late. Tell me we've got something so that I can send Morrison home happy.'

Seamus Baxter propped his hip on a corner of a desk. 'I've been looking into anything I can find on our four priests. Jeffreys, Maher and Dillon have been in the parish for several years. There's nothing out of the usual with any of them. McComb has been more difficult.'

West raised an eyebrow. The Catholic Church had been wracked with scandal, allegations of cover-ups over child abuse claims. He hoped they weren't going down that road: child abuse was a harrowing crime to investigate.

Baxter ran a hand through his ginger hair causing it to stand up in spikes. 'McComb has only been in the parish for a few months. Before that he was in Clontarf for six months, before that in Donabate for a little over a year, and before that in Rathmines for eight months.' He looked up from the sheet of paper he was holding. 'I could go on. Bottom line is, he never stays long in any one place.'

Did it have something to do with the murder in the church? Or was it one of those annoying details that needed to be followed up but went nowhere. Until they looked into it, they couldn't be sure. 'Okay, leave that with me, I'll have another word with Father Jeffreys. As the parish priest, he's bound to know McComb's story. It might be nothing to do with what happened.' He looked to where Sam Jarvis and Declan Foley were standing. He could tell by their expressions they'd nothing to add.

'You spoke to Miss Summers?'

It was Foley who answered. 'We were in luck, she was on a half-day from her job in the library. She wasn't too pleased to see us, said she was trying to put it all behind her.'

'When we told her that Ian Moore had been killed, she didn't look surprised, in fact, she looked a bit odd. I thought we were onto something,' Jarvis chimed in.

Foley took over with, 'She said she was sorry he was dead–'

'And she looked genuinely sorry–' Jarvis said.

'But it turns out her sorrow was only because she dreamed about killing him herself and now she'd never be able to,' Foley finished.

West held up his hand. 'Please, one of you tell me the rest and save the double-act for another day.'

Jarvis grinned. 'There's not much else to say. Her parents live in Portugal. She's an only child. She swears there's no boyfriend on the scene.'

'She was quite bitter when she said the last,' Foley added.

West wasn't surprised. Moore had had an eight-month prison sentence, hers, as always was the way, was a lifetime one. 'Tell me you learned something in Mountjoy,' he said to Andrews, anticipating his headshake. Had there been something to tell him, Andrews wouldn't have been able to keep it quiet till then.

'Moore was a model prisoner, kept to himself, didn't get involved with anything or anyone. The administrator wasn't sure if he'd been in contact with the prison chaplain. I left a message for him to contact me when he gets back from the retreat he's on.' He lifted some of the papers from the pile he'd pulled from the attaché case. 'I don't think we're going to find much of interest here either. Seems to be every utility bill he's ever had. Apart from this.' He handed a sheet of paper to West.

West read it with a frown that quickly cleared. 'Ian Moore's birth certificate. Mrs Moore will be pleased.' He looked up at his team. 'Inspector Morrison won't be though. Okay, first thing in the morning, Baxter and Edwards, you two head out to our vic's place of work. I want everyone he worked with spoken to. I'm surprised they kept his job for him while he was in prison, find out why. Question his employer, workmates, customers if necessary. I want to know who this guy is. Someone has to know something.' He reached into his pocket for the address the landlord had given him and handed it to Jarvis.

'You and Allen look into this reference he gave the landlord eight years ago. Our vic didn't simply wake up one morning and decide to change his name.' He waited for their nod before turning to Foley who was standing to one side with a hopeful expression. 'Unless something dramatic happens in robbery, stay here and do a search on the real Ian Moore and see what you can find on him.'

He pointed towards The Wall. 'Tomorrow, I want that filled with information. Now, go home, you don't want to hear Inspector Morrison's screams of frustration.'

Grinning, the team headed off, leaving West and Andrews standing staring at the photo of their victim. 'A strange one,' West murmured.

'Another strange one,' Andrews said. 'You always say you like complicated cases: seems like you've gone and got another one.' He perched on the side of a desk. 'You want me to go to the post-mortem with you in the morning?'

West shook his head. 'There's no need. I'll be back by mid-morning. I'll leave you here to protect Mother in case any of the clergy call around.'

13

West had been joking but a short conversation moments later with Inspector Morrison told him that his or Andrews' presence in the station was going to be necessary while this case was ongoing.

'I don't want to be bothered with their sanctimonious clap-trap,' the inspector said. 'Especially since I've nothing to tell them.'

Since this was a dig at their lack of progress in the case, West bit back a groan. Sometimes, it suited Morrison to forget he'd worked his way up the ranks.

'I'm heading to the post-mortem in the morning, but Andrews will be here. He has a close relationship with the church.' The last was an exaggeration but he didn't want Morrison to insist that he stay in the station while Andrews went to the post. He'd not left a much more lucrative job as a solicitor to sit behind a desk doing paperwork, not even to make Morrison happy. He kept his expression carefully neutral as the inspector's hairy eyebrows met in a frown as if trying to decide if wool was being pulled over his eyes.

Finally, the brows parted and he nodded slightly. 'Fine, get some damn answers so we can get this case closed. As soon as, okay?'

Yes, West would work miracles and conjure information out of nowhere. He swallowed his irritation, assured the inspector he'd do his best to have the case sorted as early as possible and left the office.

Back in the main office, West wasn't surprised that Andrews had gone. He gave The Wall a final glance before nodding a greeting to the late shift and heading for home.

Outside his house, a sense of contentment sneaked over him and pushed away the stresses of the day. His life was good, probably better than it had ever been. Andrews wasn't the first to have dropped hints about marriage; his mother had been making pointed remarks, his sister, always less subtle, asked him what he was waiting for.

He'd brushed her off with a careless laugh but he knew what his answer was – he was waiting for a period of peace and stability. Ever since he and Edel had met it had been one catastrophe after the other; kidnapping, murder attempts, poisoning. They'd survived it all; it had probably made them stronger. But the mundanity of living together, day after day, the sameness of it all, could they survive that? He had to be sure before taking the next step. Overly cautious, perhaps, but it was the way he was.

A smell of food drifted towards him when he opened the front door. His stomach growled in response, reminding him that he'd once again missed lunch. 'Hi,' he said, pushing open the kitchen door, smiling to see Edel's intense concentration on whatever it was she was stirring so rapidly.

'Sauce,' she said, lifting a wooden spoon. 'If I stop for even a second it will end up lumpy.'

West kissed her lightly on the cheek. 'Can I do anything to help?'

'You can open the wine,' Edel said, tilting her chin to where a bottle of red stood on the counter.

West picked it up, an eyebrow rising when he saw what it was. 'Very nice.' Edel seemed brighter, more animated than she'd been in a while. He didn't have to be a detective to know she was bubbling with news. 'You sounded excited on the phone. Are we celebrating something?'

'Wait till we're sitting down,' she said, removing the pot from the hob and pouring the sauce into a jug. 'It's all ready. Sit.'

Doing as he was told, he sat at the table and opened the wine. 'Very nice,' he said when a plate was put in front of him. Fillet steak. So that was his favourite!

'And pepper sauce.' Edel placed the jug within reach and took her seat.

Edel considered how she would tell her tale. It seemed better to skip her fear at seeing the man on her doorstep and cut to the good news. 'Remember I said I'd been getting emails from Owen Grady but hadn't bothered to answer?' She waited for the nod before continuing. 'I decided to visit him today. A spur-of-the-moment decision. I wanted to put that part of my life behind me.'

She saw his expression flicker a little. He was probably thinking that she'd had to do that so many times. That her life was a series of catastrophes that any sane woman would want to forget. But instead of commenting, he cut into his steak, jabbed a fork into the meat and held it there, waiting for her to continue.

She shook off the twinge of irritation. It was probably the same way he dealt with criminals he was interviewing... giving them space to hang themselves. 'It seems,' she explained, 'that I'm still under contract. Owen wants to remain as my agent.'

That did bring a reaction. 'Really? I thought he wasn't interested since you wouldn't publish under a pseudonym.'

'He's not a well-regarded agent for nothing.' Edel poured a tiny puddle of sauce onto the corner of her plate. 'He had an idea. That's why he's been emailing me but because I'd never read them, I wasn't aware of what he was doing.'

'Which was?'

'He'd spoken to my publisher, Hugh Todd and the managing director of Books Inc–'

'Elliot Mannion?'

'Yes, I forgot you'd met him. Anyway, Owen went to them both with a proposition. They gave it some consideration and decided it would work.' She cut a piece of her fillet and pushed it through the sauce before putting it into her mouth, chewing slowly. The idea was so simple, she was surprised she hadn't come up with it herself. She'd promised to keep using the name Johnson in memory of the man who lost his life because of her late husband. Now it seemed she'd be able to keep that promise and still have a career as a writer. 'It's easy really,' she said with a smile. 'Owen suggested I use the initials of my first and middle name. E.M. Johnson.' Her smile grew wider. 'It will work even better, actually, since I've decided I'm finished with writing family sagas. I want to write a crime series.'

His horrified reaction was what she'd expected. 'I thought you didn't want to write crime, that you wanted to escape from the reality of it all.'

It was almost exactly what she'd said. Edel speared a piece of carrot, swirled it around the sauce and popped it into her mouth. 'That was after that awful experience with Adam Fletcher but since then...' She placed her cutlery carefully on the plate and pushed it away. 'I've nearly been killed twice and met some terribly dangerous and some extraordinary people. It's made me think about the secrets they hide and the crimes they commit.' She tilted her head to look at him. 'Perhaps I see now why you love being a detective – you solve a puzzle. But I can go one better, Mike, I can make up the crimes, then solve them.'

She reached a hand out and laid it on his arm. 'You're worrying that you won't be able to talk about your work when you come home, that I might use it in my books. I won't, Mike, I promise. I have enough of an imagination to be able to make up my stories.'

Doubt coloured his eyes, making them hard. The cheerful, celebratory atmosphere was going to be ruined if she didn't lighten the mood.

'Oh, I almost forgot,' she said, squeezing his arm. 'There was something else Owen wanted to tell me. He and Aidan, they're getting married.' That's why Aidan had been on their doorstep. He'd wanted to come around to deliver the invitation in person and to beg forgiveness for his jealousy.

She smiled at West. 'They want us to come to the wedding.'

14

———

Next morning, West negotiated the roads to Connolly Memorial Hospital for the 8am post-mortem, amused at his quick change of heart after hearing Edel's news. He had been worried how they'd manage when their life became mundane and conventional. He should have guessed: it never would.

It was a little before eight when he turned into the hospital car park. He put Edel firmly to the back of his mind, paid the extortionate car-parking charge and hurried to the far side of the extensive hospital grounds where the morgue was situated in a low-lying building that so far had managed to escape the renovation that had gone on all around it.

Five minutes later, on the dot of eight, he was sitting in the viewing area of the post-mortem room. It was the first of the day, and on time as a result.

West had no sooner sat than Dr Niall Kennedy pushed through the double doors, easily recognisable despite the mask and eye shield. For a small man, he had a powerful presence. He looked up to the viewing area and lifted a hand in greeting. 'Morning,' he said, his voice coming loud and clear through the

85

speaker beside West's head. Too loud and clear. West shuffled up a few seats.

There was no hanging about: Kennedy started work as soon as the body was wheeled in and positioned on the table.

Twenty minutes later, West was drumming his finger on the arm of the chair. So far, he'd not learned anything that was going to help their investigation. The victim, whoever he was, had been in the best of health. Didn't smoke. There were no needle marks to suggest he had a serious drug habit. He wasn't overweight, not malnourished.

'He should still be alive,' Kennedy said.

Since at this stage, the pathologist was in the middle of removing the victim's lungs, West had to bite back the retort that it was as well he wasn't. He took a breath and let it out slowly. Something killed the man: he needed to know what.

The lungs were weighed and put to one side. West leaned forward as Kennedy examined the puncture wound, using tweezers to remove something.

After a few minutes examining the wound, he straightened. 'The wound is approximately 100 millimetres deep, the original puncture to the skin approximately three millimetres in width. I've found microscopic particles of red cellulose acetate on the skin.' He looked up to where West sat. 'I can't be one hundred per cent certain but I'd be fairly sure we're looking at a screwdriver. It was rammed in, to the end of the shaft, the handle leaving that microscopic residue on the skin.'

A screwdriver. 'The residue: could it be matched to a specific screwdriver?' He'd take anything at this stage.

Kennedy shook his head. 'You know how I hate to disappoint but it's likely to be a common or garden type, I'm afraid. Most handles of that kind of tool are made from the same cellulose acetate. However–' he shrugged '–if you find a likely screwdriver, there might be microscopic particles of blood to be found where the shaft fits into the handle.'

West groaned. A screwdriver. Probably one of the most common tools there was. Even he had one, and he wasn't into DIY.

'The puncture wound didn't kill him though,' Kennedy was saying. 'He was dead before this insult was offered.'

'So, what did kill him?' West couldn't hide the frustration in his voice.

'I've sent off blood, skin and hair samples to toxicology, plus fragments of cotton from the skin around his mouth.'

'From around his mouth? A gag or something?'

'Not something used to keep him quiet, no, that's not what I meant.' Kennedy rested his gloved hands on the table as he explained. 'Sergeant Maddison informed me they found a substance on the mesh that separates the priest's and penitent's confessional.'

'Toxicology will show up whatever it is, won't they?'

'Yes, it should do. There are a couple of things that might have been used,' Kennedy said. 'I'd guess gamma-Butyrolactone, or GBL. At high doses, it causes rapid death. It's a colourless fluid, widely used as an industrial solvent. Unfortunately, it's hydrolysed to gamma-Hydroxybutyric acid and will be completely gone from the body after two or three hours.'

'That's GHB, isn't it,' West asked. The classic date-rape drug. 'It won't show up in a tox screen.'

'That's correct, it's undetectable after two, three hours max. But generally, it's used to subdue and manipulate, not kill. If I had to give an opinion based on what we know so far, I'd say the GBL was mixed with something and sprayed into our victim's face in sufficient quantities to render him unconscious within a few seconds. From the fibres around his mouth, it looks as though the perpetrator then applied a pad soaked in the drug over his mouth and nose ensuring inspiration of a high enough concentration to be lethal. Death would have been almost instantaneous.'

West frowned in thought. 'The perpetrator would have needed to take precautions.'

Kennedy looked up at him, head tilted in thought. 'A good mask and a quick retreat from the vicinity would have been sufficient. But I would have expected a tall man like this to have made rather a clatter when he fell.'

'The penitent's box is small. If he were there intending to make a confession, he'd have been on his knees, there wouldn't have been much space to fall anywhere.' But West would have to check with the church, see if the sacristan heard anything, check if there were any other people in the church after mass was over. Churches were quiet places, someone must have heard something. He'd keep pulling at all the strings in the hope that one of them would untangle the case.

With a wave and a muttered *thank you* to Kennedy, West took his leave. An hour later he was turning into the car park in front of Foxrock station.

15

Detective Garda Seamus Baxter had arranged to pick up Detective Garda Mark Edwards first thing that morning and go directly to the garage where their victim had worked both before and after his arrest for rape.

Baxter had recently moved to Gorey with his girlfriend, Tanya, and was still adjusting to the longer drive in the morning. One of those people who hated to be late, he tended to arrive too early as a result and pulled up outside Edwards' Clonskeagh home fifteen minutes before the agreed eight o'clock pickup. Switching off the engine, he climbed out. It never crossed his mind he wouldn't be welcome at such an early time and he pressed the doorbell whistling off-tune.

The plump, pretty woman who opened the door didn't seem surprised to see him. 'Morning, Seamus,' she said, standing back to allow him in.

'Morning, Mrs Edwards. Sorry, I'm a bit early.'

'You always are,' she said, her voice resigned rather than annoyed. 'When Mark said who was picking him up, I guessed you'd be here way before you said, so I have coffee made if you fancy a cup.'

Baxter, who had left home without breakfast, accepted happily and was munching a slice of toast and drinking coffee when Edwards came through to the kitchen ten minutes later.

'Is that my toast you're eating,' he said by way of greeting to Baxter.

'There's plenty made,' his mother said, pouring him coffee. 'Sit and have your breakfast.'

Edwards finished knotting his tie and sat. 'You know where this garage is?' He slathered butter onto the hot toast, took a bite and wiped melted butter from his chin with his hand.

'I used to live in Raheny,' Baxter said, putting his empty mug down and standing, impatient to be on the way. 'I know the northside pretty well. We'd best be off: the traffic will be a nightmare.'

With a couple of gulps, Edwards finished the last of his coffee. 'Okay, let's go then,' he said, turning to give his mother a kiss on the cheek. 'Thanks, Mum, someday the Garda Síochána will pay you for feeding their waifs and strays.'

'Ha, I wouldn't hold your breath, Mrs Edwards,' Baxter said, kissing her other cheek. 'Thanks, it was what I needed. Mark here doesn't realise how lucky he is.'

'Lucky!' Edwards said, climbing into the passenger seat and fastening his seat belt. 'I need to move out before they drive me nuts.'

Baxter indicated and pulled into the line of traffic. 'Why don't you rent somewhere?'

'Have you seen the rents they're charging for even the pokiest flats?'

Baxter had been lucky. He'd used a small inheritance to buy his apartment in Rathmines at a time when they were relatively cheap and had sold it several years later for a good price. He and Tanya had discussed the option of getting a big mortgage and buying close to the city or moving further out and having money to spare. They were still trying to decide when Tanya saw a vacancy advertised for a ward nurse in the hospital in Loughlin-stown. When she got it, it made their choice easier, looking first in Arklow, then finding the perfect house a bit further in the booming town of Gorey. Less than an hour's drive for her and slightly more for him.

'A guard's salary doesn't get you far in Dublin,' Edwards complained.

Baxter raised an eyebrow but said nothing. There was no point at all in stating the blinding obvious that if Edwards spent less on holidays, it would be easier to save for a deposit.

'This is an odd case,' Baxter said, deciding it was better to focus on their investigation rather than the state of Dublin's inflated housing and rental market. 'It would be nice if we could get some concrete information.'

The conversation stayed, to Baxter's relief, on the case for the rest of the stop-and-start journey through Dublin's crazy rush-hour traffic.

It was after nine before they pulled up in the visitor's car park of Tedford Motors, a large, sprawling, new and second-hand car dealership.

'That's not a bad price for a service,' Edwards said, nodding towards a large sign.

'You get what you pay for,' Baxter said. 'Looks dodgy low to me.'

The two men approached the service office just as an over-weight man wearing a T-shirt stretched over a grossly rotund belly pulled the door open and came out, ignoring them as he passed.

Inside the office, a middle-aged woman with a head of spiky purple hair stood behind a waist-high counter. She was flicking the pages of a diary backwards and forwards, a frown between her eyes and didn't look up as Baxter and Edwards stepped up to the counter.

Baxter slid his identification across the top, the blue and gold of the Garda Síochána emblem catching the light.

She looked up then, her eyes sharp. 'As if my day wasn't bad enough.' A long sigh. 'What can I do for you?'

'We'd like to see Ronan Tedford, please.'

'You did,' she said with a jerk of her head to the exit. 'That was him. His office is at the back. Off you go.' Dismissing them, she started flicking through the pages of the diary again, looking up impatiently when they didn't move away.

'We're here about Ian Moore,' Baxter said.

'We heard,' the woman said.

'From who?' Edwards asked. Since they hadn't been able to find a next of kin, his name hadn't been released to the press.

'His landlord, some snooty-voiced woman called Laura something or other. She wanted to know if we knew a next of kin to clear his stuff out.'

'And do you?'

She shook her head.

'But you did know Ian Moore?' He'd worked in the garage for over eight years; Baxter would have expected to see some sadness at his passing, but if the purple-haired woman were grieving, it wasn't obvious.

She shrugged a beefy shoulder. 'As much as I know any of the mechanics. I keep myself to myself. They come in when they need to. Otherwise they keep to themselves and don't bother me.'

'A friendly place,' Edwards commented as they left and followed her directions to the office building at the back. They couldn't miss it. A flat-roofed, ugly building, with two small windows and a brown metal door with the word PRIVATE painted large across it in white paint. Baxter's knock rattled the door but did little else. With a sigh of frustration, Edwards hammered on it with his fist, the sound echoing around the area and resulting in the unlocking and opening of the door.

'What the f–' the rotund man they'd passed earlier started to say, biting the end off the last word, his eyes narrowing. 'Guards?' At their nod, he stood back and let them in.

Inside, in contrast to the shabby exterior, the office was remarkably comfortable. A large wooden desk almost filled one corner. Behind it, the office chair Tedford had been occupying, was swinging softly. He collapsed back onto it, waving a hand to the two chairs on the far side. 'Sit. I assume this has to do with Ian Moore.' He reached a hand up and rubbed the back of his head roughly, the movement stretching the T-shirt over his extended abdomen.

Unlike the purple-haired woman, the garage owner did seem affected by Moore's death. He took a surprisingly white handkerchief from his trouser pocket and wiped it over his face, rubbing his eyes and blowing his nose before looking across the desk to the two men. 'Terrible, terrible,' he said, putting the handkerchief away. 'When his landlord rang to tell us, I was stunned, stunned.' He fished out the handkerchief again and rubbed it over his eyes. 'Whatever I can do to help.'

'Can you tell us about him?' Baxter asked, taking out his notebook.

'Where do I start? He was a good lad, hard-working, a good timekeeper, conscientious, friendly. Customers liked him. The other mechanics liked him.'

'The lady in reception didn't seem particularly keen,' Edwards said.

'Shirley hates everyone,' Tedford said dismissively. 'Ian Moore was one of the best mechanics we've had.'

He was making Moore out to be a saint. Baxter tapped his notebook. 'You know about his prison sentence?'

Tedford's expression changed, his mouth twisting in a grimace as if he'd eaten something rancid. 'A miscarriage of justice, that was.'

'He was tried and convicted of rape.'

'It was nonsense. Nonsense, I'm telling you.' Tedford rocked back and forth in his chair. 'Listen, I saw that Summers one, flaunting herself.'

Expecting to hear a misogynistic *she got what she deserved*, Baxter was taken aback when Tedford's eyes welled. 'Ian was besotted with her, she'd stroll by twice almost every day, slowing down as she passed the garage, wiggling her ass for effect. I saw her do it myself.' He pushed the chair along the desk until it was in front of the computer screen and turned it towards the Gardaí. 'There are CCTVs outside.' He clicked a few keys on the keyboard and the screen suddenly showed four windows simultaneously.

'The top left is the street outside to the left of the forecourt and the one on the top right is the street to the right. I noticed her almost from the beginning, three months before her alleged rape. She'd be walking briskly, then slow down as she passed by the forecourt, tossing her hair, wiggling her backside, staring into the garage trying to catch the lads' attention.'

'Moore in particular?' Edwards asked.

'Not at first, but one day he was out talking to a customer who left as she was walking by, and he said hello to her. That was it. They chatted for a bit, then she left. Over the next few weeks, I noticed he'd make any excuse to be outside at the time she walked by. The other mechanics started to tease him about it. I heard them telling him to ask her out, but he never did. He was a shy lad, you know, not like the others always spouting off about their latest bird. In fact, I never, in all the years he'd worked here, heard him talk about a girlfriend.'

'But he did ask her out eventually,' Baxter said.

Tedford shook his head, the chair squeaking loudly with each movement. 'I think she did the asking, about a month after he first said hello to her. I was in the garage that Saturday afternoon, I heard the lads teasing him. He looked slightly stunned to be honest, as if all his Christmases had come together. Then on the Monday we heard he'd been arrested.'

'It must have come as a shock to hear he'd been arrested for rape.'

'I didn't believe it then, I don't believe it now. She said they'd been drinking and he wouldn't stop when she asked him to.' He leaned over the desk as far as his distended abdomen allowed and looked from Baxter to Edwards. 'In all the years he worked here, the only complaint the other mechanics made about Ian was that he wouldn't have a drink. Ever.' He sat back. 'So, answer me this, why would he suddenly start when he was out with a bird he'd been dreaming of for weeks?'

'Maybe he needed some Dutch courage,' Baxter said.

'He insisted he was drinking soft drinks all night, but she said he was drunk and pushing drinks on her. The jury believed her.' Tedford shook his head. 'She's a little bit of a thing, maybe only four ten and slight with it, has one of those irritating little girl voices and she speaks in a breathy whisper. Ian is... was... six feet tall and brawny. I could see why the jury was swayed by her.' A long sigh hissed between his teeth. 'Hell, I almost believed her myself.'

'But only almost,' Baxter murmured. 'You allowed him to keep his job.'

The answer was an abrupt, 'Yes.'

'He'd been with you over eight years so he'd have been what? Eighteen when he started?'

'About that. He'd finished school and wanted to work in a garage. Came around every day for weeks, hanging around the garage, lending a hand when he was let. Eventually, I caved in and offered him a couple of hours work. It didn't take me long to see that the lad had a natural inclination so I encouraged him to take it seriously and offered him an apprenticeship here. He took to it like a duck to water and got his National Craft Certificate in four years without any problem. I thought he might leave us then, you know, get a bit more experience elsewhere, but he stayed and I was glad to keep him. He was a good lad.' The regret in his voice was genuine.

'And there was no problem getting him sorted with tax?'

Tedford frowned. 'Why would there be? What are you getting at?'

Unsure of how much to tell him, Baxter waited a moment. 'Okay, it's going to come out eventually but we'd appreciate if you'd keep what I'm about to tell you to yourself for the moment.'

'I can keep my mouth shut when it's necessary.'

'Ian Moore isn't who he said he was.'

Tedford gave a short laugh, then shook his head in disbelief. 'What're you saying?'

'The real Ian Moore, the man who owns the PPS number your mechanic was using, lives in Dubai.'

'That's impossible!' Tedford glared at him. 'I remember distinctly because I was surprised it was his first job. Most of the youngsters we get applying for apprentices have worked summer or weekend jobs over the years.'

'But you didn't question it.'

'What was to question? He gave me all the paperwork I required to set up his taxes.'

'The real Ian Moore lived in Dun Laoghaire; what address did your lad give?' Edwards asked.

Tedford pulled the screen around and his sausage-like fingers sped across the keys. 'When Ian started, our personnel files were paper but I had them all computerised a couple of years ago.' He pursed his lips as he worked, then let his breath out in a puff. 'Okay, yes, he gave Patrick Street in Dun Laoghaire as his parents' address but he was living in an apartment in Booterstown. He was there the whole time he worked for me, got the DART here every morning.'

'He didn't have a car?'

'No, never did. If he needed to go anywhere, he'd borrow one from here.'

'What about references?'

Tedford peered at the computer but Baxter saw it as the ploy it was and wasn't surprised when the man shook his head. 'Looks like they forgot to update the files with that info,' he said. 'Probably didn't think it was worth worrying about after all this time.'

'Are you sure you got any?'

'Maybe not, I can't remember. He was coming to do an apprenticeship. What did I need references for? I'm a good judge of character: that's a good enough reference as far as I'm concerned.'

They spent a few more minutes talking but there was nothing else to learn from the garage owner so Baxter and Edwards asked to speak to the other mechanics.

'No problem,' Tedford said. 'You can speak to them in the staffroom behind the service office.'

An hour later, Baxter and Edwards were done and headed back to their car. They'd spoken to the three other full-time mechanics and knew nothing more about their victim than they had at the start of the day.

'I'm surprised our vic never moved nearer to here,' Edwards commented.

'Probably afraid to chance his arm with more paperwork. Not everyone is as trusting as our kindly garage owner.'

Edwards turned to look at him. 'You think there's something fishy about him?'

'I don't know. Second-hand car dealerships aren't renowned for their trustworthiness, are they, and yet Tedford took our vic on without as much as checking a reference.'

'Seemed fond of the lad.'

Baxter started the engine. 'Yes, but why? Because he was a genuinely nice guy? And in that case why was he arrested, charged and prosecuted for rape? Or because he was an obliging lad and always did what he was told?'

'You're thinking something dodgy like car clocking?'

Changing the odometers on second-hand cars was one of the more common illegal practices in second-hand car dealerships. 'Something like that.' Baxter pulled into traffic and headed down Philipsburgh Avenue to Fairview Strand. Instead of indicating right, he indicated to change to the left lane and turned onto Fairview Strand, heading for Marino.

'Where we going?'

'Something I want to check,' Baxter said. A minute later, he waved a hand towards the building on the left. 'That's Marino Library where Laetitia Summers works – or worked at the time of her rape anyway.'

'Yes.' Edwards looked towards the building and back to Baxter with a frown. 'So?'

'She lives on the Marino end of Griffith Avenue, doesn't she? So why would she walk past the garage to get home? That's well out of her way when she could either go straight ahead and join the end of Griffith Avenue further up or – and this would be much faster – go via Marino Park Avenue.'

'You thinking she went past the garage deliberately?'

'I don't know, but it seems a bit odd. And I don't like odd.'

'Might be worthwhile talking to the investigating officer,' Edwards said.

'My thoughts exactly. Clontarf Garda Station isn't far. Let's go and see what we can find out.'

16

———

Two minutes later Baxter indicated to turn into Strandville Avenue, then into the car park in front of the attractive building that housed their Clontarf counterparts and squeezed into a space between two squad cars.

'Beats Foxrock station,' Edwards said, getting out and staring across to the sea. 'You're from around here: you never thought about coming back to the northside?'

Baxter shook his head. 'I moved from here when my parents died. Too many memories.' He shook them off and waved towards the front door. 'Let's see if we can find the investigating officer.'

They had to hang around for almost an hour waiting. They filled their time chatting to other detectives, comparing notes, crimes, exchanging gossip.

'There's your man,' one said, as a door opened behind them and both Edwards and Baxter turned at the same time to greet the detective who came through, his eyes searching the busy office, stopping when he saw them and nodding.

'Don Mitchell,' he said, extending a hand. 'I heard you were looking for me.'

'We're investigating a murder and it's crossing with a case you handled. We were hoping you could give us some information.'

'Sure, if I can, glad to help.' Mitchell checked his watch. 'We can use one of the interview rooms unless they're needed.'

The room he led them to was small and muggy. They sat on standard-issue chairs and leaned on the scarred and scratched table.

'Okay,' Mitchell said. 'Ask away.'

'We've been chatting to Ronan Tedford of Tedford Motors,' Baxter said. 'One of his mechanics, a lad who went by the name Ian Moore, was found dead early Monday morning.'

'The body in the church?' Mitchell frowned. 'I know him, of course. He's not out of prison that long. You said *went by the name of*?'

'He wasn't who he said he was. The real Ian Moore is working in Dubai. We've no idea who our victim is. Not yet anyway.' Baxter took out his mobile and brought up a photo of the crime scene. 'This is the murder scene. Someone was making a point, but we're not sure what it is.'

Mitchell stared at the photo, making it bigger and peering closer. 'Pretty gruesome.'

'Ronan Tedford seemed quite fond of the lad. He was convinced he was innocent of that rape charge, seemed to think it was all Laetitia Summers' doing.'

'Tedford gave Moore a good character reference at his trial.'

Baxter heard something in the man's voice, a tinge of regret perhaps. 'Did you think Moore was guilty?'

'Ours isn't to ascertain guilt or innocence, ours is to collect the evidence and present it in a professional manner to allow the director of public prosecution to do their job,' Mitchell said in a dull monotone. He sat back in his chair and looked at Baxter. 'False accusations of rape are rare and I've never come across one in all my years as a guard. In this case, whereas Moore was adamant that sex had been consensual; she was equally adamant it hadn't. In the courtroom, his size and build made him look guilty, in the same way as her tiny physique made her look innocent.' He sighed loudly. 'To answer your question... I don't honestly know.'

'Did she say why she walked along Philipsburgh Avenue to get home when it would have been much quicker to go another way?'

'For the exercise,' Mitchell said. 'She said she liked to walk at least twenty minutes after work.' He held a hand up. 'Before you ask, no, I didn't believe her. I think she went that way to ogle the mechanics in Tedford Motors. You may not know this but a little over a year ago, four of the mechanics, Moore included, did a charity calendar. It brought them some attention for a while. Too much, I think: they never did another.'

'Did you ask her about it?'

Mitchell sniffed. 'She looked at me with her big eyes and spoke in that irritating girly voice and said she'd never seen it, that it wasn't the kind of thing she'd have looked at. Almost as if I'd been suggesting she watched porn.' He lifted his hands and let them drop to the table with a clunk. 'She stuck to her story, never wavered even a little so maybe she was telling the truth.'

'Or she was a very good liar?'

'What did Moore say about it?' Edwards asked.

'It was all very odd, you know,' Mitchell said. 'According to Moore, he woke up in his flat the next morning and couldn't remember getting home. He insists he wasn't drinking. We tracked down the taxi he'd taken and the driver remembers him being so drunk that he didn't want to let him into the cab but it seems Moore climbed in and wouldn't get out so he decided to give in.'

'Tedford says he didn't drink. Did someone slip him something?'

'His defence argued that someone did, and even pointed a finger of blame at Laetitia but–' he shook his head '–it sounded like they were trying to come up with any reason to get Moore off and you could tell the jury didn't believe a word.'

'What motive would anyone, even Laetitia, have for slipping him something?' Baxter tapped his finger on the table. 'Unless it has something to do with who he really is?'

There was silence as all three men thought of this possibility.

'Someone set him up?' Mitchell frowned. 'Then she'd have to be in on it, wouldn't she?'

And if she were, maybe she knew who Moore really was. 'It looks as though we're going to have to look into Laetitia Summers a bit more,' Baxter said.

'Anything I can do to help, let me know,' Mitchell said, pushing back from the table. 'Let me know how it turns out: it's an interesting and challenging case.'

Back outside, Baxter stood leaning on the car looking out to sea. 'We need to speak to the Summers girl again, but I think we should go back to the station first and lay this out for West. It's getting a bit complicated and might get a bit sticky.'

Edwards agreed. Neither of the men minded *complicated*, but *sticky* involved the inspector and both were happy to let West deal with Mother Morrison.

17

Detective Garda Mick Allen was already in the station car park when Detective Garda Sam Jarvis pulled up at 8.45am. The two men had wildly different backgrounds, Allen growing up on his parents' farm in Tipperary, Jarvis the Black-rock College-educated son of a doctor who'd hoped he'd follow in his footsteps and who tried, without much success, not to look at his son as an oddity. But different as they were, Allen and Jarvis had quickly become friends and Jarvis was pleased to be working with him this morning rather than the intimidating Baxter or the too-smart-for-his-own-good Edwards.

'You want to drive?' Jarvis greeted Allen as he parked alongside.

'Don't mind either way.'

'Climb in then, no point in me getting out.'

Ian Moore's previous address was in Sallynoggin, only a few kilometres from Foxrock but traffic was heavy and it was twenty minutes later when they pulled up outside Casa Mia, an Italian restaurant above which Moore was supposed to have lived. The address of the referee was the restaurant itself.

To their surprise, Casa Mia was open. A chalk board sitting

at a precarious angle outside proclaimed that they sold the best coffee and croissants in the city.

'Might be easier to ask questions over a coffee,' Allen said, lifting his chin and sniffing the air.

The aroma of coffee was tantalising. Maybe it would be easier to ask about Moore with a coffee in hand.

Inside, the restaurant was like every Italian restaurant Jarvis had ever been in. Red-and-white-gingham tablecloths, Chianti bottles decorated with melted wax from the half-used candles sitting at drunken angles.

A door at the back of the restaurant opened and a small, dark-haired man hurried out, hands extended. '*Buongiorno, signore,*' he said. 'You want coffee, something to eat?'

Jarvis looked at Allen's hopeful expression and smiled. 'Coffee and croissants for both of us, please.'

'Cappuccino, Americano, latte?'

'Cappuccino for me,' Allen said quickly.

'And for me.'

'*Perfetto*, take a seat. It will be ready in a moment.'

It was, in fact, several minutes before he returned with two of the biggest croissants Jarvis had ever seen.

'Fresh from the oven,' the man said, putting a plate in front of each of them. He hurried away and returned with small pots of jam and butter. 'And now the coffee,' he said, and disappeared once more.

'Wow,' was all Allen said, pulling off a piece of his croissant and spreading jam on top before popping it into his mouth. 'Wow, these are amazing.'

Jarvis shook his head at the groans of pleasure coming from Allen and broke a piece off his own croissant. He had to admit, it was very good. As was the coffee when it arrived moments later.

By unspoken agreement, the men ate their croissants and drank their coffees before embarking on the reason they'd come.

'More coffee?'

Jarvis shook his head. 'No, thank you, although it's particularly good coffee. Actually,' he said, reaching for his identification and handing it over. 'We're here as part of an investigation into a man's death. I'm Detective Garda Jarvis and that's Detective Garda Allen.'

There was no change in the man's jovial expression, in fact his smile grew wider. 'I thought as much.' He went away and came back with two more coffees. 'On the house,' he said, pulling a chair from a nearby table and sitting down. 'I'm Luca Esposito.' He waved a hand around the room. 'I own this wonderful place. There's little that gets by me. I took you for policemen as soon as you come through the door.'

Jarvis smiled at the man's disarmingly friendly manner. They weren't always greeted that way. 'The man who died went by the name Ian Moore. We're trying to find out more about him, where he came from, whether he had family, anything really. Before he moved to Booterstown eight years ago, he lived in the apartment above this restaurant. He gave a man by the name of Giovanni Ricci as a reference.'

The name worked like a switch. Esposito's expression turned stern and closed. 'Him!'

Jarvis's eyes flicked to Allen. Maybe they were onto something here. He waited.

The restaurant owner shook his head sadly. 'Giovanni is my wife's nephew. Trouble from the day he arrived on a business class flight from *Roma*.'

Sensing that the man intended on releasing a catalogue of woes about the nephew, Jarvis guided him back to the information they needed. 'Why didn't Moore ask you for a reference?'

'Because he never lived in the apartment upstairs. Me and my wife, Mia, we've lived there since we bought this place nearly fifteen years ago.' He shrugged. 'Now and then we talk about moving but we both love the restaurant and it is good to be close.'

So Moore had lied.

'Does the name Ian Moore ring a bell?'

Esposito laughed. 'Names, pah, they go in one ear, shoot out the other.' He must have noticed Jarvis' crestfallen expression. 'But Giovanni, he is here, maybe he can tell you about this man and why he lied for him.'

Jarvis exchanged glances with Allen. Maybe they weren't going to go home empty-handed after all.

Giovanni Ricci answered his uncle's yell after a second louder one made the glasses on the shelf behind the counter rattle. He pushed through a door behind, a sullen tilt to his mouth, a hard look in his eyes.

'These men want to ask you some questions,' Esposito said, standing and kicking the leg of the chair so that it slid across the floor towards the approaching man. 'Sit and answer whatever Garda Jarvis and Garda Allen ask.'

Ricci's eyes sharpened and flicked from Jarvis to Allen, assessing.

Esposito smirked. 'Maybe you're going to get your comeuppance at last, eh?'

The animosity between the two men was palpable and it wasn't helping their cause. 'Perhaps we could speak to your nephew alone,' Jarvis said politely.

'Better that I don't have to listen to his lies.' Esposito disappeared through the door, taking some of the tension with him.

'He has never liked me.' Ricci was clearly the type of person who blamed everyone else for his failings and a sneer curled his lips as he looked the detectives up and down. 'It doesn't help when the police come calling.'

'We're sorry to add to your woes,' Jarvis said. 'Unfortunately, a man has been murdered and your name has come up in the course of our investigation.'

This was enough to demolish Ricci's aggressive manner; he wilted, his shoulders drooping. 'I don't know anything.'

About anything. Jarvis and Allen knew the sort; Ricci wasn't going to be helpful if he could avoid it.

'Ian Moore,' Jarvis said bluntly. 'Remember him?'

'Never heard of him.'

'You gave his landlord a reference. Eight years ago. You said he rented the apartment above this shop and was a model tenant, paid his rent on time, kept the apartment in good order. Do you remember now?'

The question resulted in the rapid blinking of unusually-long eyelashes, but Ricci's lips stayed firmly shut.

'Your uncle says the apartment was never rented, so we know you lied,' Allen said, drawing the man's eyes towards him.

'And if you lied about that, what else did you lie about?' Jarvis added.

Ricci looked from one to the other. 'Listen,' he said, leaning forward, his voice dropping to a conspiratorial whisper, a *we're all in this together* kind of camaraderie that sent the hairs on the back of Jarvis' neck standing to attention. 'Okay, yes, I remember the man. He came in here a few times for pizza, always on his own. If it was quiet, I'd sit with him, maybe have a beer if Luca was out of the way.' He looked behind as if to check his uncle hadn't crept behind him to listen. 'Then, one night, he asked if I'd give him a reference. He wanted to move into an apartment and his new landlord was looking for one.' Ricci narrowed his eyes as he thought back. 'He must have known I'd say yes; he had the letter with him. All I had to do was sign it and stamp it with the restaurant stamp.' He sat back in his chair. 'I never saw him again.'

'You did that out of the goodness of your heart?'

Ricci shot Allen a dirty look but said nothing.

Jarvis wondered how much Moore had had to fork out for this worm of a man to lie for him. More importantly why did he have to? He wasn't sure there was any point in asking but he did anyway. 'Do you know where he was living? Why he couldn't ask for a reference from his landlord? Or was he still living at home?'

Ricci's uninterested shrug didn't surprise him.

'Do you know if he drove here or walked?'

Ricci lifted his shoulder to shrug again, then stopped, his eyes suddenly alert. 'What's it worth?'

'It's worth you not being prosecuted for lying on a legal document,' Jarvis said, guessing rightly that Ricci would have no idea that he was stretching the truth considerably. 'Now tell us what you know.'

'One night, it was raining heavily. I commented that he would get wet and I remember him saying he'd run home, that it wasn't far.'

That was it. All they got. Moore always paid cash according to Ricci and until he'd signed that letter, he didn't know his name.

'There was no reason to know it,' he admitted. 'He was a customer. In and out. I forgot about him as soon as he left, never thought about him again.'

And he wouldn't have remembered him but for the money he earned for the signature on that letter. Jarvis finished his coffee and stood. 'We may have more questions for you at a later date,' he said. He didn't think they would but there was no harm in putting a scare up the weasel.

They settled their bill and Jarvis insisted on paying for the second coffees.

Outside, he eyed the row of shops. 'I wonder if it's worth getting a clear photo of Moore and asking around?'

'The only photo we have is the one on his prison record. Eight years is a long time at that age. He was a boy when he was here, eighteen maybe. He'd have changed quite a bit. Filled out, bulked up.'

'Might still be worth it,' Jarvis said, unwilling to dismiss the idea completely. 'Let's go back, see what West says.'

18

When West strolled into the station after the post-mortem, Andrews was on the phone and Foley was peering at a computer screen. Otherwise the room was empty. The coffee percolator bubbled away in the corner. West hoped whoever had made it that morning had emptied out the previous days rather than topping it up. He poured a cup and tasted it and knew they hadn't bothered.

He took it with him anyway. It bore scant resemblance to coffee but it was caffeine.

A minute later, he was grimacing at the taste when Andrews appeared in the doorway. 'Learn anything interesting?'

West put the mug down and sat back. 'Kennedy thinks the puncture wound was caused by a common screwdriver. There were fibres found around his nose and mouth. Looks like our perp disabled the vic by spraying something in his face, then finished off the job by holding something over his nose and mouth. We'll need to wait for forensics to see if they can be more specific as to what was used. If it's GBH though, we may not be lucky. It's metabolised very quickly, as you know and some metabolism takes place after death. Let's hope we're lucky.'

Andrews nodded. Unfortunately, they all had enough experience with date-rape drugs for him to recognise the name. 'We might be getting close to the how, but we're a long way from the why and the who.'

West didn't need to be told, but he bit his tongue. 'Any word from the chaplain?'

'I was on to Mountjoy Prison: he's back this afternoon. I've left a message asking him to ring.'

'Hopefully, he won't feel the need to come here,' West said with a grin. 'I think Morrison would have a coronary if we told him more priests were on their way.' He checked the time. 'Let's have a meeting at four, see where we are.'

'Right, I'll let everyone know,' Andrews said and turned to leave.

'Oh, by the way,' West said, waiting until Andrews turned back before waving him to a chair. 'Sit for a second, I have some news.' He saw Andrews' suddenly arrested expression and shook his head. 'No. It's not that! Edel has decided to write crime novels.' He hoped his voice sounded enthusiastic. 'Her agent has come to an agreement with the publisher. She'll publish as E.M. Johnson.'

'But you're not crazy about the idea?'

West was about to lie, to insist that of course he was pleased for her but he knew the lie would be heard. He never could manage to hide the truth from Peter Andrews. 'I'm wondering about conflict of interest, you know, if she accidentally uses things she'd heard or seen.'

Andrews ran a hand over his short hair. 'I've said it before but I'll say it again, you take yourself way too seriously. Lots of people write crime books, they don't come to us and ask for a story to use, they use their imagination, and so will Edel. Forget all that legal hocus-pocus you learned and let the poor girl write whatever she likes.'

'Woman,' West automatically corrected. He hadn't realised he was tense about the whole crime-writing thing until he felt himself relax. Andrews had a simple way of looking at things that always seemed to put things into perspective. Hocus-pocus... perhaps he was right.

Andrews got to his feet. 'You're hungry. I'll get you a sandwich from the canteen.'

A cardboard-tasting sandwich with unidentifiable rubbery filling wasn't likely to make West feel much better but he nodded anyway and picked up the phone to ring the forensic lab.

Stephen Doyle answered his extension number on the first ring.

'You must have been waiting for my call,' West said.

'I wasn't, and if I'd known it was you, I wouldn't have bloody well answered.' Doyle's gravelly voice was unusually testy.

'We're lost here,' West admitted, hoping for the sympathy vote.

'Well, we're snowed under here.' A long-suffering sigh drifted down the line. 'Sorry, Mike, I've had a hell of a morning.' The distinct sound of glass clinking against china, told West coffee was being poured. He'd been in Doyle's office: it was small and untidy with the constant aroma of good coffee. His mouth watered at the thought; he could almost smell it. He pushed his half-drunk mug with its acrid contents further away. A moment later, a clunk and thump told him Doyle was sitting in his chair, then a loud slurp and a sigh. 'God, I needed that. Okay, yes, I heard about your macabre death but I've no results for you yet.'

West wasn't surprised but he was still disappointed. He quickly gave Doyle a precis of the post-mortem results and their current running theory about what had happened.

'Hmmm, okay,' Doyle said, 'it sounds interesting. I'll get the team to prioritise samples taken from the confession-box mesh and the fibres from around the victim's mouth. But it's going to be tomorrow at the earliest.'

It would have to do. Thanking him, West hung up.

Andrews arrived a few minutes later with a carrier bag from a local deli that made West's stomach rumble. The faint aroma of coffee made him more hopeful.

'Coffee and a sandwich. You'll feel way better after both,' Andrews said, lifting a takeaway coffee from the bag and peering at the lid. 'This is the without-sugar one.'

He sat in the chair opposite and for a few minutes both ate and drank in companionable silence.

'No forensic results yet,' West said, wiping a hand over his mouth.

'Didn't think there would be,' Andrews said, balling up the sandwich wrapper and tossing it in the bin. He missed and reached for it with a shrug.

'Doyle has promised to prioritise the confessional and the fibres around his mouth. Maybe by tomorrow evening, we'll have the how he was killed right and tight.'

Chatter coming from the general office told them that some of the team had returned. West checked his watch. 'We can have a meeting as soon as they're all back. It'll give me a chance to speak with Morrison before he heads off.'

It was another twenty minutes before Andrews told him that everyone had returned.

'I hope they've something to tell us,' West said, getting to his feet. His hopes weren't raised by the rather subdued air. No backslapping or loud congrats. With a sigh, he stepped up to The Wall. 'Please tell me you got something.' He looked around hopefully. 'Okay, I'll settle for anything.'

Jarvis and Allen exchanged glances. 'We did find out something,' Allen said. His Tipperary accent was always more pronounced when he was nervous, the words coming out in a sing-song, melodic way, the vowels stretched. 'Not much, but a start. We were debating on whether to go back with a photo and canvass the area.' He stopped, grinned and pushed a heavy fringe back from his forehead. 'Perhaps I'd better start from the beginning.' He gave a quick summary of their meeting with Ricci.

'Okay,' West said at the end. 'As you say, it's not much but it's something. That Ricci character, does he have a record?'

'One arrest for assault several years ago,' Jarvis said. 'He got a suspended sentence. Nothing else.' He hesitated before asking, 'What do you think about going back, maybe canvassing the area?'

'Sallynoggin is a well-populated residential area,' Andrews said. 'And you're talking about eight years ago. Plus, the only photo we have of Moore is a recent one, he'll have changed a bit.'

'I agree,' West said. 'Also, he'd acquired his new identity by this time. He was hardly going to stay in an area where he was known by his old name.' He saw the look that passed between Jarvis and Allen and guessed that there'd been division over whether it was worthwhile. 'Having said that, it wouldn't do any harm to canvass the rest of the shops along that strip. If my mind serves me correctly, there are a few.'

'Six in total. Plus a pub,' Jarvis hurried to explain.

'Okay, take a photo and check them out but don't waste time on it.' He turned to Baxter. 'How did it go in Tedford Motors?'

Baxter gave them a quick rundown of their chat with Ronan Tedford. 'All the other mechanics agreed that Moore didn't drink. And also that Laetitia Summers was definitely slowing down and looking intently at the garage as she walked past, trying to draw attention to herself.'

'Moore's attention?'

Edwards shook his head and told them about the calendar.

'Tedford thought it was a case of Moore being the first to speak to her but it's hard to know.'

'We went to Clontarf Garda Station to speak to the investigative officer on the rape case. I got the impression he wasn't convinced of Moore's guilt. Basically, it was a case of her word against his, and she, by all accounts, is a petite, girly girl and he was a strapping lad. Plus the taxi driver gave evidence that Moore appeared to be drunk getting into his cab.'

'What about his blood alcohol levels,' West asked, frowning as he tried to remember what he'd read of the case.

'She didn't report the rape till the Tuesday. According to Mitchell she was too distressed and only reported Moore on the advice of a friend.'

'So there was no DNA evidence then?' Jarvis asked.

'No, she'd been so distressed she hadn't washed any of the clothes she was wearing either. They were all available for forensic testing and Moore's DNA was found.'

'All very convenient,' West muttered.

Baxter and Edwards nodded in tandem. 'We think maybe Moore was set up, maybe because of who he really was. If so, it may be that Laetitia Summers knows the truth.'

Instead of the case becoming clearer, it was fast becoming more and more tangled. West tapped the side of the desk he was leaning against. 'We need to be incredibly careful here. Unless, and until proven otherwise, she's a victim not a perpetrator.' He looked from Baxter to Edwards. 'If things are going to go haywire, it's best if I take the flack, so leave her to me, okay?'

It wasn't a request, both men knew it, but as this was the outcome they expected, they were neither surprised nor disappointed.

'Right and finally, the post-mortem results,' West said. There wasn't much to tell them so it didn't take long. 'We're waiting for forensics to see if we can identify what was used. When we do, it might give us a lead.'

'If we're going with the theory that someone sprayed something through the mesh in the confessional,' Allen said, his tone of voice clearly sceptical, 'wouldn't someone have heard or seen something? I mean that would take time and be noisy, wouldn't it?'

Jarvis backed him up. 'It sounds a bit unbelievable. The guy in the priest's box would have to come out and go into the penitent's box and shut the door behind him. I'm not sure two men would fit.'

West hadn't given the logistics of their theory much thought; he did now. Jarvis had a point. He checked his watch. 'The technical team are still processing the scene but they're finished with the confessional. We could go and put our theory to the test.'

'Moore was tall, well-built,' Jarvis said. 'You could double for him, Sarge.'

'If the guy wielding the poison was working alone, he had to have been equally tall and strong,' Baxter said. 'You'd probably fit the bill, Peter.'

There was silence for a few seconds before grins crept over the four men who stood watching West and Andrews as they considered trying to fit into a penitent's box.

'Well, I suppose it was my idea,' West said, resigned to making a fool of himself.

Thirty minutes later, three cars pulled up outside the church and the entire team scrambled out, nobody wanting to miss the sight of West and Andrews jammed into one small box-sized space. Even Foley, who'd been called back to robbery early in the afternoon, managed to sneak away when he was told what was happening.

The technical team were working at the altar end of the church so the area around the confessional was free for their re-enactment.

Edwards opened the priest's box. 'Here you go, Father Andrews.'

Andrews smothered a sigh and stepped inside, sitting on the small wooden chair. Although tall, he wasn't bulky but he still managed to fill almost the entire space.

'And one for you, Sarge.' Jarvis opened the penitent's box where Moore had been found. The technical team had obviously given the go-ahead to clean it. There was no sign of blood and a faint smell of bleach lingered.

West peered inside. The space was tiny, barely room to stand. He shut the door behind him, the space becoming dark and soundless. Awkwardly, he knelt as Moore would have done. 'I can barely see a thing. Is this as it would have been when Moore was here?'

'There's a light over my head. It's on, so I assume so,' Andrews said from his seat. He pulled back the curtain that covered the mesh from his side and looked through it. 'I can see there's someone there but I wouldn't be able to tell it was you.'

'Same here, I can make out your outline, I wouldn't be able to identify anyone. I suppose the anonymity makes it easier for people to confess their sins.' West, who hadn't been to confession since he was a child, shivered at the thought of kneeling here and telling a stranger of the sins he had committed. 'Never again,' he muttered.

'What?' Andrews put his nose to the mesh. 'Did you say something?'

'No, but let's get on with it. Okay, so you spray something, and I collapse.' West tried to fall back, but the space was so small, he didn't manage to move far. 'Best I can do is drop back onto my calves and slump either to my right or left.'

'Okay, so then I come out of the priest's box and go in with you,' Andrews said, appearing in the doorway.

With West slumped to his left, Andrews stepped inside and pulled the door after him. It was a squash but it was doable. 'I'd need to be quick, to get a pad over his mouth before he came to.' Andrews pushed the door open and stepped outside. 'I'd also need to be very quick or be overcome by fumes myself.'

'He could tie something around Moore's mouth and nose, step outside and leave it to work,' Edwards said, as if they were discussing baking a cake. 'Since confessions weren't being held that night, nobody would go in. All he had to do was sit down in a pew and wait.'

'He'd have done research, found out how long it would take,' Baxter said. 'Easy enough to find out those kind of details on the internet.'

West climbed out and stretched. 'It's doable, and there wouldn't necessarily have been any noise to alert anyone. There's really nowhere to fall in there.' He looked around the church. 'We need to get in touch with the sacristan. See if he remembers seeing anyone around the confessional that night. Or if there were any regulars who might remember something.'

'I'll take care of that,' Andrews said with a nod.

'Good.' West looked at the others. 'Look into both Tedford Motors and that Italian restaurant more closely. I want to know everything there is to know about Ronan Tedford and every mechanic who works there, and both Luca Esposito and his nephew. Someone knows more than they're telling. They have to. I refuse to believe Moore kept his secret all these years without letting something slip. Find out. Meanwhile, I'll visit Laetitia Summers and see what I can find out from her.' He checked his watch. 'Okay, go home. Start early tomorrow.'

Baxter held a hand up. 'Before you all go,' he said, the colour flooding his cheeks, clashing with his ginger hair, 'It seems appropriate to tell you in a church that we're getting married. Tanya and me, obviously. Not till next year, but on Saturday we're going to have a bit of a celebration to mark our engagement and christen the new house at the same time. And you're all invited.'

'A wedding! Now that will be nice,' Andrews said. 'And you know what they say about weddings, don't you.'

'What?' Allen said.

West was about to say something cutting but he saw Allen's blank expression. He really didn't know. No doubt the others would hurry to enlighten him.

Baxter did the duty. 'They say, going to a wedding's the making of another.'

West glared at him. 'Well I don't know what *they* say but I know what Inspector Morrison will say! He'll say, "When are we going to solve this case?" so let's concentrate on that, shall we?' And without another word, he turned and left

19

West drove back to the station. Most of the others would have taken his *go* at face value and headed for home but when he stopped at the traffic lights, he wasn't surprised to see Andrews' car behind him.

They were two of a kind in their approach to their work. He shouldn't be too surprised that Andrews wanted their similarity to spread to their personal lives too. He had been happily married to the lovely Joyce for several years, and he seemed to think it was what West needed. Maybe it was. But the timing wasn't right.

Back in the station, he decided it would be best to approach Mother Morrison directly. He gave a thumbs up to Andrews who pulled into the car park seconds after him and saw his nod and grin.

Morrison was standing outside his office door. He saw West and raised his eyes to the ceiling. 'You better be coming to see me with good news,' he said, pushing the door open. 'Well?' He sat behind his desk and glared.

West had been going over what they knew on the short drive back to the station and had come up with a theory. He laid it out for the inspector. 'We think that Moore was set up for the rape to punish him for something he did before he acquired the Moore persona. He only served eight months so maybe whoever set him up didn't think it was sufficient punishment–'

'And decided to make sure this time by killing him,' Morrison interrupted. 'You do get involved in the most complicated and far-fetched cases, West, but I'm inclined to think you might be onto something. We need to find out who our victim was.'

Why didn't I think of that? 'We're going to look into everyone involved with the garage and restaurant. I think someone must know something.' West leaned tiredly against the wall. One of these days, he was going to bring a chair with him when he came to see the inspector. 'They may not even know they know so it's going to be a slow, laborious process.'

A faint smile appeared on Morrison's thin lips. 'Sounds like policework to me.'

West nodded. It was the typical hard slog of investigative work. The questioning of every person with the remotest link in the hope that somewhere in the recesses of their brains they knew something important. 'I'll pay a visit to Laetitia Summers tomorrow. She's the best bet. If Moore was set up for her alleged rape, she must have been complicit.'

'I don't have to tell you to tread carefully, Mike,' Morrison said.

West smiled. 'No. Rest easy, I'll be cautious.'

Andrews was on the phone when he returned to the main office. He waited until he was finished, perching on the side of his desk.

'That was the chaplain,' Andrews said, hanging up. 'He remembered Moore quite well. Said he was a troubled boy. It appears the chaplain offered confession but Moore refused.'

'Damn! That makes our theory about him being lured into the confessional unlikely.'

Andrews smiled. 'No, I don't think so. The chaplain saw Moore not long before he was released. Again, he offered him confession. He remembers that Moore refused, but he did ask something strange. He asked if confession would cover sins in his past, things he'd never told anyone before.'

A smile lit West's expression. 'That's more like it. Looks like we're right. Something he did as a young man of–'

'Eighteen,' Andrews said. 'Something so bad he ran and hid from it.'

'But someone found him.'

'And tried to punish him, but eight months wasn't enough so they decided to finish it.'

It was exactly what West had decided on the drive back. He wasn't surprised to see Andrews coming to the same conclusion. They were like clones.

West tapped the side of the desk. 'A crime bad enough to have caused such a desire for revenge, it has to be on the books. Get the lads to start looking at every crime committed...' he rocked a flat hand to and fro '...start at the date of the Moores' burglary and work backwards for a year.'

'What're they looking for?'

'Any crime where the perpetrators were young men. And you better make it solved and unsolved cases. If it was a gang crime, some of the perpetrators may have been arrested but not all; some may have remained unidentified.'

'We'll get on it in the morning,' Andrews said, standing and stretching. 'Time for home, dinner is calling.'

West sat behind his desk, switched on his computer, and waited for it to power up, thinking about the case. He tapped a few keys and brought up the details of the rape Moore had done time for. There was nothing that the team hadn't told him. He reached for the phone and dialled a number. It was answered almost immediately.

'Ms Summers, my name is Detective Garda Sergeant Mike West. Would it be possible to meet with you?'

There was silence on the line before a soft, high-pitched voice replied with one word. 'Why?'

He didn't want to tell her the details over the phone. Long experience had taught him that people's facial expressions often revealed as much as their words. He went for the vaguely mysterious, 'I'm afraid I can't discuss it over the phone but I'm happy to meet whenever and wherever it suits.'

There was the distinct sound of fingernails tapping. Finally, on a heavy exhale, she said, 'I've a morning off tomorrow. Here at ten.' A tinny titter drifted down the line. 'I assume you know where that is.'

'Yes, Ms Summers, I do. Thank you. I'll see you tomorrow at ten.'

Edel looked up from the email she was writing when she heard the key in the front door. She'd finished it and shut her iPad before the kitchen door opened. 'Perfect timing.' She looked towards the oven. 'It's almost ready.'

'Good, I'm starving,' West said, leaning down to kiss her lightly on the lips. 'Did you have a good day?'

'Very good indeed,' she said. 'I'll tell you about it over dinner.'

Edel dished up the fish pie she'd made and put a plate in front of him. 'Do you want a glass of wine?'

'No, water is fine,' West said, then tilted his head. 'Unless we're celebrating again. Are we?'

She laughed. 'No,' she said, sitting in the chair beside him.

'But I do have news. Owen asked me for a brief synopsis of the first book in the crime series I'm planning to write. I wrote it this morning and sent it off. He was back to me within the hour.' Excitement coloured her voice. 'He loved it, Mike. Said it was the best thing he'd read in ages.'

West put down his cutlery and leaned forward to kiss her. 'Of course he did. You're amazing. Tell me about it.'

Edel pushed her plate away, propped her chin on her joined hands and gave him a summary of the book she planned to write. 'And that's book one,' she said. 'I've an idea for book two but haven't got it completely in my head yet.' She saw his flicker of relief and laughed. 'Seriously! You really thought I was going to base a story on one of the ghastly experiences I've been through, didn't you?'

West had the grace to look embarrassed. 'I suppose I was a bit worried about that, yes.'

She shook her head. 'What is it Peter often says about you? Oh yes, "you take yourself far too seriously sometimes!" Relax, Mike, I have enough imagination to come up with plenty of crimes without touching on reality.' She sat back, a smile lingering. 'And now that we have that out of the way, tell me how your case is going.'

He finished his dinner and sat back. 'Okay,' he said. 'I always did like talking things over with you.' He filled her in on the case, the theories they'd come up with, his meeting with Laetitia Summers the next morning.

'Sounds like a complicated case,' Edel said when he'd finished.

West laughed. 'Morrison thinks I attract them.'

'And you've no idea who this poor man is?'

'Not yet. I'm hoping Laetitia will be able to give us somewhere to go.'

Edel had met so many horrible people in the last year, she

really shouldn't be surprised by the depths some would stoop to. 'You really think she helped set him up? Cried rape when it was anything but?' Adam Fletcher came to Edel's mind and she shivered. *How could anyone pretend something so terrible?*

'It's a theory,' West said and as if he read her thoughts, he reached out to hold her hand. 'Based not only on what Ronan Tedford said but also on what the investigating officer said. But it's still a theory. Until we know otherwise, she is still a victim.'

For the next few minutes, while they cleared away and went into the sitting room where West switched on the TV to catch the nine o'clock news, Edel was thinking about Moore.

She was frowning when the news was over and West turned to her with some comment about world affairs which she dismissed with a casual wave. 'I was thinking about Moore,' she said, and watched his eyebrows rise. Before he could say anything, she lifted a hand to stop him. 'Hear me out. When Cyril Pratt stole Simon Johnson's identity and married me, he didn't abandon his old identity, he lived a double life, right?'

With obvious reluctance, West murmured agreement.

'Well I was thinking: if your victim stole Ian Moore's identity, what happened to the old identity? He was only a boy, wasn't he? Seventeen or eighteen. Maybe,' she said, 'whoever he was, he was reported missing?'

She saw West's eyes widen and smiled. He hadn't thought of that.

20

West was annoyed that he hadn't thought that someone might be missing the lad who became Ian Moore. Because, of course, it made sense. For someone to acquire a new identity, if they weren't living a double life – as Edel's first husband had done – the first identity had to be killed off. The victim had been eighteen when he'd acquired Ian Moore's identity. Someone had to have missed him.

'You should have been a detective,' he said and smiled at her look of pleasure. He leaned closer and kissed her. 'I have no doubt that your books are going to be a huge success. I hope your crimes don't give anyone ideas.'

'It's quite fun trying to think up a crime,' she said. 'I think perhaps I understand now why you love what you do. It's the whole puzzle of it.'

He put his arm around her shoulder and pulled her close. 'Yes, it is. For instance, if Moore, as we'll still call him, did something wrong when he was eighteen, why did someone wait until he was twenty-seven to get revenge?'

'They couldn't find him?'

'Exactly. So, how did they find him now?' West frowned.

There was something at the edge of his mind, something tanta-lising. 'Someone said something today,' he murmured.

'I'll make a cup of tea,' Edel said, uncurling from his arms and getting to her feet. 'Tea and biscuits, guaranteed to get your brain working.'

The TV was showing some current affairs programme but West tuned out. What was it? Who'd said it? His mind went back over the conversations of the afternoon. It was something Edwards had said. His frown eased. *The calendar!* That was it, he was sure of it. The stupid lad had posed for a calendar. And what was it Edwards had said? It had got them much more attention than they'd expected and they'd never done another.

Maybe it had got Moore the wrong kind of attention. A blast from his past. When Edel arrived back with two mugs of tea and a packet of Kimberley biscuits, he told her.

'What an idiot,' she said, tearing the packet open with her teeth. 'He goes to all the trouble of acquiring a new identity, then poses for a calendar. Why would he have been that stupid?'

West took a biscuit from the packet, bit into the ginger and mallow centre and sighed. 'He was young when he started in the garage. He kept his head down, didn't drink. Maybe for a short time, he wanted to be one of the lads. They probably coaxed him into it, maybe even told him it wouldn't be seen by many.'

'But it was seen by the wrong person.'

Two biscuits later, West drained his mug and put it down. 'Baxter and Edwards thought Laetitia Summers walked past the garage because she'd seen the calendar and fancied her chances with one of the mechanics.'

Edel had reached for her third biscuit. 'I really should stop buying these,' she said, biting into it. 'You think she was looking for Moore in particular.'

West linked his hands behind his head. 'Yes, I think she was.

I think someone from his past saw the calendar and recognised him. Someone who'd been looking for him.'

'And lured the Summers woman in to help.'

'Yes, Tedford wasn't enamoured with her, I gather. Maybe he had reason.' He dropped an arm around Edel's shoulder and pulled her to him. 'With me investigating crime and you writing it, it looks as if we're going to have some criminally good conversations.'

'Maybe I should come with you tomorrow when you meet her,' Edel said. 'Give you another woman's perspective.'

West tightened his hand on her shoulder. 'You know I can't do that, and before you say it, yes, I know you tagged along on that case on Clare Island but they were different circumstances.'

She pushed away from him and turned to look him in the eye. 'I was joking.' She shrugged. 'Kind of. I don't think you should go alone.'

'You're thinking of Fiona again, aren't you?' West laughed when he saw her nod. 'Well relax, I'm going to bring Peter with me. This case is getting too knotty for my liking and he's a good one for seeing through lies and mistruths.'

'I like Peter. In fact, I like all your team.'

He remembered the party. 'Good, Baxter has invited us to a housewarming-stroke-engagement party on Saturday.'

Edel sat forward. 'A party! Excellent, I've been looking for an excuse to go shopping. Now I can buy a new dress, and a housewarming-engagement present. What should I buy, do you think?'

West had no idea, but he happily joined in a conversation about household appliances and paraphernalia that had nothing at all to do with crime and he felt the last of the tension ebb away. It was going to be all right.

21

———

West, as usual, was in the station sitting at his desk when the rest of the team ambled in.

'Listen up,' he said, standing in his doorway. 'I was talking to Edel last night and she came up with an interesting take on our case.' He filled them in, watching as their eyes widened.

'Why didn't we think of that?' Jarvis said.

'I suppose,' Baxter commented, 'she had up close and personal experience with identity theft.' His cheeks reddened. 'No offence meant.'

West shook his head. 'None taken, you're right, she looked at it from a different viewpoint and came up with something we should have thought about.' He strolled over to The Wall, stared at a photo of the crime scene. 'This case is developing legs.' He told them his idea about the calendar.

Jarvis perched on the desk behind and folded his arms. 'I thought of something last night too,' he said, drawing all eyes to him. 'It was something you said, Sarge, about maybe Moore coming from elsewhere. I don't think Ricci or his uncle would have noticed a regional accent but maybe Tedford, the other mechanics or Laetitia Summers might have done.'

'Good point. I'm seeing Ms Summers this morning. Baxter and Edwards, you two follow up Jarvis' idea since you were there yesterday. Jarvis, you and Allen start searching the data banks for crimes committed as we discussed... going back a year from the Moores' burglary.'

'That's going to be huge,' Baxter said with a shake of his head.

West turned to look at the murder-scene photo again. 'Whatever he did, our perp didn't think eight months in prison was enough.' He turned back to Baxter. 'Start with crimes that resulted in death of a family member, loved one or child where there was more than one perpetrator. If Foley gets free from robbery, get him to start the search on missing persons, same time frame. While you lot are doing that, Andrews and I will see what we can gently squeeze from Laetitia Summers.'

He was in the office preparing to leave when his desk phone rang. He picked it up, expecting to hear Morrison, surprised to hear the deeper voice of Sergeant Blunt.

'Hi Tom, what can I do for you?'

'It's Mrs Bennet, we had to bring her in again. She was blocking the Parsons' driveway.'

West sat on the seat behind him and swore softly under his breath. 'I'll come out and have a word,' he said. 'Is her husband on the way?'

'He said he'd be here in fifteen minutes.'

West hung up. Some cases were sad for all involved. This will have been the fourth time in the last couple of months that the Parsons had rung. They'd recently applied for a barring order against Mrs Bennet. West knew it wasn't going to have any effect. In October, Mrs Parsons had knocked down and killed Mrs Bennet's only child, her son, Milo Junior. Mrs Parsons' legal team refused to allow her to be charged, saying she was suffering from post-natal depression and was unable to answer questions. She'd spent several weeks in a psychiatric clinic before being released but was still under the care of doctors who refused to allow her to be questioned, insisting she was incapable of pleading.

Meanwhile, the family of the boy who had died were falling apart. Desperate for justice, Mrs Bennet started calling upon the Parsons, begging Mrs Parsons to confess what she'd done and to take responsibility for Milo Junior's death.

There was no happy outcome for either family.

West stopped by Andrews' desk. 'We'll head off soon. Mrs Bennet is out in reception. I'm going to go and have a word while they wait for her husband to arrive.'

'I thought the Parsons were going to take out a barring order against her.' The corners of Andrews' mouth turned down. 'Not that that's going to stop Mrs Bennet turning up outside their house. There's no solution to this, is there?'

'None,' West said, and left to meet the bereaved woman.

Mrs Bennet, dressed in a heavy brown coat, flat shoes and a thick scarf, looked as if she was dressed for the elements, for standing outside the Parsons' home for hours. In reception, she looked lost.

West sat beside her, drawing a slight smile of recognition. 'Sergeant West, it's nice to see you again.'

'You promised me that you'd try and stay away,' he said, reaching out to take the woman's hand. It was cold. She'd forgotten to wear gloves.

Her smile faded. 'I did try, but I didn't succeed.'

'Joanne!' The tall, pale man who pushed through the door had sad eyes and a downturned mouth. He looked like a man who bore the sorrows of the world on his slumped shoulders. He glanced at West but said nothing, merely taking his wife's hand and pulling her gently to her feet. 'Come on,' he said gently, 'let's get you home.'

West knew he should stop Mr Bennet and warn him, yet again, that his wife couldn't keep going around to the Parsons' house, or accosting Mrs Parsons in the street, or in the shops, all of which she'd done at one time or another over the last few months. Instead, he let them go, making a mental note to ring the grief counsellor Mrs Bennet had been attending.

'How was she?' Andrews said, closing the computer programme he was using.

'She looked dreadful; Mr Bennet looked worse.'

'Do you think it would have made any difference if Mrs Parsons had pleaded guilty.'

West jangled his car keys as Andrews grabbed his coat and pulled it on. 'Mrs Bennet thinks what she wants is justice but what she really wants is her son back. Nothing Mrs Parsons does now is going to change what she did that day.'

They reached Griffith Avenue slightly before ten. The front gate of the Summers' home stood open. A Micra took up half the parking area in front leaving enough room for West to park alongside.

'Nice house,' Andrews said, and climbed from the car. 'She lives with her parents, doesn't she?'

'According to the file, yes,' West said, shutting the car door.

The half-glass front door had a doorbell on the side. One push sent a chime pealing within. It was ten o'clock, on the dot. They expected the door to be answered promptly but after a minute, when there was no sound of movement from within and no sign of anyone coming to answer, West grunted in annoyance and pressed the bell again, twice.

They were both peering through the glass several minutes later when they heard a breathy laugh behind and turned to see a petite woman in Lycra running clothes wiping a hand across her forehead. 'Am I late?' she said. 'I'm so sorry, I must have been slower than usual.'

She took a single key from a pocket on the side of her leggings, holding it up to them as if she'd found it by surprise.

It was a deliberately choreographed act, as was her late arrival. West took an instant dislike to her.

'Come in,' she said, pushing the front door open. She waved them towards another door at the end of a narrow hallway. 'Straight through, I'll make us a cuppa.'

The door lead into a small, tidy galley kitchen. A window overlooked an overgrown back garden, tall trees blurring the boundaries. West and Andrews stood as Laetitia hummed under her breath, filled the kettle and took down mugs. 'Tea or coffee?'

West would have preferred to refuse but if it helped her to treat their visit like a social one, maybe she'd find it easier to talk. 'Coffee,' he said. 'Milk no sugar.'

'Coffee with three sugars and milk for me.'

'I go running every morning,' she said, spooning coffee into three mugs. 'I go earlier some mornings.' She chatted about the route she took while the kettle came to the boil. Nothing she said required an answer.

It was inane, meaningless nonsense. It came to West suddenly, that she was playing a role. The dizzy blonde with a breathy, light voice. She'd have succeeded but for the sharp calculating glances she was giving them from the corner of her eyes.

'We can have it through there,' she said, handing them their coffee and indicating the door behind them.

This was a bigger, brighter room, sliding doors leading from it onto a patio where several pots held skeletons of the previous year's summer flowers. The only furniture in the room was a square mahogany dining table surrounded by four matching chairs but indents in the carpet near the wall told West that some furniture had been removed.

'You've been redecorating?' he asked, taking a seat and placing his mug on the coaster she hastily pushed towards him.

She looked at him, puzzled.

He pointed to the telltale flattened marks on the carpet. 'Something is missing.'

Her titter was irritating. 'I'm not keen on mahogany,' she explained. 'There was a sideboard there. I sold it.' She slid her hand over the surface of the table. 'This too, they're coming back for it later. I prefer something more modern.'

'Your parents don't mind?'

Laetitia picked up her coffee and sipped. 'They're living in Portugal most of the time. They're happy for me to make some changes.' She tilted her head to the wall behind her. 'I'm going to have the wall knocked down and make this one big kitchen-diner. Much more modern, don't you think?'

West did, it was exactly what he had done when he bought his Greystones house. But it was his house; this belonged to her parents, didn't it? They'd need to look into the Summers family a little deeper.

'I'm sure you're wondering why we are here,' he said. Her expression didn't change. As if it was quite normal that two detective Gardaí would call on her. He had expected to have to approach the subject obliquely, to have had to tread carefully around a woman who was herself the victim of a crime. But he knew, with instinct borne of his years in the Gardaí as well as his years as a solicitor, that there was no need to pussyfoot around this woman. 'I know you spoke to Detective Garda Foley and Jarvis but the investigation into the murder of Ian Moore is ongoing and we've a few more questions to ask.'

She nodded as if she'd expected this.

'Were you shocked by his death?'

Laetitia sipped her coffee slowly, as if taking time to answer, then her mouth twisted, making her look older, harder. 'No, I wasn't. Men like him who cause such pain and devastation are bound to meet a sticky end eventually.'

'You said you'd both been drinking,' Andrews said, holding his mug between cupped hands. 'Can you remember what?'

'Distinctly. I was drinking gin and tonic. He was drinking vodka and coke.'

'And he bought all the drinks?'

'Yes.'

'You didn't buy even one?'

'I offered, but he insisted.'

'His boss, and the other mechanics said they'd never seen him drink alcohol, never mind get drunk.'

She shrugged. 'I remember what they said. It didn't change what happened. He got drunk and raped me.'

Andrews looked at her. 'In a laneway.'

'That's right.'

'And you got a taxi home afterwards. Didn't tell anyone until the following Tuesday?'

Laetitia folded her arms across her chest. 'I've been through all of this. Nothing has changed. He was found guilty and sentenced to five years, serving a miserable eight months of that. Eight months,' she said, her voice scathing.

'And now he's dead,' West said quietly. 'Murdered.'

'You hardly expect me to be sorry, do you?'

West looked at her. Beneath the surface prettiness, there was something hard and unpleasant. There was no sorrow. Was there satisfaction? Did she have a hand in the man's death? 'You were the victim then, Ms Summers; he's the victim now. Obviously, we'll be looking at anyone who had a motive for killing him.'

She laughed. 'You think *I* might have murdered him? I don't know how he died, but I'm four-foot-ten, he was six-two. How do you think I'd have managed it?' She stood and glared at them. 'If that's why you've come, you've wasted your journey.'

'Sit down, please,' West said.

When she didn't, standing there with her arms folded and an irritated crease between her eyes, he said, 'Ian Moore wasn't his real name. Did you know that?'

He saw the lie in her eyes before she spoke. 'No,' she said. 'I didn't. What was his real name then?'

'That's what we are trying to ascertain. Do you still have a copy of the calendar the mechanics made?'

Laetitia blinked. 'No... no, I don't.'

Not *what calendar* or *no, I never had one*. He saw the confusion in her eyes as she wondered if she'd said the wrong thing.

The calendar had been brought up at the trial. She'd stated that she'd never seen it, didn't even know of its existence. West knew now, with complete certainty, she'd lied.

He stood abruptly, startling her. 'Thank you for seeing us, Ms Summers. We may have more questions for you at a later date.'

Back in the car, he and Andrews exchanged glances. 'You think what I'm thinking?'

'That she's a conniving so-and-so that I wouldn't trust as far as I'd throw her?'

West started the engine. 'I was thinking that she's lying through her teeth, but that'll do.' He waited for a gap in the fast-moving line of traffic on Griffith Avenue, pulling out at a flash of lights, raising a hand in thanks as he took off in the direction of home. 'She looks to be spending a lot of money on a house that isn't hers,' he said. 'I think we need to look into her parents and their move to Portugal.' A minute later, he indicated and turned off the main road.

'We going somewhere?'

'I thought we'd call in to the library and see if we can find out a little more about Laetitia Summers.'

There was a small car park beside the library and they were in luck: there was one space available. Pulling into it, West switched off the engine. 'I want to know more about her,' he said. 'From someone neutral. Who better than her boss?'

'Won't she want to know why you're asking?' Andrews said.

'I'm sure she will. I'll wing it.'

The library was quiet. A couple of people were perusing the bookshelves; an elderly woman sitting in an armchair was reading a newspaper; one other younger woman was reading the noticeboard. A long desk at the back was manned by a young, bespectacled male with a straggly goatee. West and Andrews approached and stopped in front of him and waited for him to look up from the book he was reading.

When he did, he looked at them with a dreamy smile. 'Such a good book,' he said, waving a hand in apology. 'Sorry, what can I do for you?'

'I'd like to speak to the librarian, please.' West hoped not to have to show his identification, the more discreet their presence the better.

But the goatee-wearing man didn't as much as ask his name.

'Sure,' he said. 'Hang on and I'll give her a buzz.' He picked up the phone and dialled a two-number extension. It was answered immediately. 'Someone here to see you,' he said, and immediately hung up. He was back in the pages of his book before the clickety-click of high heels crossed the library floor.

'I'm Debbie Long, the librarian. You wanted to see me?' A small, plump woman with an anxious crease between her eyes looked from West to Andrews. 'Is there something wrong?'

'Is there somewhere we could talk,' West said. 'Somewhere private.'

The crease between her eyes deepened, and her rather narrow lips tightened. She looked like a woman who was used to hearing bad news. 'My office,' she said, waving back the way she'd come. She looked down on the bent head of the young man behind the desk. 'Hold any calls for the moment,' she said to him.

Her office was a small windowless room. No effort had been made to personalise it; the furniture was standard office fare, the bookshelves jammed willy-nilly with books. Only the framed photograph on the wall beside her desk said something about the librarian. It was a family photo of a relaxed quartet... the librarian, a smiling man, an older boy wearing a football jersey, a pretty girl and two younger, scruffy-looking boys.

West brought his focus back to the woman who'd taken her seat on the far side of the desk.

'What's this about?' she said, her voice tight, then, as if remembering to be professional, she gestured to chairs behind them. 'Please, sit,' she said.

West and Andrews sat in the grey utilitarian chairs. 'Nobody's in trouble,' West said, sliding his identification across the desk. 'We're looking for information about one of your staff.'

The librarian picked up the identification and looked at it

for far longer than either man thought was warranted. When she put it down, she looked across the desk. 'One of my staff?'

'We need the utmost discretion,' West said, leaning forward. 'The person in question isn't in any trouble, it's simply that her name came up in relation to a case we're investigating. We've discovered from experience that the more we know about every person who turns up in the course of an investigation, the easier it is to solve. Links and connections,' he added vaguely.

Debbie Long sat back and folded her arms. 'I'll do what I can to help, of course, as long as I'm not breaching any of my staff's privacy.'

'I won't be asking for any details that would be classified as private,' West reassured her.

'Okay, so what do you want to know?'

'What can you tell us about Laetitia Summers?'

A flicker of surprise was followed by a second's panic before Debbie assumed a carefully neutral expression. 'Laetitia? She's worked here for six years. Diligent, hard-working. Customers and the other staff like her.' Her hands were clasped on the desk in front of her, the pad of one thumb rhythmically rubbing the nail of the other. 'Laetitia rarely takes a sick day either. Obviously,' she said, 'she took a few days off last year with all that went on.'

'You know about that?' West said, wondering exactly how much she knew.

'That Laetitia was raped? Yes, of course. She rang me in tears and told me what had happened. I was shocked.'

West waited and when she didn't elaborate, said, 'It must have been difficult for her to return to work. Tedford Motors isn't far away.'

Long looked at him with a raised eyebrow. 'It's far enough, and the mechanics have never used the library.'

'And I suppose Ms Summers didn't have to pass it on her way home, did she?'

The librarian looked at him blankly. 'Why on earth would she need to? She lives the other direction.'

'Do you use Tedford Motors for car servicing?'

'You wanted to know about Laetitia. What interest would you have in where I get my car serviced?'

West held a hand up. 'I wasn't involved in the rape case so I never got to meet the man responsible. I simply wondered if you had done, if you'd met him. To get your take on him, I suppose.'

She frowned. 'I didn't need to meet him to get a *take* on him. Laetitia is a tiny, slight woman, he was a big man, over six foot. She hadn't a chance. Anyway,' she said, lifting her wrist to glance pointedly at her watch, 'not that it's any of your business but I live in Swords and get my car serviced in a local garage. Now, that's all there is to say, really. Laetitia recovered from her ordeal as far as I could tell. She does her work. I don't know anything more about her. I don't see her socially. We're not big into work outings here.' She pushed the corners of her mouth up into the semblance of a smile. 'In fact, I don't think I've ever seen her at a social event.'

'Not even at a Christmas party?' Andrews said, surprised.

Long's smile wavered and faded away. 'I don't like Christmas.'

West was hit by the sadness in the words, and by the desolation that flickered in her eyes before vanishing, her eyes hard as she tapped her watch. 'Well, if that's all, I really do have a lot of work to do.'

'Thank you, yes,' West said, getting to his feet. 'You've been most kind, that's all we really needed to know.'

'And Laetitia isn't in any trouble?' She tried a smile; it didn't work. 'She runs the early readers group: I need to be certain she's not a risk to them, or any of our customers.'

'As I explained, her name came up in connection with another case, that's all.' He smiled reassuringly. 'It's the tedious nature of our job to follow up all the links and connections we find and eliminate every one.'

West and Andrews left her sitting behind her desk and made their way through the library to the exit. 'Let's grab some lunch,' West said. 'I saw a sign for a café before we turned off.'

The café was busy but, as usual, Andrews spotted a couple who were getting ready to leave. 'We'd take your graves as fast,' he said with a grin, standing beside them.

'No problem, enjoy your lunch,' the departing woman said with an answering smile.

A young woman in black leggings and a baggy black T-shirt hurried over and cleared the table. 'I'll be back to take your order in a sec,' she said, taking the tray of dirty dishes away. She was true to her word, back with a pen and pad in hand before they'd even looked at the menu.

Both hurriedly scanned it and gave their order.

West sat back and looked around. 'Nice place,' he commented.

'Going to the library was a good move,' Andrews said.

'You caught it?' West asked, unsurprised when Andrews nodded. Little escaped him. It had been something small, almost unnoticeable. When Debbie Long had described Ian Moore, she'd said *was* not *is*. So how did she learn of his death? From Laetitia, a woman she didn't socialise with, or from someone else?

They'd hoped to find some answers that morning. Instead, they'd found more questions.

23

Lunch over, West looked across the table. 'Since we're out this way...'

'We may as well, I suppose,' Andrews agreed without waiting for him to finish.

'Honestly,' West said with a grin, 'I swear you read my mind.'

Andrews stood and pulled his coat on. 'No, we're like an old married couple, we think alike. It makes sense to speak to Tedford, see if Baxter and Edwards did a good job.'

They decided to leave the car and walk to the garage. The day was cold with a biting wind blowing but it was dry, the sky a sapphire blue, and it was good to be outside for a bit. Ten minutes brisk walk brought them to Tedford Motors.

The service office was busy, a purple-haired, middle-aged woman behind the waist-high counter arguing loudly with a customer about the price of a service, two other customers behind listening and smirking as she lambasted the man. West and Andrews had no choice but to wait, no choice, too, but to listen. Finally, it was their turn. She looked them up and down. 'Guards,' she said. It wasn't a question. 'What can I do for you?'

'We'd like to speak to Ronan Tedford,' West said.

She picked up a phone and stabbed the keys. 'Coppers to see you,' she said. Listening a moment, she grunted and hung up. 'You can go round. Out the door, follow the wall around the back. It's the flat-roofed building. You can't miss it.'

'When people say that, I find it's usually somewhere impossible to find,' Andrews muttered.

'And you call yourself a detective,' West teased. 'Anyway, this time she was right.' He lifted his hand and pointed. 'There it is.'

The door opened as they approached, an overweight man staring their way. 'More questions?' He stood back and waved them inside.

'Just a couple,' West said, taking the seat he was offered. 'I gather from the officers who spoke to you yesterday that you were very fond of Ian Moore.'

'I was, but I understand I was also fooled by him,' Tedford said. 'That doesn't sit easily with me.'

'His assumption of a new identity obviously wasn't done to fool you, Mr Tedford. You were happy, after all, to keep him employed even after his prison sentence.'

Tedford linked stubby fingers on the desk in front of him. 'He always struck me as a nice lad, a bit soft... if you get my meaning.'

West cocked his head. 'It would be helpful if you'd elaborate, Mr Tedford. Soft in what way?'

Tedford puffed. 'He wasn't like the other lads: kept himself to himself, didn't swear much or chat about girls. Now and then there'd be a bit of argy-bargy between the lads. Ian always kept out of it. I remember one of the lads called him a coward once when Ian walked away from a confrontation but instead of getting annoyed, he simply said, "Walking away doesn't bring regrets, staying does".'

'You didn't think that was a strange thing for a young man to say?' Andrews asked.

'In my line of business, you get to meet all sorts, hear all sorts.' He shrugged. 'I did think it was a bit odd, I even asked him later what he'd meant.' Tedford smiled at the memory. 'Ian laughed, said he was trying to sound profound, that it didn't mean anything, but... I didn't believe him.'

'He never mentioned trouble in his past?'

'He didn't mention his past full stop,' Tedford said. 'He was eighteen when he started here, what reason could he have had for needing to change his name?'

A thought crossed West's mind. 'Did he have an accent?'

'An accent?' Tedford looked puzzled. 'You mean was he foreign?'

'No, I was thinking more of a country accent. Especially when he came here first.'

Tedford gave the idea some thought, a fat index finger tapping the desk. 'He always spoke very softly, slowly even. I remember thinking when I first met him that he was a bit... you know... slow. He wasn't: he simply thought before he spoke. So, I'm not sure about any accent. Most of the mechanics we've had over the years have been Dubs, northsiders, some have strong Dublin accents, but Ian didn't.'

'Okay, thank you,' West said. 'And one final thing, by any chance, do you have a copy of the calendar the mechanics made?'

Tedford pushed back from his desk, turned in his swivel chair and pulled open the lower drawer of a metal filing cabinet. 'Here you go,' he said. 'Ian was February, June and October.'

West took it, flicked to February and held it out for Andrews to see. The photo they had at the station of Ian Moore didn't do him justice. The man who posed bare-chested behind a motorbike was extremely handsome. 'I can see why it was popular.' West smiled, looking through the rest. The photos were well done, posed to show off the physiques of the men without tipping over into salacious sleaze.

Tedford laughed. 'It was crazy for a while. The charity they did it for were more than happy with the proceeds.'

'What about Ian? Was he happy with the attention?'

'I think they all thought it was funny for a while, but then women, girls, auld ones started hanging around and staring.' Tedford grinned. 'It was a turnaround for the lads. They were used to being the ones doing the gawping, you know.'

'Whose idea was it?' Andrews asked, curious.

'Toby, one of the mechanics – it was his girlfriend, Suzy's idea. She's a photography student and wanted some practice; thought doing a charity calendar would be good fun and give her exposure. She said it would only work if all four mechanics did three months each. I think she guilted Ian into it, to be honest.'

'How many were sold?'

'She made a hundred initially, then another hundred. A local paper heard about it and did an article on it so that boosted sales. I think the final number was two thousand.'

West caught Andrews' eye. For someone who had gone to the trouble of changing his identity it must have been a nightmare. Not only the calendars but a newspaper article. 'Was there a photo in the paper?'

Tedford grimaced. 'There was and none of the lads were happy but it appears the girlfriend had copyright for the photos so she could do what she liked with them. I think she and Toby split up over it.'

There was nothing more to be learnt and taking their leave of Tedford, West and Andrews headed back to Foxrock.

Frustratingly, there was nothing new from any of the team either. West added the Summers' family and the librarian to the growing list of people whose background needed to be checked and went to update Morrison, trudging up the stairs one step at a time.

'Nothing?' Morrison said when West had filled him in.

'So far, we seem to have stirred up more questions than answers.'

Morrison scowled. 'I'd hoped to have this solved quickly. The bishop has been in touch with his cronies. You know the way it goes.'

West did. The bishop would go straight to the top and speak to the commissioner and the commands would come swiftly down the rank. 'It's a complicated case,' West said. He had a vague idea he'd said the same thing before. It hadn't changed.

'Well, uncomplicate it,' Morrison said brusquely. 'Preferably before the bishop decides it would be better to come here himself.' His mouth twisted at the thought and he waved a hand at West in dismissal.

Back in the main office, West looked around. Everyone was either glued to a computer screen or on the phone. There was no point in him telling them they were under pressure to get results. If the results were there, they'd find them.

Back in his office, he sent Edel a quick text to say he'd be home at six. There was only so much he could do with nothing.

He held a brief meeting before the end of the shift. If he'd hoped to have any enlightenment, he was destined to be disappointed.

'Nothing yet,' Baxter and Edwards said almost in unison. Jarvis merely shook his head when he looked in his direction.

'I found out something about Laetitia Summers,' Allen said, drawing all eyes to him. He held a hand up as if to hold them back. 'Don't get too excited, it's not much. Her parents moved to Portugal a year ago. They bought a bungalow in a place called Cascais.'

West frowned. He knew the place. Very nice, and very expensive. 'They didn't sell their house here, though, so how did they fund it?'

Allen shook his head. 'All I can tell you is that they bought a place there and have been there since.'

'Do some more digging,' West said. 'Tomorrow. Go home, let's pick it up again in the morning.' He wasn't surprised when Andrews followed him back to his office.

'Mother not happy?'

West sat behind his desk with a grunt of frustration. 'He wants results. The bishop has been making waves.'

'We'll get there,' Andrews said calmly. 'We always do. We've got all the pieces, now we need to see how they fit together.'

'One of these days, we're going to fail, you know that.'

'Not this time. We need to find out who that lad was before he became Ian Moore and then everything will fall into place.'

West laughed. 'Oh, that's all, is it? So easy.' He was still smiling when he climbed into his car, watching as Andrews sped from the car park. Not for the first time, he thanked his lucky stars that he had him as a partner.

Edel heard the car pull up outside. One final word, she saved her work and switched off the computer. It had been a good day. At this rate, she'd have the first draft written in about six weeks.

'Hi,' she said, coming down the stairs as the front door opened. 'All the criminals in Dublin locked away?'

'Almost all,' he said, leaning in to plant a kiss on her lips. 'Something smells good.'

'Lamb casserole,' she said, opening the kitchen door. 'One of those handy dishes that you can throw in the oven and leave it to cook for hours.' She checked the dinner, watching from the corner of her eye as West took off his jacket and tie, rolled up his shirtsleeves and unbuttoned the top button of his shirt. It amused her: it might make him feel more relaxed, but he still looked every inch the policeman.

'How's the case going,' she asked, putting a large helping of the casserole in front of him.

'Peter and I went to look for answers today, came back with more questions.'

Edel laughed. 'Well that's no surprise! Honestly, you two can't help but complicate things.' Her laugh faded and she reached across and laid a hand on his arm. 'I hope Inspector Morrison knows how lucky he is to have you and Andrews, men who don't take the easy road, who will keep going despite everything until they get to the truth.'

West jabbed a fork in a piece of lamb. 'I think he'd be happier if we got it solved. He's not keen on the clergy.'

'Tell me about the woman you went to see, Laetitia Summers.' She tilted her head. 'A great name, by the way, shame I can't use it.' She smiled at the look in his eyes. 'Relax, I'm teasing you, Mike! But tell me about her anyway.'

By the time they'd finished their meal, Edel knew as much as there was to be known about the woman. 'She sounds like a caricature of a very feminine woman with the breathy voice and her tiny size, but you make her sound hard, tough even. Quite a contrast.'

West put his cutlery down and pushed the plate away. 'I didn't take to her.'

Edel wanted to ask why, wanted to know more about this woman who'd taken her fancy but she saw a wariness creep over West's face. 'I'll throw these in the dishwasher,' she said, standing and picking up the plates. 'Would you like a coffee?'

He shook his head and left and a moment later she heard the TV. He'd watch the news, waiting for any reference to his case and would take any criticism personally. They wouldn't care that he gave heart and soul to his job.

As she cleared up and switched the kettle on to make herself a cuppa, her thoughts were on Laetitia Summers and she was still thinking about her when she took her tea into the lounge to sit on the sofa beside West. 'Anything about it?'

'No, luckily for us some politician was caught out in a financial fraud so the murder of one ex-con was never going to compete.'

She put her empty mug on the coffee table and reached for his hand, feeling his fingers close over hers, hearing his quiet sigh of contentment with a smile.

Perhaps West wouldn't have been quite so contented if he'd known her mind kept drifting back to Laetitia Summers.

24

When Edel sat to write the next morning, her fingers froze over the keyboard. The main characters in her new crime novel were two private investigators, each with a complex background. They were easy to write and, thanks to her experience of the last year, she'd no problem with writing bad guys either. But the main baddie in her story was going to be a young woman... she thought about Fiona Wilson and shook her head, she'd been a cow but she wasn't *bad* enough.

Mike's description of Laetitia Summers intrigued her. If she could see her, maybe speak to her, it would be such a help. It would fill out the character in her story, giving her body and three-dimensionality.

'Don't be daft!' she muttered, reading back the last paragraph she'd written. But her brain wouldn't co-operate. She sat back and chewed her thumbnail. Marino Library. She knew exactly where it was, right beside Wrights fish shop in Fairview. A DART from Greystones would take her directly there; she could visit the library and be back home in a couple of hours... maybe three, tops... then she could get back to work with a clear mind.

She was wearing her writing clothes. Stretchy sweatshirt and pants. Switching the pants for jeans, she slipped on a pair of lace-ups, grabbed a coat and was ready to go. In Greystones DART station, she decided it was karma that she found a parking space straight away and she was smiling when she jumped on the DART five minutes later.

There were plenty of free seats. She took one at the window. The track hugged the coastline most of the way as it trundled past Bray and Dalkey. When it passed Booterstown, she craned her neck to look up Booterstown Avenue. She'd lived there once, a long time ago, years before she bought a place in Drumcondra, a long time before Simon.

All that was behind her. She was in a good place now. A happy place, with a man she loved. *Who would be very annoyed at what she was doing.* She batted that thought away. She was going to look, that was all.

It would have made sense, of course, to have rung and checked Laetitia was working that day. Libraries were open late some evenings and she might work shifts. But Edel was on her way; it was too late now to be clever.

It was over an hour before the DART stopped in Clontarf Road station. It had been bright and sunny when she left Greystones. Here, a light rain was falling. Dark clouds low in the sky made the day dim and gloomy and told her clearly that heavier rain was on the way. Her umbrella was languishing uselessly in the boot of her car. She pulled up the collar of her coat, hunched up her shoulders and made a dash along Clontarf Road for the library.

As she dashed down the laneway to the entrance, the rain started to fall in straight rods of cold grey. She pushed through the wooden door and turned to look back at the rain. She'd planned to stay for only a few minutes, but she could linger and look at some books until it stopped. Maybe check out the competition. The idea made her smile.

The customer service desk was manned by a skinny young man. Edel glanced around. Some of the bookshelves were tall, the petite Laetitia, if she were working, could be behind any of them. Edel wandered up and down the aisles, picking up a book now and then. *Undercover.* A giggle bubbled at the thought.

This had been a crazy idea! She reached the crime section and all thoughts of Laetitia vanished as she took out one book after the other, reading the blurb, checking out the covers, narrowing her eyes as she compared one to the other, looking for trends. Women in raincoats and abandoned houses featured prominently on many. She decided she'd have neither on hers.

One book blurb really caught her attention. She was nodding at how well it was phrased and searched in her pocket for a pen to write the author's name down so she could read it again later. Unfortunately, her pockets held a glut of paper tissues but no pen.

It was at that auspicious moment that a young woman holding a tall pile of books came around the edge of the bookshelf. Edel didn't need to guess, a large name badge prominently displayed on her right chest declared the owner to be Laetitia.

Edel watched from the corner of her eyes as the petite woman dexterously shelved the books she was carrying; balancing and bending, her movements fluid and graceful.

'I wonder if you had a pen I could borrow to write down the name of this book,' Edel said as Laetitia straightened from putting the final book in its right place.

'A pen? Yes, of course.' She slipped one from the pocket of her shirt, handed it over and waited.

Colour flushed Edel's cheeks. What was she going to write on? 'How stupid of me,' she said. 'I don't have paper either.'

She expected the woman to laugh, a mutual understanding

of how we can all be a bit dotty at times. But Laetitia didn't laugh and although the corners of her mouth tilted upwards in what Edel supposed constituted a smile, it was patently false, as fake as her helpful, 'So you need some paper too.'

'No, it's okay,' Edel said, handing the pen back. 'I'll remember the name.' West's description of Laetitia had been accurate, she was a very feminine-looking woman, her voice almost irritatingly breathy. Edel remembered commenting that he made Laetitia sound hard which was a contrast to how he described her. Now, having met her, Edel knew why. There was something unsettling about the juxtaposition of the feminine appearance and the hard, cold eyes.

Curiosity made her decide to extend the contact. 'Perhaps I could photocopy the back of it,' she said, as Laetitia turned away. 'That's permitted, isn't it?'

'Yes, of course. The photocopier is beside the desk.'

Edel gave a throaty laugh. 'I'm useless with technology, do you think you could do it for me?'

Customer training had done its best. Laetitia put the same fake smile in place. 'Of course, if you can't manage it, it's no problem.'

Her mouth might have been saying *no problem*, but her eyes were saying *why can't you do it yourself, you stupid cow.*

According to West, the librarian had said Laetitia was well-liked by the customers. There was no reason for her to be any way suspicious of Edel, so this unfriendly, unhelpful manner was obviously the way she always was. The librarian had lied. Edel wondered why.

As they approached the desk, Edel saw a change in Laetitia's manner. Her smile grew warmer and more genuine.

'Marcus,' she gushed, resting her small hand on the desk in front of the skinny young man with a goatee who was tapping the keys of a computer keyboard without enthusiasm. 'Would you be a darling and look after this customer for me.' She didn't wait for an affirmative, handing over the book and with a nod to Edel, walked away.

Marcus looked after Laetitia with cow eyes before looking down at the book in his hands, then up at Edel with a genuine smile. 'What would you like me to do?'

'I'd like the blurb photocopied, please,' she said. It was tempting to say she could do it herself, but Laetitia might drift back as suddenly as she'd gone. Anyway, maybe she'd get a chance to find out more about her from this obviously smitten man.

She followed him to the photocopier. 'Thanks for doing this,' she said.

'No problem,' Marcus said. 'It's been switched off, though, so it'll take a minute or two to warm up.'

'That's okay, I'm not in a hurry.' She looked around to see if Laetitia was within earshot before saying, 'It must be nice working in the same place as your girlfriend.'

Colour chased up his neck into his cheeks. Even his rather protuberant ears went red. 'We're not–'

'Gosh, I'm so sorry,' Edel rushed in, feeling guilty for embarrassing the young man. 'I jumped to the wrong conclusion.'

The photocopier chose that moment to clank and whirr into life. By the time Marcus had put the book into place and started the process, his colour had returned to normal. He must have noticed Edel's sympathetic expression; leaning towards her slightly and in a hushed voice, he said, 'I really like her but even though we're the same age, she says I'm too young for her and too unsophisticated.' He held his hand out to catch the photocopy as it slid from the machine. 'But I'm hoping she'll eventually realise we'd be good together – if I play my cards right.'

As he took the book out, Edel wanted to grab his arm and warn him that the only thing that was being played was him. A manipulative woman was keeping him dangling for her own benefit. But she said nothing, handing over the money to pay for the photocopying and taking the sheet from him with a smile. 'Thank you. I hope everything works out for you.'

She hoped he got wise before he got hurt. Laetitia struck Edel as the kind of women who had her eye on the main chance, not a woman who'd be remotely interested in dating a poorly-paid library assistant.

Hoping for one more look at Laetitia, Edel hung around the noticeboard for a few minutes, taking leaflets at random. A few were interesting and might give her inspiration for her stories. She folded them and slid them into her pocket alongside the photocopy. She'd turned to leave when she saw Laetitia coming from a room at the back. Edel hurriedly picked up another leaflet, pretending to be engrossed in it while she watched her from the corner of her eye.

Laetitia ignored Marcus, picked up a pile of books and took them to the other end of the library where she was out of view. With a last glance after her, Edel folded the leaflet she'd taken and put it into her pocket beside the others. It was time to leave.

Outside, the sky was still dark but the rain had stopped and she took her time walking back to the station.

She was glad she'd come, glad she'd met and spoke to Laetitia. The character of the evil, murdering female in her crime novel was going to be easy to write now.

25

In Foxrock station, the detective unit was busy. Calls were being made, fingers flew across keyboards, frustrated hands pushed through hair or rubbed strained eyes.

West alternated between sitting in his office and going from desk to desk trying to see some connection, some missing link or jigsaw piece that would make it all come together. This was the job, the long hard, often thankless trudge down one blind end after the other until suddenly you found yourself heading in the right direction.

But that hasn't come yet.

It was almost four when he heard voices raised slightly. He cocked his head to listen, hoping it wasn't an argument. Stress tended to strain patience. He stood when he heard the pitch of the voice. It wasn't annoyance, it was excitement. In the main office he saw Baxter, thumping Edwards on the back. The only thing that could make them this excited was a breakthrough. 'This better be good,' he said, moving closer.

'It is, it is.' A grin almost split Baxter's round freckled face in half. 'We've found him.'

Their noisy excitement attracted everyone's attention and

soon they were surrounded by the rest of the team.

'Get on with it,' Andrews said, nudging Baxter with his elbow.

Baxter wasn't a man to be rushed, especially when he had the limelight. 'Well, as you know I was doing a search for serious crime with multiple offenders in the year before the Moores' home was burgled.' He jerked his head to where Edwards was standing. 'When I said to Mark that it was going to take forever to go through all the reports, he suggested we cross-reference with the search he was doing, the one for missing men in the same time period.'

'It made sense,' Edwards butted in. 'My search turned up over thirty men missing in the same period.'

'And it worked?' West didn't want to rain on their parade but if they had information, he could tell Morrison. Make his day.

'It worked.' Baxter picked up a sheet of paper. 'Three months before the burglary, there was a fight outside a nightclub in Wexford. There were several youths involved. One of them smashed a bottle and used it as a weapon.' Baxter looked up from his notes. 'Eighteen-year-old Gary Bolger died at the scene. Three youths were arrested but one was witnessed fleeing the scene. From all accounts, it was the lad who got away who wielded the bottle.'

West frowned. 'Did they get fingerprints from it?'

'Nope, the bottle was never found. The nightclub is right beside the river. They guessed it was thrown in when the lad absconded.'

'The three who were arrested didn't give up his name?' Jarvis asked.

'Yes, and what about CCTV?' Allen added.

Baxter waved the sheet of paper. 'The three who were arrested were in Wexford for a weekend celebration, staying in a hostel. They didn't know the lad who died or the lad who got away. They also didn't remember what the fight was about.' He looked down at the sheet of paper. 'Their blood alcohol level was almost off the scale and there was a suggestion that drugs were also a factor.'

'A month later,' Edwards cut in, 'seventeen-year-old Cormac Furlong was reported missing by his family. Despite TV and radio appeals, they never heard from him again.' He reached for the photocopy that lay on his desk and handed it over to West. 'This is him.'

It was a family photo. An older couple and three teenage children. A ring had been drawn around the middle child. A sullen-faced skinny boy with the acne-troubled complexion of youth, he was still recognisable. Andrews scrabbled through a pile of papers on his desk to find the photo they had for their victim and held it beside the photocopy. The years had been kind to Cormac: the skinny boy had grown into a well-built, handsome man.

'I spoke to the Garda station in Wexford. They have DNA on file for the missing lad. Forensics are going to do a comparison; they've promised us results by tomorrow.' He tapped the edge of the photocopy. 'Not much doubt, though, is there?'

'So what are we thinking?' Allen asked. 'That he was the one who wielded the broken bottle that killed Gary Bolger, and what? He ran away?'

'I spoke at length to Garda Sergeant Sinnott who remembers the case well,' Edwards said. 'The two families, the Bolgers and the Furlongs, lived on the same street, a few houses away from each other. Gary and Cormac were best mates, had been in school together right through since infant school.'

'There were never any rumours that Cormac was involved in his friend's death?' West asked.

Edwards shook his head. 'Not according to Sinnott. Cormac's mother confirmed that he had come home at least an hour before the attack on Gary Bolger because he'd found the night-club boring. Cormac was, by all accounts, devastated at his friend's death and blamed himself for leaving without him.

'After the funeral, Gary Bolger's mother had a breakdown. There were younger children, a seventeen-year-old girl and ten-year-old twin boys. The father couldn't cope, and the twins came to live with a sister in Dublin.'

A whole community torn apart. 'Then Cormac went missing?'

'Yes. His parents thought at first that he'd run away; that he'd hear the appeals and come back. But when weeks passed, they began to suspect a different scenario.'

'Suicide?' Andrews said with a grimace.

'Yes. He was known to be devastated by his friend's death, it seemed to be a logical enough conclusion.'

'But now we know better,' West said, handing the photocopy back. 'Well done, both of you. At least I can tell Inspector Morrison that we're making progress.' The tension that had grown had relaxed a little. 'Finding out our victim is Cormac Furlong is a big step in the right direction. Now we need to know who killed him and how he got his hands on Ian Moore's ID.'

It was almost to a word what Morrison said a few minutes later.

West smiled to himself as he shifted his shoulder against the wall. 'It's a big piece of the puzzle.'

'We seem to be missing a few facts,' Morrison said, steepling his fingers. 'You're only theorising that Cormac Furlong left Wexford because he killed his friend.'

'Cormac came to Dublin and took on a whole new identity. I think it's reasonable to consider he had a good motivation for doing so.'

'Reasonable,' Morrison said, his mouth twisting as if it were a dirty word. 'I don't want reasonable, West, get me facts.'

26

———

Andrews was waiting when he got back and followed him into his office.

'Don't ask,' West said, dropping onto a chair.

'Don't tell me,' Andrews said with a grin. 'He said *is that all you have?*'

West laughed. 'Not quite, but near enough.' He ran a hand over his head. 'He's right, of course, it's great to know who our victim really is but it doesn't get us much closer to knowing who murdered him.' He leaned back, tilting the chair onto its back legs.

'You won't be able to do that for much longer,' Andrews remarked. 'They're replacing all the chairs with proper, ergonomically-designed chairs. Something to do with health and safety or some such nonsense.'

West brought the front legs of his chair down with a bang. Ignoring the discussion about chairs, he picked up a pen and tapped it on the desk. 'We'll need to speak to everyone again. See if anyone recognises the name. I know St Monica's clergy can't break the sanctity of the confessional but maybe they know the name Cormac Furlong from elsewhere.'

'I'd thought of that, plus the Moores might recognise it – or maybe their son, Ian. It would be worth getting them to ask the next time they speak to him. Furlong had to have known Ian Moore in some capacity.'

'Knew him and burgled his house to get the documents he needed to allow him to take his identity.' West sighed loudly. 'It's all speculation, Peter. We need to get some facts.'

'We will,' Andrews said calmly. 'It's early days. Don't let Morrison get to you. He knows as well as we do that cases like these are a long trudge to the end.'

'It suits him to forget.' West threw the pen down and pushed to his feet. 'Let's get out of here, Pete.'

'Are you going to Baxter's party tomorrow?' Andrews asked as they walked to the car park.

'Yes, Edel is looking forward to it. We can pick you up, if you like? No point in us all driving.'

Andrews shook his head. 'Thanks, but no thanks. Joyce has already said she wants to drive. We don't like leaving the babysitter too late so we'll probably head home from it early.'

West stood. 'I think I'll head back to Fairview in the morning. Surprise Ms Summers and see if she recognises Cormac Furlong's name.'

'You don't need me to come?'

'No, you can have the clergy.' West grinned.

'I'd a feeling that would be my penance,' Andrews said. 'Tell Edel I said hello.'

There was a time West used to envy Andrews heading home to his wife and child. A time when he'd try to drag him to the pub for a pint rather than facing the long evening home, alone. He sat into his car with a smile. Now he was in that same state, or almost. For the first time, he wondered what it would be like to be rushing home to Edel and a child. They'd never discussed the future, or children. Maybe it was time.

Edel was in the kitchen when he got home, humming along to a song playing on the radio, the volume loud enough to drown his arrival. He stood in the doorway watching her.

'Hi,' he said, raising his voice to be heard over the combined noise of the radio and the extraction fan.

Startled, she dropped the wooden spoon and whirled around on her heels. 'I was in a world of my own,' she said with a laugh.

'Thinking about the book you're writing?' he asked, kissing her on the cheek before sniffing loudly. 'Smells good.'

'Me or the food,' she said, turning to kiss him back.

He slipped his hands around her waist. 'My heart says you, my belly says whatever it is you're cooking.' Guilt flickered. 'You know you don't have to cook every night, Edel. We could go out or get a takeaway.'

She shook her head. 'I like to cook. It relaxes me; sometimes it helps get a story tangle untangled.' She waved a hand to the table where an open notebook was surrounded by papers and pencils. 'My muse even responds to the sound of bubbling rice. I jotted down a few notes while it cooked.' She turned to switch off the oven. 'It's almost ready.'

'I'll move your notebook,' West said, reaching over to close it. The scraps of paper and leaflets that were strewn willy-nilly over the end of the table made him smile. She really was very disorganised. He gathered them together and opened the cover of the notebook to slip them inside when something caught his eye. Not the leaflet itself, but the stamp on the back of it. *Marino Library.*

He remembered how interested Edel had been in hearing about Laetitia Summers and felt a leaden weight in his chest as he looked across the room to where she stood dishing up the dinner.

'You went to the library.' It wasn't a question, he didn't need to ask. Where else would she have found it.

She looked up, startled, sauce dripping from the serving spoon to the counter, her eyes flitting to the leaflet he held in his hand. He watched the colour drain from her cheeks, the slight tremble in her lower lip, her eyes darting from right to left as if looking for a way out. Signs of guilt he'd seen so often in the course of his work, it wasn't something he wanted to see at home. Not something he wanted to see on the face of the woman he loved.

He put the leaflet on the table and walked from the room, shutting the door quietly after him. Slamming the door and dramatically storming from the house wasn't his way; anyway, it wasn't really anger that surged through him, more a deep disappointment.

Tyler was curled up on the sofa. West poured himself a large Jameson and sat beside the little chihuahua who opened one protuberant brown eye to look at him before guessing it wasn't a good time to ask for attention and closing it again.

Half the whiskey was gone before the door opened.

'I'm sorry.'

He didn't look at her. 'Sorry for going or sorry for my finding out?' He heard her quick indrawn breath and waited for the apologies, the excuses.

'I'm not sorry I went,' she said, surprising him. 'I'd decided to make the bad guy in my first crime novel a young woman... mainly because it was away from everything I'd experienced. Remember, I said I wasn't going to write about anything close to what I'd been through.' She moved to perch on the sofa beside Tyler, her hand sneaking out to caress the dog's head. 'Problem was, I found I couldn't see the character in my head. I kept seeing Liz Goodbody and if I managed to shoo her out of my head, Fiona Wilson popped in.'

West turned to look at her. Liz had tried to kill her, Fiona had tried to destroy her. She'd not had much luck with the women she'd met recently. What on earth dragged her to see Laetitia Summers?

'When you told me about Laetitia,' Edel said quietly, 'you made her sound fascinating and I knew I could build her into the kind of character I wanted.' She reached a hand out and rested it on his arm. He could feel the warmth of it through his shirt. 'I wanted to see her, to drive out the other women.'

'Did it work?'

Edel picked Tyler up and put him on her lap, sitting back on the sofa with a sigh. 'I may as well tell you everything,' she said.

There was more? The tension that had started to ease ratcheted up again. 'I think you'd better.' The sooner he knew, the faster he could do some damage limitation. He tried not to think of Morrison's tight-lipped annoyance if he heard.

'I asked her to photocopy something for me. I don't know whether she thought it was beneath her or whether she simply couldn't be bothered but she quickly passed me on to another library assistant. Turns out he'd do anything for her, totally smitten. I'd say he hasn't a chance in hell.'

West waited for more and when she stayed silent, he turned to look at her. 'That's it?'

Annoyance jerked her upright. Tyler did what any sensible dog would do, he jumped off and headed for some food. 'What did you think?' Edel said. 'That I'd gone to her and said Detective Garda West had mentioned she seemed to be a bad 'un and I was curious as I wanted to have a young woman like her in my next book?'

He wasn't sure what he'd thought. Truth was, it had been such a shock to see the leaflet with Marino Library stamped across it that he'd reacted rather than thought. He sipped the whiskey, tapping the glass against his teeth. Rather than answering her question, he asked, 'What did you think of her?'

There was silence for a few seconds. Then with a loudly exhaled breath, Edel rested back against the sofa. 'I thought she was absolutely perfect as a model for the devious, manipulative young woman who is the guilty party in my book.'

West finished the whiskey. 'Yes, there's something about her that struck me as being a little–' He hesitated. The word *evil* wasn't one he liked to use.

'Wrong?' Edel suggested.

Wrong? It would do for the moment. 'Yes. I didn't believe her story about being raped. Not a bit of it.'

'That library assistant, Marcus, obviously fancied her. His eyes followed her all the time but he said he hadn't a hope, that he was too young and unsophisticated for her. But if that's the case, why would she have gone out with Ian Moore? He didn't sound in any way sophisticated from what you said.'

'Cormac Furlong,' West said, smiling to see her puzzled expression. All tension had gone. She'd not done anything wrong. As Andrews said all too frequently, he needed to stop taking himself so seriously. 'I hope you didn't throw out that dinner,' he said, reaching for her hand.

'It's in the oven,' she said. She leaned forward and kissed him on the cheek. 'Does that mean I'm forgiven?'

'For the moment, it means my hunger outweighs everything else,' West said. Getting to his feet, he reached a hand down for hers and pulled her to her feet. 'Over dinner, I'll tell you all about Cormac.' Why not? They'd spoken about cases before and she'd been involved in some of the recent ones. It was how they met. Maybe it was the way it was meant to be.

Over dinner, he told her about Cormac Furlong and his possible involvement in Gary Bolger's death. 'It's all so much guesswork and theory so far though,' he said, pushing his empty plate away and reaching for the wine.

'It strikes me that it's always that way,' Edel said. 'Remember on Clare Island, more information kept turning up, pointing you in different directions, then it was the person you least expected who was guilty.'

Clare Island. How could he forget? 'There we had a surfeit of suspects. Here we've none.'

'But you think, somehow, it's tied in with that daft calendar?'

West took a swallow of the wine and put the glass down. 'For almost ten years Furlong lived a quiet life, kept himself to himself, didn't drink or get involved in fights. Then he's persuaded to do the calendar and within months this unassuming man is imprisoned for rape.'

'You're thinking he might have been set up by Laetitia?'

'She didn't report the crime until three days after the fact. Too late to do blood alcohol levels on Moore. He insists he'd not been drinking but the taxi driver who picked him up insisted he was.'

'He could have been drugged.'

'That's what his defence team argued but the jury weren't convinced. Baxter and Edwards spoke to the investigating officer in Clontarf who said he wasn't convinced of Furlong's guilt.'

'But he was found guilty,' Edel said, horrified.

A long sigh was West's only answer as he reached for his glass. Miscarriages of justice were, unfortunately, not as rare as they'd like. 'He was a model prisoner which was why he was released early.' He tapped a fingernail against the side of the glass. 'It seems like someone felt he hadn't been punished enough.'

'And decided to finish the job by killing him.'

West smiled at her wide eyes. 'Maybe you shouldn't write

novels about crimes. Maybe you should join the Gardaí and help solve them.'

'Now wouldn't you love that,' she said with a grin. 'I'll stick to writing about them.' She lifted her wine glass and clinked it against his. 'It's fun being a sounding board for you, though.'

'You know you're more than a sounding board, Edel. You've a keen mind. It was your idea to look for missing people, remember, and thanks to that we were able to find out our victim's identity.'

She smiled, pleased at his praise. 'I like to hear about your work and I think it's good for you to be able to talk about it, too.' Pouring more wine into both of their glasses, she lifted hers and sipped, her expression serious. 'What are you going to do next?'

West's eyes hardened. 'I'm going to turn over a few rocks to see what crawls from underneath.

27

―――――

West left the house early next morning. The roads were Saturday-morning quiet and it was a pleasant drive across the city to Marino. He turned on the radio, increasing the volume when he heard 'Nessun dorma', relieved that Andrews wasn't there to demand he switch to something more his style. It was too early to listen to Johnny Cash.

It was almost nine before he arrived at Summers' house. She wasn't expecting him and the gates were shut. The Micra he'd noticed on his previous visit was in the same position. He could have opened the gate and parked beside it, instead he pulled up onto the wide pavement and stopped there. He got out, stretched, and looked around. Griffith Avenue was one of the prettiest streets in the city. In the summer, the trees that lined its length were lushly green; this early in the year they were bare, their knotted and gnarled branches stretching out dramatically. They suited his mood.

He'd half-expected to find that Laetitia had gone for a run and was prepared to wait but looking up at the closed curtains of the bedroom windows he thought perhaps it was other exercise she was having that day. An older, more sophisticated boyfriend, according to Edel's chat with the other library assistant. Or was that the impression Laetitia wanted to give?

There was something *wrong* about her had been Edel's conclusion. He'd thought it apt, but if Laetitia were somehow involved in what had happened to Cormac Furlong, perhaps his first choice of word might have been more correct. *Evil.* He'd long come to understand that such people did exist.

The front gate opened without a sound. To his surprise, the doorbell was answered almost immediately. Laetitia stared at him, her fingers tightening the belt of a silky robe. 'Was I expecting you?' Her tone wasn't friendly.

He tried a smile. It wasn't returned. 'I'm sorry to arrive unannounced,' he said. 'I was at an early meeting in Clontarf Garda Station and I thought I'd call on the off-chance you'd be here.' The lie was believable but he could see by the glint in her eye that she knew he wasn't telling the truth. She was a much sharper woman than the impression she liked to give. 'If I could come inside for a few minutes, there's a couple of things I wanted to ask.' When she didn't reply, he added, 'Unless, of course, you have visitors.'

'No,' she said, then as if remembering the wisdom of staying on the right side of the Gardaí, she pasted an unconvincing smile in place and stood back. 'You must forgive me,' she said, running a hand through her hair. 'I've had a very restless night. Insomnia is a curse.'

West followed her into the kitchen.

'Coffee?'

'Please.' He stood, his hands jammed into his coat pockets while she filled the kettle and spooned coffee into two mugs. She didn't ask him if he wanted sugar or milk, handing him the black coffee and going through the door into the other room without a word.

West, following her, watched as she sat on a chair near the

French doors and stared out across the garden. She raised the mug to her mouth, blew on the hot coffee and slurped noisily. He sat on the nearest chair, put his mug on a coaster and waited for her to turn his way.

She kept her gaze fixed on the garden. 'Ask away.'

He'd have preferred to be able to see any change in expression, but he'd learned to make do. 'Does the name Cormac Furlong mean anything to you?' West kept his eyes fixed on her hands, saw the automatic tightening of her fingers, knuckles white against the dark-blue mug.

'No,' she said. 'Should it?'

They hadn't had DNA confirmation yet, but in West's head there was no doubt. 'It was the real name of the man who assaulted you.'

She turned to look at him then, eyes widened, her mouth a perfect O, a masterclass in feigning a look of surprise. 'His name wasn't Ian Moore?'

'No, it wasn't.'

'How odd.' She lifted the mug to her mouth again and slurped.

West picked up his coffee and took a sip. It was good coffee, easy to drink black. 'Do you get to visit your parents often?'

If she was surprised at this change in direction, she didn't say, merely shrugging a shoulder that sent a ripple down the fabric of her gown. 'I've been a few times. It's a bit too hot in the summer for me, too boring in the winter.'

'But they're happy there?' When she didn't answer, he sipped his coffee. 'I've often thought about buying something there myself, but a guard's salary doesn't run far. What was it your father did?' The question lacked any subtlety so he wasn't surprised when her eyebrows rose into her hairline. He laughed and held a hand out, palm up. 'Sorry, nosiness becomes a habit. I suppose I'm jealous: as I said, it's something I'd love to do.'

Her eyebrows lowered a little, her lips curving in an unattractive sneer. 'Perhaps you should look at cheaper places, parts of Spain perhaps.'

'Perhaps,' he said, unoffended. She hadn't told him what her father did. It didn't matter. It was something he could easily find out for himself.

As fishing exercises went, it wasn't catching him much. He finished his coffee, put the mug down and stood. 'Thank you for your time.'

'Perhaps, if you feel the need to come again, you'd do me the courtesy of phoning first?'

'That's my wrist well and truly slapped,' he said. 'Don't get up, I'll see myself out.'

He didn't rush, stopping in the hallway to fasten his jacket, his head cocked to listen for sounds from above. If there was someone there, they were being remarkably quiet. A free-standing, ornate coat stand in the corner caught his eye. It was exactly what he'd been looking for for his home and he took a step closer, admiring it while his detective's brain was assessing the two coats hanging there. The pink raincoat was most likely Laetitia's; but not the long, heavy grey coat that would have swamped her.

West would have liked to have gone through the pockets, but a multicoloured scarf was stuffed into the one nearest him. With a sigh of regret, he opened the door and left temptation behind.

He had reached his car when he had the distinct impression he was being watched and glanced up to the bedroom window. There was nobody to be seen but he'd swear the curtain twitched. No more than anyone, he didn't like being spied upon and lifted a hand in a wave. The curtain stayed motionless.

Laetitia was entitled to a private life. Entitled to a boyfriend, lover, whatever. But, as he stared up at the window, his sense that there was something suspicious about Laetitia Summers went up a notch. More theories and suspicions. He hadn't learned anything new and still had no hard facts. A smile flickered when he thought of what Morrison would say if he knew. But the inspector didn't need to know everything. He sat into his car, pulled out his phone and rang the station.

'Forensics got back to us with confirmation. Our vic is definitely Cormac Furlong,' Andrews told him.

Confirmation was good, but it wasn't a surprise. 'Nothing else?'

Andrews must have heard the frustration in his voice, his own more than usually calm. 'It's early yet, the team is chipping away.'

'I didn't learn anything new from Ms Summers,' West said. 'Who's looking into her and her family?' He heard a rustle of paper before Andrews came back to him.

'I have Jarvis on it.'

'Good. Okay, I'm heading to speak to the Moores.' He checked his watch. 'I should be with you late morning. Anything else I should know about?' He listened to the details of a minor domestic that Edwards and Baxter were dealing with. 'That shouldn't take them long,' he said, relieved. He needed all their focus on this case.

'And Mrs Bennet was brought in again,' Andrews said. 'I had a word with her and her husband when he came to fetch her. The Parsons want it to stop.'

'I bet they do,' West said with a weary sigh. 'Dammit, I meant to ring the bereavement counsellor Mrs Bennet's attending to give her a heads-up and it went out of my mind. I'll ring her later.' Hanging up, he sat for a few minutes thinking about Ella Parsons, guilty of a crime she might never serve time for, and Joanne Bennet, a grieving mother looking for justice. Sometimes, the law was an ass.

There was nothing he could do for either except make that phone call. This time, he wouldn't forget.

Before West drove away, he made a quick call to the Moores' house. 'If I could have a few minutes of your time,' he said when the call was answered.

'We're not doing anything more exciting,' Ben Moore said.

It wasn't exactly inviting. 'Thank you,' West said. 'In about an hour if that's convenient.'

'As convenient as any other,' Moore said and hung up.

The journey across the city was slow but uneventful. Slightly later than the promised hour, West turned onto Patrick Street. There was no parking directly outside the house, nor on the rest of the street and it took a few minutes of journeying up and down side streets to find a space. He checked his phone for messages. There was nothing new from Andrews, but his expression brightened to see one from Edel. *My crimes are getting solved quickly, hope yours are too!!!!*

I wish, he answered, adding a *love you* before sending it. He imagined her smiling when she got it.

Heavy rain hammering a beat on the windscreen wiped the smile away. It was a few minutes' walk to the house; a dripping, sodden man arriving on their doorstep wouldn't endear him to the Moores. He grabbed a raincoat from the back seat and shrugged it on.

Ben Moore's earlier unenthusiastic response hadn't led West to believe that he'd be greeted warmly so he was surprised when Eve Moore answered the door with a bright smile. It faltered when she saw his rain-drenched figure.

'Oh dear, you're soaked,' she said, standing back. 'Come in quickly.' Leaving him to step inside, she hurried away and returned holding a fluffy towel that she pressed into his hands.

West blotted his face. 'Thank you. I couldn't get parking outside.'

'Parking around here can be a nightmare,' she said, taking the towel from him. 'Hang up your coat.' She indicated the coat rack behind him. 'I made some scones. They're waiting to be eaten.'

West followed her into the cosy living room where Ben Moore was slouched on a sofa, a newspaper folded in his hands, spectacles perched on the end of his nose. 'Come sit near the fire,' he said without standing. 'It's turned a nasty day out there.'

West unbuttoned his jacket and sat. The fire hissed and crackled in the hearth. Eve Moore fussed around, mother-hen-like, Ben Moore directing her actions from his chair, and soon there was teas, scones, butter and jam on a low table.

The tea was strong, the scones delicious. 'Have another,' Eve said, pushing the plate towards West.

He'd already eaten two. Tempted though he was, he couldn't manage more. 'Thank you, I won't, but they were probably the best I've ever tasted.'

'Silver-tongued,' Ben said with a shake of his head. 'I told her you were.'

'It isn't always easy, telling the tales we need to tell,' West said with an apologetic shrug.

'Hmmm,' was the reply. 'Well, you'd better tell us what you've come to tell us this time then.'

West put his cup on the saucer, reached into the inside pocket of his jacket and took out a folded document. 'I thought you might like to have this back.' He handed it to Eve.

She took it, unfolded it, and gasped. 'Ian's birth cert.'

'We found it among paperwork in the victim's apartment. It seemed a good idea to return it to you.'

Her eyes shone. 'Thank you. This means a lot.'

'I'd like to say it was the only reason I came, but unfortunately it isn't,' West said with a smile. 'Does the name Cormac Furlong ring a bell?'

Ben Moore quickly showed he was no fool. 'That was the man's real name?'

'Yes. He'd been reported missing by his family ten years ago. For reasons that are not as yet clear, he chose to change his identity. We'd obviously like to know why he chose your son. He must have known he was going away for a long period of time.'

'But originally Ian was going to come home after a year or two,' Eve said.

West saw her husband's eyes flicker. He needed to know the truth. 'Is there something you want to add, Mr Moore?'

Ben's cup clattered on the saucer as he put it down. 'Ian thought it would make it easier if he told you that,' he said. 'But he confided in me that Dubai was his dream job, that he was going to stay as long as they wanted him.'

West reckoned there'd be words between them when he'd gone, but he needed to know more. Someone apart from Ben Moore knew about Ian's plans. 'Who else would have known the truth, Mr Moore?'

His answer was a slow headshake.

Frustrated, West sat forward. 'Maybe Ian might recognise the name? You say you speak to him on Skype. Would it be possible to get him now?'

Ben checked his watch. 'Maybe. I could try.' He stretched behind him for the iPad that sat on a shelf. 'Let's see if he answers.'

West was in luck. Seconds later, a cheerful Ian appeared on the screen. 'Hey, Dad, you're early.'

'It isn't me who wants to speak to you, son,' Ben Moore said. 'It's the detective who was here telling us about the dead man. He wants to have a word. Your mother and I will talk to you later.' With a wave, he turned the iPad around so that it faced West.

'Mr Moore, I'm Detective Garda Sergeant Mike West. I'm sorry if this is inconvenient but you might be able to help us solve a crime.'

'Sounds intriguing.' Ian Moore was suntanned and relaxed. His smile was reminiscent of his mother's but his sharp eyes were inherited from his father.

'We pinpointed the man who used your identity as Cormac Furlong. He lived in Wexford and was reported missing before you went away. He would have been eighteen at the time. I know it's a long time ago but does the name ring any bells?'

But it was Ben Moore's voice that cut across the silence. 'You didn't mention Wexford,' he said sharply. 'We used to have a house in Wexford. In Kilmuckridge to be exact.' He slid the iPad back. 'Remember, Ian, you used to go to the pubs and clubs in Curracloe?'

A laugh boomed across the miles. 'Remember! God, we had some craic there!'

Ben Moore frowned. 'You spent a week there the summer before you went away.' He turned to address West. 'We'd put the house on the market. We weren't using it as much as we used to and we knew once Ian went away we'd never go down. It had seemed the sensible thing to do.'

'When did you go?' West asked. This was it. It had to be. He sat, curbing his impatience as Ian wandered back through the memories of that summer. Finally, he heard the words he'd been waiting for.

'After that, Tim and I headed down to Kilmuckridge for a final week of fun before I went away.'

A week before Gary Bolger was killed. Two weeks before Cormac Furlong disappeared.

Ian was still reminiscing. 'We spent most of our days hanging about on the beach at Curracloe, then we'd head to the pub for drinks. There are a couple of clubs, we went once or twice but mostly we stayed in the pub chatting.'

'Talking about your future plans?' West saw Ian's eyes focus. He wasn't a stupid man, he knew where the question was coming from. 'Yes, of course,' he said with a shake of his head. 'We talked of nothing else. Not just me and Tim either, but others joined in. Local lads who were heading to Dublin to university, other visitors talking about starting various jobs in different parts of the country. We never thought to be careful about what we said, so we weren't.'

Of course they weren't. Young men full of the promise of their future. Probably Cormac and Gary were among them, talking about their own plans.

'There's something else,' Ian said. He ran a hand over his suntanned face. 'The house had gone on the market a few days before. I remember saying... jokingly... that if any of them wanted to buy a house nearby that ours was going up for sale soon. I only remember because some of the foreign students... German, I think... wanted more details so they could tell their parents about it. I thought I was being helpful.' He looked towards his father. 'You'd complained about the commission the estate agents were going to charge. I thought that if these Germans bought it from you directly that you'd be saved that.' He stopped as if embarrassed at how stupid his younger self had been.

West, who was never too surprised at how idiotic people could be, said, 'You gave them your contact details?'

A regretful nod filled the iPad screen. 'The Germans were staying in Wexford for another couple of weeks before heading to Dublin. I was heading home the next day. I wrote down our address and phone number and told them to call around.'

'Did they?'

'No, and to be honest, I never gave them another thought.' A door opening behind his computer drew his attention away from the screen for a few seconds. 'Sorry, I need to go, there's a meeting I should be at. I'm so sorry, Mum and Dad, it looks as though the burglary was my fault.'

Hurried reassurances from both parents that he wasn't to blame made Ian smile before he lifted a hand in farewell and closed the connection.

'So that's how that young man knew all about Ian's plans, and how to find us,' Ben Moore said.

'It looks likely,' West said. 'We can't prove anything, of course, but the timeline works. When Gary Bolger was killed a week later, Cormac may have been looking for an escape and remembered those words. It wouldn't have been hard to find the Germans, and if they had kept the details, why would they have refused to share? And it wouldn't have been hard to find out who Ian was and where he lived. People talk. Nor would it have been difficult to find out where in Dublin you lived.'

'Our security then was pretty bad,' Ben Moore said. 'The windows were wooden and rotten in parts. There's a laneway at the back. The burglar hopped over the wall when the house was empty and used a screwdriver to open a back window.' He pointed to the window behind. 'They're all uPVC now, maybe not as aesthetically pleasing but safer. Plus, they're all alarmed and we have Sinbad.' A smile appeared suddenly. 'Shutting the gate after the horse has bolted, eh?'

'I'd say you learned a valuable lesson,' West said.

'So more like, *fool me once, shame on you; fool me twice, shame on me?*'

'Exactly.' West got to his feet. 'Thank you both for your time and help, and for getting through to your son for me. I shouldn't have to bother you again.'

Eve stood and held out her hand. 'You got Ian's birth cert back to us. Someday, when he finds the right woman, he'll be looking for it to get married.'

It crossed West's mind as he was walking back to his car that he'd no idea where his birth certificate was. Perhaps he'd better ask his mother.

29

It had fallen to Andrews' lot to deal with the clergy again. He didn't mind, he was a churchgoer but he didn't stand in awe of the priests. At least not when he had a job to do.

He understood the sanctity of the confessional, that the priests would be unable to tell him if they'd seen Cormac Furlong there. But it was possible they'd seen him elsewhere, somewhere they weren't tied by the same restrictions. He also needed to clear up the mystery about Father McComb. Because a priest moving from parish to parish every few months was unusual.

Father Jeffreys agreed to see him at 9.30 in the sacristy of St Monica's. The Garda technical team had finished their investigation and the church was reopening for business. It wasn't how the parish priest had phrased it, but Andrews guessed that's what he'd meant when he said they were once more able to offer customary services and devotions.

Andrews parked in the car park, walked to the back of the church and rapped on the door. It was answered almost immediately, the sacristan Joe Ryan pulling the door open and waving him in.

'How are you doing, Mr Ryan?' Andrews asked. He hadn't seen him since their original call-out. The man had looked pale then, he looked paler now. Death had a far-reaching impact.

'It hasn't been easy,' the quietly-spoken man said. 'I suppose you're used to it, but I can't get the image out of my head. It's keeping me awake at night too. Millie wants me to retire, says I've done enough.'

Andrews saw the slight tremor in the man's hands, the dark circles under his eyes. 'Have you spoken to anyone? Your GP maybe?'

'Millie said I should but–' he shrugged '–it seems a bit silly. I'm not sick after all.'

'You saw something dreadful,' Andrews said. 'I've seen death many times but I've never got used to it. Certainly, I've never become numb to its effect. I don't want to either. Seeing something so terrible can cause damage, Mr Ryan. You've been injured, there's simply no visible sign. And if you speak to someone who knows about these things, they can help the healing process.'

Ryan's chin trembled.

'Think about it. There's no shame in admitting you need help. Now,' he said, raising his voice a little. 'I'd better go in: Father Jeffreys is expecting me.'

The sacristy door was open. It was a small, cluttered room that appeared to have multiple uses. A table in one corner held a kettle and tea and coffee-making paraphernalia. In the other corner, a small desk held a computer. Father Jeffreys was hunched over it, his fingers flying over the keyboard with what Andrews, a two-finger tapper, thought remarkable speed.

'Good morning, Garda Andrews,' the priest said with no noticeable slowing of speed. 'Forgive me, I must finish this, I'll be five minutes.'

'I might take a wander around the church,' Andrews said. He

retraced his steps and took the door that led into the body of the church.

It was quiet. One elderly man was kneeling in one of the pews, another younger man making the Stations of the Cross. Andrews walked quietly down the side aisle to the main doors, then turned to look back to where Cormac Furlong had hung. He wondered how long it would be before that image faded.

'Good morning.'

Andrews hadn't heard the footsteps behind and turned, startled, to find Father McComb standing there. 'I didn't hear you,' Andrews said, annoyed at being taken by surprise.

Father McComb smiled. 'You get used to moving about in a stealthy fashion so as not to disturb people.' He looked towards the altar. 'Are you here for mass? I would be happy to have a member of the Garda Síochána in the congregation: we're both on the same side after all.'

Andrews wasn't sure he understood the comparison but he smiled as if he did. 'Unfortunately, I'm here to see Father Jeffreys and under severe time constraints.' He was pleased with that expression, thought it sounded like something West would say.

'I'll say a prayer for you,' Father McComb said and with a gentle nod, he headed up the main aisle to the altar and disappeared through the door to the back.

Andrews waited a few seconds before following.

'Sorry for the delay,' Father Jeffreys said when Andrew returned. 'Please take a seat.'

There wasn't a chair free from clutter but Andrews was used to making do. He took an untidy pile of leaflets from one chair, shuffled them together and put them on the corner of the desk before sitting.

'Now,' Father Jeffreys said with a sigh as he shut the laptop. 'How can I help you this morning?'

'During the course of any investigation, we end up chasing a lot of what turns out, in the end, to be unrelated facts.' Andrews watched the priest's lips tighten as he wondered what was coming. 'Unfortunately, we don't know they're unrelated until after we've investigated.' He met the priest's gaze. 'Tell me about Father McComb.' To his surprise, Father Jeffreys laughed.

'Oh dear,' the priest said, wiping his eyes. 'I'm sorry, you must think me so rude. I thought you were going to tell me something terrible, not ask me about Kevin.'

Andrews felt a surge of relief. Whatever the reason for McComb moving from parish to parish, it wasn't the one he dreaded. 'It's unusual for a priest to move as often as he does. When he was asked, he simply said he went where he was told.'

'Indeed, he does,' Father Jeffreys said. He waved a hand towards the kettle. 'Let's have a cuppa and I'll tell you about him.'

The tea was strong, the milk on the turn. Andrews wasn't fussy and sipped it as he waited to be told the mystery behind Father McComb.

Father Jeffreys took his seat behind the desk and blew gently on his tea before taking a drink and putting it down. 'Father McComb is an incredibly intelligent, diligent man of great faith. He is also very intense. Too intense, I'm afraid and his sermons... well.'

Andrews had heard him once. All fire and brimstone, hell and damnation. 'Not exactly uplifting, from what I remember,' he said.

'Exactly!' Father Jeffreys said. 'To be honest, he scares people to death. The archbishop decided it was best if he didn't stay too long in any parish, so he's moved on every six months or so. This posting has been his longest. The archbishop is hoping that perhaps he has learned to be–' He stopped, searching for the right word.

'Kinder?' Andrews suggested.

'That and more compassionate,' Father Jeffreys said. 'I hope that puts your mind to rest that there is no mystery attached to poor Father McComb.'

'I'm relieved,' Andrews said. He saw a resigned look in the priest's eyes and knew he didn't have to say more. 'The other reason I came was to ask if the name Cormac Furlong meant anything to you?'

'Cormac Furlong? No, it doesn't ring a bell.'

'It's the real name of the man murdered here. Perhaps, if you would be so kind, you could ask the other priests if the name means anything to them.'

'Certainly.' Father Jeffreys' rather lined face creased further. 'But it will be a slim chance, Garda Andrews, we meet so many people but we rarely know their names.'

Andrews stood. 'It's worth a shot. Sometimes,' he said with a smile, 'we get our leads from mysterious places.'

There was no sign of the sacristan as he left. He hoped he'd get the help he obviously needed.

It was nearly midday. He took out his phone and rang West's number. 'Nothing here,' he said when it was answered. 'Father McComb was red-herring material and Father Jeffreys didn't recognise Cormac Furlong's name. He said he'd ask the other priests but I think we've hit a dead end here. What about you?' He listened as West filled him in on his conversation with the Moores.

'Young idiot,' he said when he heard Ian Moore had given his address and phone number out to virtual strangers. 'It seems safe to bet that's how it went down.'

'Yes, but it's still all supposition, Pete, and it's not getting us any nearer to knowing who killed him.'

'It hasn't been a week. We'll get there,' Andrews said calmly.

A frustrated grunt came down the line, followed by, 'Well,

I'm volunteering you to go and tell Morrison that on Monday morning.'

'Monday's a long way away,' Andrews said placidly. 'There's nothing else we can do today. It's Saturday. There's no point in either of us going back to the station and mulling over things or standing looking at the scant information on The Wall. I'm heading home to spend the afternoon playing with Petey. Maybe if we both relax inspiration will come to us.'

30

'Ready?' West shouted up the stairs as he checked his watch: 7.30. It was over sixty kilometres to Gorey. They'd get there a little after eight if they left soon.

'Coming.' Edel's voice floated down. It was what she'd said five minutes ago.

There wasn't much point in standing in the hallway peering up in hope. Instead, West headed back into the lounge, switched on the TV, and stood listening to a political debate that didn't really interest him. His brain was still in work mode. Even an afternoon in a local garden centre with Edel hadn't put Furlong out of his head. He liked complicated, challenging cases, but this one was driving him crazy. Everything was too airy-fairy. He needed one concrete fact to be able to bring to Morrison on Monday. A smile flickered. Maybe he should make good on his threat and send Andrews.

He heard footsteps on the stairs and checked his watch again: 7.45pm. He switched off the TV and turned as Edel came into the room. 'Wow,' he said, giving a low whistle of appreciation.

'You like?' She twirled around, the silk dress floating, then settling on her curves.

'I like very much,' West said. He put his hands on her waist and drew her close. 'You smell nice too.' She was warm and comfortable in his arms. Suddenly Gorey seemed too much of a bother. 'We could stay home,' he whispered into her hair.

Edel laughed and pulled away. 'Seamus would be upset and, anyway, we'd miss all the fun.' She turned to pick up the wrapped gift that was sitting on the coffee table. 'Let's go or we'll be late.'

There didn't seem to be any purpose in pointing out that he'd been waiting for the best part of thirty minutes. He grabbed his keys and within a few minutes they were on the road to Gorey.

Baxter's new home was in a small housing estate on the far side of the town. West followed the satnav directions to the entrance of the estate and Baxter's directions from there to a neat semi-detached house. 'That's the one,' he said, passing by the line of cars parked along the road. He drove on and found parking a few minutes away.

Baxter opened the door at the first ring of the bell. 'Hello, welcome to my castle!'

'Congratulations,' Edel said, handing over the gift. 'A little something to mark the occasion.'

Tanya appeared at Baxter's shoulder and he reached an arm around to bring her forward. 'I don't think either of you have met my lovely fiancée. Tanya, this is the famous Mike West you hear me talking about all the time, and his girlfriend, Edel.' He handed her the wrapped gift. 'And look, another housewarming present.'

Tanya, a petite brunette with slightly protuberant brown eyes, smiled. 'That's very kind, thank you.' She pointed up the stairway behind. 'You can drop your coats up on the bed in the spare room while I get you a drink. What would you like?'

'White wine would be lovely,' Edel said, taking off her coat.

West asked for a beer and followed Tanya through to the kitchen while Edel vanished upstairs. He knew quite a few of the people crowded into the house; Allen and Edwards were deep in conversation on the far side of the room, Andrews and his wife, Joyce, speaking to an older woman he guessed to be Tanya's mother. 'It's a good crowd,' he commented, taking the glass of beer Tanya held out.

She smiled. 'Seamus invited everyone under the sun, and everyone came.'

The doorbell rang, the noise barely audible over the sound of voices and laughter. West sipped his beer and waited for Edel to return. 'Here you go,' he said, handing her the glass of wine. 'Let's squeeze through and speak to Peter and Joyce.'

'This is Tanya's mother,' Andrews said when they joined him.

West smiled and shook the older woman's hand. 'I guessed,' he said, 'she's very like you.'

They stayed chatting for a while, joined by others from Foxrock station until, as was often the way it went, the crowd divided into work friends, school friends, and old family friends.

West smiled as Edel and Joyce got their heads together. 'I bet I know what they're saying,' he said to Andrews.

'That we always end up talking shop,' Andrews said. 'They know us too well.'

A shout of laughter came from the far side of the room followed by Baxter's loud, slightly inebriated voice.

'I hope he'll sober up by Monday,' West said, taking a sip of his beer, wishing he could have another. But he knew even if he weren't driving he wouldn't have drunk any more. The same reason Andrews would stick to only one even though Joyce was driving. Neither man liked to let their guard down in front of the rest of the team.

There was food; a chicken curry and a vegetarian curry. West and Andrews ate and talked about the case and about the team. It was pleasant, relaxing.

When the food was cleared away, Tanya and Baxter opened their gifts, laughing at the funny ones, genuinely grateful for the suitable, if boring, ones. They laughed when they opened Edel and West's gift. He hadn't seen it. In fact, he didn't even know what it was until Tanya opened it.

'This is great,' she said, punching Baxter's arm. 'You will have to divide your allegiance now!'

Edel had bought a tea cosy and egg cosies in the Wexford colours of purple and gold. It was the perfect gift for the GAA-mad Baxter, who frequently wore a scarf sporting the Dublin colours of blue and navy.

The Gaelic Athletic Association encouraged support of county teams. It wasn't something West had ever been interested in, he knew the Dublin colours thanks to Baxter, but other counties' colours were an enigma to him. He picked up the tea cosy. Did people really use such a thing anymore?

'I'll use it every day,' Tanya said, answering his unspoken question.

West put it down beside the smaller egg cosies. Purple and gold. He frowned. They were striking colours. Where had he seen them recently? It danced around the corner of his brain, tantalisingly close. Ignoring the hullabaloo that surrounded him, he thought back to all the places he'd been over the last few days. The Moores' house? No, despite their link to Wexford, it hadn't been there. It hit him then, Laetitia Summers' house. The coat hanging on the coat stand. With the scarf stuffed into the pocket. The multicoloured scarf in purple and gold.

Like most detectives, he didn't believe in coincidence. Andrews had drifted away and was chatting to some men West recognised as Gardaí but didn't know. He made his way to his side. 'I think I have something,' he said, drawing him away. He told him about the scarf.

Andrews raised an eyebrow. 'If you're going into Morrison on Monday with that, give me warning so I can take cover!'

'Think about it,' West said. He knew he was on the right track. 'Laetitia Summers is involved with a man from Wexford. Where Furlong is from. Where we're pretty sure he committed a crime and got away with it.' He recognised Andrews' scepticism. He'd seen it there before. 'I know I'm onto something,' he insisted. 'We need to look into Bolger's family. Didn't Edwards say that twin brothers came to live in Dublin?'

'Yes, they'd be twenty now.'

'Maybe one of them hooked up with Laetitia Summers to plot revenge.'

'You're determined to tie her into this, aren't you?'

'I think she's involved somehow,' West said. 'You've met her, Pete, she's a tricky character.'

'We need to check out the Bolger family anyway,' Andrews said with a shrug that indicated he wasn't convinced it was necessary. 'The twins may not even be living in the city anymore.'

'We need to find out. And where the sister is too.'

'Enough, you two,' Edel said, coming over and pushing them apart. 'Honestly, you've done nothing but talk shop since you arrived.'

For the remainder of the night, West made an effort to chat with everyone he knew, and a few he didn't. He laughed when he needed to, kept an arm around Edel when one of the Gardaí he didn't know made it quite clear he found her attractive, and tried to put the case out of his mind.

But the purple-and-gold tea cosy kept drawing his eye. He knew he was onto something. But he wasn't sure what.

31

Sunday was a lazy day. West and Edel enjoyed breakfast in a local pub, the newspapers spread out over the table, snippets shared and discussed. Relaxing conversation about nothing at all. Then a long walk along the seafront, hand in hand; not much was said, there being no need to make conversation, relaxed as they were in each other's company.

It wasn't until later in the afternoon, sitting near an open fire in a pub they both liked, that Edel asked what was on his mind. 'And don't say nothing,' she said with a smile. 'I know you too well.'

He picked up his Guinness and took a mouthful, leaving a trail of white foam on his top lip that he licked away. It rankled that Andrews hadn't thought much of his theory. Maybe Edel would be more receptive. He told her about the scarf, his idea that maybe Laetitia was involved with one of the twin brothers of Gary Bolger. 'Andrews didn't think much of the idea.'

Edel sipped her glass of wine, a slight crease between her eyes. 'I'd like to believe she's involved somehow. On paper, you'd think butter wouldn't melt in her mouth. She's tiny, pretty, and that irritating breathy voice would probably appeal to many. But when you meet her, there's something about her eyes. They're cold. Hard. Mean even.'

'You didn't like her either.'

'No, I didn't.' Edel thought a moment. 'Marcus… that other library assistant… said Laetitia wasn't interested in him because he was too young. I don't know how old he is exactly, but I'd have put him around twenty, maybe a little older. The same age as the twins would be, so that wouldn't gel with your theory.'

'I wonder if that was an impression Laetitia wanted to give, a young woman who older men fall for? Making herself out to be mysterious.'

Edel didn't look convinced.

West reached for his pint. 'Andrews will be pleased if I'm proved wrong. He didn't say it outright but I think he thought my idea was rubbish.'

'You're going to check into the twins anyway?'

'It's on the list of things to do.' West couldn't put any enthusiasm in his voice so wasn't surprised when Edel reached over and laid a hand on his knee.

'You'll get the tangle sorted,' she said softly. 'You always do. Stop worrying.'

He covered her hand with his own. 'You and Andrews have great faith in my abilities. I'm not sure Inspector Morrison will feel the same.'

On Monday morning, however, the inspector's reaction to West's shaky theory wasn't the only thing he had to worry about. The Parsons had rung to complain of damage to their property and were laying the blame squarely on Joanne Bennet. They wanted her arrested. Immediately.

'Come with me,' West said to Andrews. 'It might take our

combined endeavours to calm this situation down.' It wasn't far to the Parsons' home, West drove and filled Andrews in along the way. 'Last thing I did on Friday was to ring Cecelia O'Dea, the grief counsellor Mrs Bennet attends. She said she'd have a word when she saw her on Wednesday.'

Andrews looked at him, surprised. 'Mrs Bennet is still going to the meetings then? They don't seem to be doing her much good.'

'She goes every week according to Cecelia. Mr Bennet only went to a few, said it wasn't for him.'

'He appears to be handling his grief better than his poor wife.'

West turned down the road the Parsons lived on. The initial report passed to him hadn't specified what damage had been done but it was obvious as they approached the house. The cream, pebble-dashed wall that surrounded their garden had been graffitied with red paint.

West pulled up on the other side of the narrow road and peered out the window to read. *Confess* was written on the wall to one side of the wrought-iron gate and on the other, *Sinner*.

'To the point,' West said. He turned the car around and parked in front of the house.

Andrews took a few photos of the graffiti with his phone, then rubbed a hand over the words. 'They've used gloss paint: it's not going to come off easily.' The red paint had trickled from each letter and pooled in the angle where the wall met the foot-path. It was a mess.

The front door was answered almost immediately by a man whose face was set in angry lines. 'About time you lot got here,' Nick Parsons growled before standing back and waving them in. 'And keep your voices down. Max is asleep.'

West and Andrews exchanged glances but remained silent as

they followed Parsons into the large open-plan room at the back of the house. There was no sign of Ella Parsons.

Parsons shut the door behind them, then folded his arms and stared from one to the other. 'Well?'

Tempted to reply with a childish *well what?* West took a breath. 'We will investigate the incident which resulted in damage to your property, Mr Parsons,' he said formally. 'We're aware you have security cameras covering the front of your home. Can you show us the footage, please?'

Parsons glared at him. 'There's no point! They didn't come into the garden, did they? Did all the damage outside where the camera couldn't catch them.' He crossed the room in long angry strides, stopping at the window to rest his forehead against the glass before turning to look back at the two detectives. 'Confess sinner. All our neighbours reading that on their way to work this morning, gossiping, telling everyone else. Laughing and spreading it around. Wondering what we did to warrant such an action.' His anger faded as his chin trembled and he lifted a hand to his mouth and held it there. 'I'm sorry,' he said eventually, taking his hand away.

He waved West and Andrews to seats. 'I'll make coffee,' he said, fussing with a kettle and cafetière. He was calmer when he brought it to the table. 'The graffiti was done sometime during the night. I saw it when I was leaving for work. I had to come back in, of course, I couldn't leave it there for Ella to see when she went out.' He poured the coffee and pushed milk and sugar towards them, picking up his mug and holding it between his hands without drinking.

'I didn't want her to go out but she insisted. She was hysterical when she saw what it said.' He gave a sad smile. 'I know you lot think that we've been pushing Ella's poor mental health as a ruse to stop her taking responsibility for the death of that young boy, but we haven't, you know. She really isn't capable of answering questions about what happened. She was always emotionally fragile. The pregnancy and birth appear to have made her more so. These last few months haven't been easy. The doctors keep telling me she's doing well but she's a shadow of the women she was.'

West sipped his coffee. He'd met Nick Parsons on the day they came to arrest Ella. He'd been a pleasant-looking man in the best of health. Now he was pale, his cheeks gaunt and dark circles ringed his eyes.

Both families were suffering for Ella's catastrophic lapse of judgement.

'We've applied for a barring order to stop the Bennets coming here or approaching Ella anywhere,' Parsons said. 'It hadn't come through yet but anyway, what good will it do if they can do something like that instead? You must stop them. Please.' There was a plea in the words, tears in his eyes.

Nick Parsons, West decided, was a man at the very last fragile thread of his tether. 'We'll go around to them now,' he said. 'We've taken photographs of the graffiti for our files so you can have it removed.'

'I was lucky,' Parsons said. 'A firm I contacted were able to send someone out to sandblast it this morning.' He looked at his watch. 'They'll be here any moment.'

West took the hint. 'We'll head off and keep you informed of the results of our investigation. I know you think it was the Bennets, Mr Parsons, but we need to be sure.'

Parsons' face tightened again in anger. 'What? You think there are more people out there who hate us that much, do you?'

West waited a beat. 'We don't deal with emotion, we deal with facts. We'll speak to the Bennets and hear what they have to say.'

Parsons' lips disappeared into a compressed line.

'We'll see ourselves out,' West said. He shut the door after them and turned to Andrews with a hint of a smile. 'Let's get out of here.'

They were at the front door when they heard a shuffle on the stairs and looked up to see Ella Parsons staring down at them, a wraith of the woman West remembered from only a few months before. She said nothing, simply stood there, huge eyes in a thin, pale face.

West raised a hand in greeting. It wasn't returned.

Outside, Andrews blew a gusty breath. 'Tragic.' They went back to look at the two words that were so dramatically displayed. 'Neighbours must be having a field day,' Andrews said. 'I can imagine them saying, *this kind of thing shouldn't be happening in Foxrock.*'

'This kind of thing shouldn't be happening anywhere,' West said, taking his car keys from his pocket. He used the edge of one key to scrape a paint sample into an evidence bag. 'Okay, let's go and see what the Bennets have to say about it.'

The Bennets lived ten minutes' drive away in Cabinteely. The day of the accident their son had gone home with a friend who lived not far from the Parsons. The friend had escaped with a simple fracture when Ella Parsons' car had hit them but Milo Bennet had been left with devastating injuries from which he'd never recovered.

West pulled up outside the house. He'd visited several times over the last few months and had seen a subtle deterioration on each visit as both Joanne and Milo Bennet Senior struggled to survive the death of their only child.

It was Joanne who answered their ring of the doorbell. Once, she would have been called a pretty woman but that was before sorrow and grief had carved lines on her forehead and painted dark circles under her eyes. She'd lost weight and her clothes sagged on her frame. Straggly hair was pushed behind her ears and the white tramline down her parting said it had been too long since she'd had it coloured. 'Come in,' she said, in a lifeless voice that matched the rest. She led them into the small kitchen at the back of the house.

It had been a couple of weeks since West's last visit. Then the kitchen had been tidy, if not particularly clean. Now, the sink was filled with dirty dishes, the floor strewn with crumbs. Half-finished cups of tea sat on various surfaces. It looked as if things had got a lot worse.

'Please sit down,' Joanne said. 'Would you like some tea?'

'How about you sit and talk to Mike and I'll make us all a cuppa,' Andrews said gently. 'I'll find where everything is, don't you fret.'

She threw him a grateful smile and sat.

West took the chair opposite, smiling to himself as he watched Andrews quickly find his way around the kitchen. A few minutes later, the dishwasher was churning, the sink was empty and all the kitchen surfaces had been wiped clean.

'Here we go,' Andrews said, putting mugs of tea in front of each of them.

'You see why I bring him with me,' West said, with a smile for Joanne. 'He's a domestic god.'

'He's a truly kind man,' she said, taking a tiny sip of tea.

'Where's Milo?' West asked. Milo Bennet had taken leave from his job in the bank when his son had been killed and hadn't returned. Usually, he was there, reluctant to be far from his wife.

'I don't know.' Joanne's voice was defeated.

'You don't know?' This was unexpected. West pushed his tea aside and leaned across the table. 'What do you mean you don't know, Joanne?'

'He comes home for a few hours to sleep, then goes out again.'

Andrews reached across and patted her hand. 'That must be very worrying for you. How long has this been going on?'

She shrugged. 'A week, maybe more. I don't know really. All the days are drifting into one another.'

All the days since she lost her son. 'And you don't know where he goes?'

'No idea.' It was obvious she no longer cared.

West met Andrews' gaze. *Maybe it was Milo Bennet who'd done the graffiti, not Joanne?* 'Joanne,' he said, 'we've had a complaint from the Parsons.' He waited for a reaction but her expression didn't change. 'Someone daubed graffiti on their garden wall. Was it you, Joanne?'

'Graffiti?' She shook her head. 'Seems a strange thing to do. I simply want that woman to tell the courts what she did, that's all.'

'The words *confess* and *sinner* were painted on the walls.'

'Ah,' Joanne said with a tiny smile. 'So that's why you're here. Well, I hate to disappoint you, but it wasn't me.'

'Could it have been Milo?'

Her sigh was long and weighed with sadness. 'I would have said no, but I don't know him anymore.'

They needed to speak to Milo. 'What time does he normally come home?' West saw her shrug, knew she'd no idea. 'Is there somewhere Milo would store paint and brushes? A garden shed maybe?'

Rather than answering, she turned in her chair to peer out of the grubby kitchen window. Andrews rose to look out. 'There's a shed.' He turned to her. 'Is it locked?'

It wasn't. Andrews opened the kitchen door, crossed the garden to the shed and returned a moment later with a small tin of red paint and a paintbrush. 'The paint is already dry on the brush,' he said, holding it up. 'He won't be using this one again.'

'We can get forensics to match the paint fragments I took,'

West said. There was no doubt, but he'd do things by the book. It was safer that way.

'More trouble.' It was all Joanne Bennet had to say about the matter.

'If he comes back, get him to ring me,' West said, handing her his card. 'My mobile number is on it. He can ring me any time.'

'I'll tell him.'

'You're still seeing Cecelia O'Dea?'

'Every Wednesday.'

Her expression didn't change. She might be going every week but it didn't look as if she was deriving much comfort or solace from the bereavement counselling. West knew Cecelia to be one of the best. If she couldn't help, possibly nobody could. He was curious why she kept going. 'Is it a big group?'

Her eyes brightened a little. 'Usually five or six. Nice people, full of pain. It's good to be with people who understand, even for a short time.'

Kindred spirits. West felt a pang of sorrow for her. 'We'd better be on our way.'

'Okay. If I see Milo, I'll tell him you're looking for him.'

If? 'Okay, well, take care,' West said, getting to his feet. 'And please, stay away from the Parsons.'

Back in the car, West shook his head. 'This is starting to stink. We need to find Milo. It sounds like he's coming apart.' A second later, he was speaking to Sergeant Blunt and giving him an update on the situation. 'Have uniforms keep an eye out for him.' He tapped his free hand on the steering wheel. 'His wife says he comes home when it gets dark, so post someone outside his house from about five. I know that'll be a pain. I'll clear it with Mother when I get in, okay.'

'You think he might try something else?' Andrews said as West hung up.

'I think Milo Bennet has come off the rails. In fact, I think both he and Mrs Bennet have.' West remembered Ella Parsons standing on the stairway looking like a ghost. 'Maybe all of them have,' he said, pulling the car back onto the road to head for the station.

32

Leaving Andrews to organise sending the paint and the sample to forensics, West went to the office to see if the team had come up with anything to strengthen his theory about Laetitia and one of the Bolger twins. He needed some facts before he went to Morrison.

He wasn't expecting to be lucky and his first glance around the room at those present didn't give much room for hope. They were all Monday morning glum. Baxter looked as if he was still suffering from a hangover.

But when they saw him, their expressions changed. Allen almost bouncing on his feet.

'I hope this is something good,' West said, perching on the side of a desk. 'Come on, Allen, spill before you burst.'

Mick Allen grinned. 'You're going to like it.' He reached for a sheet of paper. 'Does the name Debbie Long mean anything to you?'

'Yes,' West said. 'She's the librarian in Marino Library where Laetitia Summers works.'

'That's not all she is,' Allen said. 'She's the sister of Kim Bolger, the mother of that lad Gary Bolger who was stabbed outside that nightclub in Wexford ten years ago. When the father couldn't cope, the twin brothers came to live with her.' He flicked over the page. 'Ashley and Aaron Bolger. Aaron died from a drug overdose three years ago. Twenty-year-old Ashley is still living with Debbie and her husband in Swords. He's done a few different jobs over the years. Nothing exciting. He's currently flipping burgers in McD's.'

Andrews arrived and Allen went through everything again while West listened patiently. He saw Andrews eyes widen and resisted the temptation to thump him on the arm and say *I told you so*. Okay, so far, they'd no proof that Laetitia and Ashley were involved but he knew he was right. He *knew* it. Andrews turned and looked at him with a shake of his head. 'Looks like you might be right, after all.'

'We need proof.' West looked around the room. 'Right, let's bring our burger-flipping friend in for questioning. We don't know that's he's guilty of anything apart from having two dead siblings, so let's tread softly.' He looked at Allen. 'See when his shift finishes and pick him up.'

West's step was lighter as he headed up to speak to Inspector Morrison. They were still a long way from solving the murder of Cormac Furlong but he was confident they were on the right path.

Morrison didn't seem convinced. 'It's all a bit airy-fairy, isn't it? Coincidences and suppositions.'

West leaned both hands on Morrison's desk. 'Inspector, Laetitia Summers, who accused Cormac Furlong of rape, works with a woman who is related to a man we think Furlong might have killed. That's a pretty big coincidence.'

'Yes, I have to admit, I do agree but we need some facts.' He sat back and twirled his thumbs. 'Sounds like you're getting somewhere though. Good.'

It was a dismissal, but West hadn't finished. 'There's something else, Inspector.' He straightened and explained about the graffiti and their visit to the Bennets. 'They're falling apart, and I'm concerned about what Milo Bennet might do next. I asked Mrs Bennet to get him to ring me but, to be honest, I'm not entirely sure she will remember even if she does see him. Sergeant Blunt is going to post a uniform outside their home from dusk and bring him in when he turns up. I'll come in, regardless of the time.' West shook his head slowly. 'I'm concerned.'

Morrison said nothing for a moment and his thumbs had stopped moving. 'A sad situation,' he said finally. 'Yes, go with that. Tell Blunt I'll approve the overtime if necessary.'

West wasn't surprised. Morrison had a decent streak carefully hidden away. He stopped by the front desk to let Blunt know the good news. 'Give me a shout when they pick him up and I'll be in.'

'Okay,' said Blunt, a man who used words as if afraid he'd run out of them.

West headed back to his office. He'd no sooner switched on his computer than Andrews appeared, a sandwich in each hand. 'Chicken or ham and cheese?'

'From the canteen?'

'No, the deli. Can't afford to poison you.' Andrews see-sawed his hands. 'Which?'

'Chicken,' West said, reaching to take it from him.

'Hang on and I'll get us some coffee.'

A minute later, the two men sat munching sandwiches and drinking coffee. West threw the sandwich wrapper into the bin. 'Did Allen find out what time Ashley Bolger finishes his shift?'

'Three. They're leaving soon. It's the one in Liffey Valley so they'll take the M50 and be back quickly.'

It was nearly four before Allen and Jarvis returned.

'He's in the Big One,' Allen said from the doorway of West's office.

'Any trouble?'

'Not a bit. But we rang our colleagues in Swords before we went. Ashley Furlong isn't unknown to the Gardaí. He's never been arrested but there have been a few warnings and a few visits to the Garda station in Swords. So, he's no stranger to being questioned. He was slightly surprised to be taken here but apart from asking if we were going to take him home afterward, he didn't seem too bothered.'

'Okay,' West said, getting to his feet. 'Let's see what he has to say for himself.' In the main office, he gave Andrews a nod. 'Take Jarvis and watch from the observation room, will you. I'll take Allen in with me.'

When they opened the door into the Big One, Ashley Bolger was slouched low on a chair. He hadn't removed his coat or the purple-and-gold-striped scarf that was wound around his neck as if he didn't plan to stay long. He looked mildly curious rather than worried.

'Mr Bolger, thank you for coming in to help with our enquiries.' West pulled out a chair, Allen taking the one beside him. 'I'm Detective Garda Sergeant West. You've already met Detective Garda Allen. For your protection, and ours, this interview will be recorded. Are you happy with that?'

A shrug of a shoulder was the only reply.

'And to keep things right and tight,' West said, coming to a decision, 'Detective Garda Allen will now read you your rights.'

This got a reaction. Ashley Bolger's eyes came out on stalks. 'What? I haven't done anything!'

'Then you've nothing to be afraid of,' West said calmly and signalled to Allen to read the suddenly nervous man his rights.

Whether it was nerves or the heat being belted out from the

radiator in the corner of the room, Bolger unwrapped his scarf, took off his coat and threw both over the back of the chair beside him.

'It's interesting,' West said, looking at the discarded items. 'The last time I saw that coat and scarf they were hanging on a coat stand in the hallway of Laetitia Summers' house.'

A wily expression crept into Bolger's eyes. 'Lots of coats and scarves like them around.'

'Maybe, but I bet if we look at your coat, we'll find a poorly-mended tear below the right-hand pocket. Am I right?'

'Well, so what? Yes, I was in Laetitia's house that day. What of it? It isn't a crime.'

'No, it's not. So how long have you been seeing one another?'

Bolger shoved his hands into his jeans pockets. 'What's this all about then? Why is it any concern of you lot who I do or don't shag?'

West waited.

'Over a year, if you really want to know.'

'Thank you. And your aunt, Debbie Long, she knows you two are in a relationship?'

'Yea, what of it?'

'Did you meet Laetitia in the library?'

'Yea, what of it?' Bolger sneered as he gave the same answer.

West took a photo from the file he'd brought with him. He slid it across the table. 'Do you know this man?'

Bolger gave the photograph of Ian Moore a cursory glance. 'Never saw him before.'

'What about this man?' West pushed a second photograph across.

A quick flick of his tongue over suddenly dry lips gave Bolger away before he spoke. 'Yea, I know that bastard all right. Cormac Furlong. The man who destroyed my family.'

'You held him responsible for the death of your older brother, Gary?'

'He *was* responsible, everybody knew it.'

'They were supposed to be best friends,' Allen said. 'Why would he have wanted to kill him?'

'I was only a kid but I heard rumours. It was something about a girl. They both fancied her but that night in the club it seems she'd decided on Gary and was all over him like a rash. That was why Cormac left the club early.'

'According to his mother, Cormac was home before the attack took place.'

Bolger sniffed. 'Yes, she probably believed he stayed there too. She didn't know that Cormac used to sneak out at night, same as Gary did. Our houses are the same and both Cormac and Gary had a bedroom in the same part of the house, one where the window overlooked the flat roof of the garage. Me and Gary shared the room and I remember Gary sneaking out when the parents thought he was in bed asleep, then he'd sneak back hours later smelling of smoke and alcohol. It would have been easy for Cormac to do the same, get out and creep back to the nightclub like the coward that he was and lie in wait until Gary came out for a fag and jump him. All because of a stupid woman.' He glared across the table. 'Afterwards, my mother fell apart and my father couldn't cope. Me and Aaron were sent to live with Debbie.'

He pressed his lips together for a few seconds and when he spoke again his voice was softer, as if he was struggling with the words. 'She did her best, you know, but we were both so shook up and shocked. She'd never had kids of her own so she wasn't sure what to do with us. We missed our parents too. We didn't see much of them over the years: Ma was in and out of hospital and eventually Da gave up and left her, went off with someone else. Debbie never forgave him for that.' Bolger's mouth twisted, his voice thickening as he spoke. 'Ma never recovered from Gary's death. She died four years ago. Aaron was devastated and started taking drugs not long after. I warned him but he wouldn't listen.'

West remembered the photo he'd seen in Debbie Long's office. He'd assumed it was her and her family. Now he understood. It was her sister and her family in a happier time. Debbie, he guessed, would do anything to protect what was left of her family... even lie. He gave Ashley a moment to recover before asking, 'When did you find out that your girlfriend had been raped by Cormac Furlong?'

Bolger shook his head. 'She told me the man who raped her had been put away. It happened a few months before we met. When I discovered that the man who raped her was the same man who had murdered my brother... if he weren't already dead, I'd have gone and done the job myself.'

'So you found out when?' West persisted.

'After you called to tell her the bastard's real name. I couldn't believe it. When she told me he'd been murdered, I was relieved. Happy.' He looked from West to Allen. 'Do you know what we did? We celebrated, that's what. Celebrated that finally someone had the balls to get rid of that piece of trash.'

'And you had nothing to do with his death?'

'Apart from celebrating it, absolutely nothing but when you find out who did, let me shake his hand.' Bolger sat back and crossed his arms, his look of satisfaction quickly disguised by a scowl.

'What about Ms Summers? She also had a reason to want him dead, didn't she?'

'You having a laugh?' Bolger sneered. 'She's a titchy little thing, he had to be over six foot. How do you think she'd have managed to–' He stopped suddenly, mouth opening and shutting.

'Managed to what?' West said.

'Kill him. That's what I was going to say. How do you think a little bit of a thing like her would be able to kill him?'

It wasn't what he'd been going to say; he'd been going to say how did a little bit of a thing like Laetitia Summers haul Furlong's dead weight from the confessional to the foot of the altar, then string him up the way he had been. And Bolger was right. There was no way she'd have been able to. Not alone anyway.

'Where were you last Sunday night?'

'Me and Laetitia went to a movie, then we went back to hers. I spent the night there.' He sneered. 'I can give you the details if you like.'

'I don't think that will be necessary.' West got to his feet abruptly, startling Bolger who reared back, eyes wide. 'That will be all. For the moment. We may have more questions at a later date. Detective Garda Allen will organise transport to take you home. Thank you for your time.'

West left without another word and returned to his office, frowning as Andrews and Jarvis joined him. 'Well?'

'I don't know,' Andrews said, sitting on the only spare chair. 'I think he was being honest when he said if he'd found out who Furlong was, he'd have gone and murdered him himself. He'd have acted there and then, not set the elaborate scene we found in the church.'

Jarvis perched on the desk. 'Yes, but I think he knew about it... that slight slip where he said she wouldn't have been able to manage, he made a quick recovery but he was lying, wasn't he?'

'I think he's involved somehow,' West said.

'But not the mastermind.' Andrews clasped his hands behind his head.

'No, I agree.' West pushed a hand through his hair and

groaned. 'For once, could we manage to get one solid piece of evidence?'

'Morrison getting to you?'

Jarvis gave a short laugh. 'It's been a whole week after all.'

'This case is getting to me,' West said, glancing at the clock over the door. 'Okay, first thing in the morning I'm going to speak to Debbie Long, see if I can shake some information from her.' He drummed his fingers on the desk. 'It'll be another fishing expedition, though, I've no idea what we're missing, but we're missing something.'

'Like, why kill Furlong in that way, and why in that particular church. Why not a church in Swords or Marino, or in fact, why a church at all?' Jarvis said, drawing two sets of eyes on him. He coloured slightly. 'If it were Bolger and Summers, working together, why would they have chosen a church? A church here in Foxrock?'

'All good questions, Sam,' West said. 'Tomorrow, find me some answers.'

33

West woke early on Tuesday morning. The only light in the room came from the luminous dial of his bedside clock. He turned his head to look at it and groaned when he saw it was only 4.30 and lay back with an arm crooked under his head. To his left, Edel snuffled softly. The murder of Furlong rolled around his brain. Sometimes, when all other distractions were shut off, clarity came bouncing in. Not today. It was no clearer now than it had been a week before.

Another worry forced its way in. There'd been no call from the station regarding Milo Bennet which meant he mustn't have turned up. It was hard to see a happy ending for the Bennet and the Parsons families.

Trying not to disturb Edel, West pushed back the duvet, took a T-shirt from the chair and headed downstairs. Coffee might clear his thoughts. He walked barefooted into the kitchen, disturbing Tyler who lifted his head and glared at him. But it was too early even for him: he curled up and went back to sleep.

The first mug didn't clear West's head, neither did the second. Restless, he picked up the previous day's newspaper and read the bits he'd missed, tutting over some of the more scandalous news, grateful there was no mention of his case.

He waited until seven before going back upstairs to have a shower and get ready for the day. It was still too early, but he was worried about the Bennets. If there was no word at the station, he'd go around and speak to Joanne Bennet again.

'Sorry,' he said, bending down to plant a kiss on Edel's cheek, her arm coming up to wrap around his neck.

'Hey, Mike.' Her voice was still groggy and thick with sleep.

'Hey, yourself. I'll grab my clothes and leave you to go back to sleep.'

'Okay. See you later.'

West kissed her again, removed the clothes he wanted from the wardrobe and headed to the main bathroom. He preferred to use it rather than the en suite. He'd spent a lot of time... and money... in getting the best he could afford when he had it put in, sacrificing the smallest of the four bedrooms for it. The original small bathroom was now the en suite to the main bedroom. Often, at the end of a stressful day, he'd spend a long time under the powerful shower trying to chase the demons away. It struck him suddenly that he hadn't had to do that in a long time.

That morning his ablutions were quick. He left the house less than half an hour later and at 7.45 he pulled into the car park in Foxrock.

The night desk sergeant looked up as West pushed through the front door. 'You're eager,' he said, stifling a yawn.

'Morning, Chad,' West said. 'Long night?'

'They're getting longer the older I get,' Chad Delaney said. 'You're wondering why we didn't ring you about Milo Bennet, I suppose.'

'I was, yes,' West said. 'Didn't he turn up?'

'He did, at four, wasted and belligerent with it. The Gardaí on the scene decided he was a danger to himself and brought him in. He's in a cell sleeping it off.'

'Good, best place for him. Was his wife told?'

'They tried her doorbell but nobody answered. I was going to ask Tom to get one of the day shift to call around to speak to her.'

'No,' West said, making a decision. 'Leave it to me, I'll head around and speak to her now. She knows me so it would be easier. Make sure they keep a close eye on Bennet, okay?' He raised a hand in apology. 'Yes, I know it doesn't need to be said.' Delaney and his day counterpart, Tom Blunt, were the solid, dependable type. Nothing would happen to a man in their care.

Ten minutes later he parked outside the Bennet home. There were curtains pulled shut in one of the upstairs windows. He hoped it was a sign Joanne Bennet was home.

He heard the doorbell peal within and waited, eyeing the dark clouds overhead with a frown as he tried to remember where he'd left his raincoat. After a minute, he peered through the frosted-glass side panels and pressed the bell for longer but there was no movement within. He stepped back and looked up to the bedroom windows. One curtain was still pulled shut. Maybe Mrs Bennet was a heavy sleeper.

Maybe she was dead.

A side passage separated the house from its neighbour. West slipped down it but a locked gate barred his path. He rattled it in frustration before returning to the front door. Swearing softly under his breath, he kept his finger on the bell. He was debating ringing for assistance from the station to break the door down when a shadow through the glass gained substance as it approached and he could make out the figure of Mrs Bennet.

Seconds later, the door was opened. 'Hello.' Big eyes in a pale face stared at him.

'Mrs Bennet, may I come in?'

Without asking why he was calling at such an early hour, she stepped back and stood to one side. She'd obviously been in bed. A terry cloth robe that had seen better days was wrapped tightly over lurid pink cotton pyjamas. The clothes swamped her. She seemed to be getting frailer by the day, disappearing from a world that had become too difficult for her.

'Let's sit down,' he said, drawing her into the kitchen. He waited until she sat across the table from him before speaking. 'I'd asked the uniformed Gardaí to keep an eye out for Milo so I could speak to him about the graffiti. When they did see him, early this morning, he was very drunk, I'm afraid. The officers were worried he was a danger to himself so they took him into the station to sleep it off. I wanted to let you know so you wouldn't be worrying about him.'

'I wasn't worrying,' she said, calmly. 'I didn't even know he wasn't home. He sleeps in the back room. And I take sleeping tablets so never hear him coming in.' She sighed; a long slow sad sound that seemed to shrink her even more.

'I'll make sure he comes home safely,' West said. It was all he could do. He had stood to go when a leaflet pinned to the cork board on the wall beside the kitchen door caught his attention. He pulled the pin out and took it down. 'Do you go to this?' he asked, turning back to Mrs Bennet.

When she looked at him blankly, he returned to the table, sat, and slid the leaflet towards her.

She picked it up, looked at it briefly and put it down. 'No, I don't. I like the counselling session I go to on Wednesdays with Cecelia O'Dea.' She gave a trembling smile. 'I'm not sure if they're helping me to come to terms with my loss but sometimes hearing sad stories from others makes me feel less alone. Milo didn't take to Cecelia so after one or two meetings he refused to go back.' Her broken fingernail tapped the leaflet. 'He started attending this group a few months ago, he wanted me to join him but I said no.'

'And he goes every week?' He wasn't surprised when she shrugged. 'Okay, would you mind if I took this with me?'

Another apathetic shrug was the only answer. Joanne Bennet was a woman who no longer cared about anything.

West slipped it into his pocket. 'Maybe you should try to get some more sleep. Don't worry about Milo, I'll bring him home.'

'Thank you,' she said, her tone of voice stating clearly she didn't even care about that.

Back in his car, West took out the leaflet and looked at it closely. He was almost certain it was the same. He took out his mobile and hit a speed-dial key, flicking the leaflet with his fingernail as he waited. 'Hi, you up?'

Edel laughed. 'Cheek! I'll have you know, right at his moment, I'm planning on how to kill Matthew Foyle.'

West smiled. 'Poor Matthew!'

'I'm sure you're not ringing me this early for an update on my book. Not that I'm suspicious or anything but what do you want?'

'It might be that I simply wanted to hear your dulcet tones.'

'Ha, why do I think that's highly unlikely?'

'Because you've a suspicious mind, Edel. But,' he said, hearing her laugh, 'I have to confess you're right.'

'Thought as much. So, go on, what can I do for you?'

West looked at the leaflet he was holding. 'Remember those leaflets you picked up in the library? Do you have them to hand?'

'I don't but I can get them, hang on.'

The old chair Edel used squeaked as she stood and a few seconds later, it squealed when she sat, then he heard the rustle of paper.

'Okay,' she said. 'I have them. Was there one in particular you were interested in?'

'Is there one called Remembrance?' He was sure he was right, but at the time it was the Marino Library stamp that had held his attention. This leaflet didn't have the library stamp, but he was sure it was the same.

'Yes,' Edel said.

'And under that, it says, *join us and talk away your pain and grief.*'

'Word for word.'

'Okay.'

'Don't you dare hang up!' Edel almost shrieked. 'You can't ring up, disturb my train of thought and leave me with this puzzle... tell me.'

'It might be purely a coincidence–'

'You don't believe in coincidences,' Edel interrupted.

He didn't. They happened, of course they did, but a coincidence that linked two cases he was dealing with, where the death of a young man was a factor in both, this coincidence didn't sit easily with him. He explained briefly what had happened.

'Goodness,' she said. 'Mind you, Mike, there could be hundreds of these leaflets around. They might be in every library in the city, never mind GP surgeries, clinics and any one of a hundred other places.'

'No,' he said, 'I don't think so. There's only one meeting place mentioned. In Sandymount. Plus, if you read it, there's no accredited organisation or counselling service mentioned. It looks almost amateurish.'

'In fairness, it does say *join us and talk* so maybe it is simply that, a place for people to chat about their experience.'

'Maybe,' West said. 'Okay, thanks for that, I'll text you later if

I'm going to be late. You can go back to killing Matthew now.' He could hear her laughing as he hung up.

~

Edel threw the leaflets to one side and pulled her laptop closer to return to her story. When she finished, she read over the scene, satisfied with what she'd written.

Her eyes slid to the end of her long desk and the pile of leaflets, reaching automatically to pick up the top one. *Remembrance.* She'd never felt the need to talk to strangers after her husband was murdered. Perhaps it was because he never had been, not really. It had been a bigamous marriage built on lies and deceit.

There wasn't a phone number on the leaflet, only an email address. Without thinking, she brought up her emails and tapped out a quick message asking about the meetings, explaining, with gross exaggeration that she was finding it hard to come to terms with the death of her husband, pressing send before she changed her mind.

Curiosity: it would be her undoing.

She went down for a caffeine boost. Coffee didn't seem enough and she searched the cupboards for something to eat, finding a packet of biscuits she'd forgotten about. She sat at the table and looked out over the garden as she drank, munching her way through almost the whole packet as she thought about her story and what she wanted to write next. It was almost thirty minutes before she returned to the small spare bedroom she used as an office.

To her surprise, there was a reply from *Remembrance.* Holding her breath, she opened it.

You've made the first step… come and join
us. We meet every Tuesday at 1pm at 22c
Seafort Avenue, Sandymount.

Today. This afternoon. Edel smiled. It was so tempting. What harm could it do? A little voice in her head said, *remember Liz Goodbody,* but she shook it away. That had been different. This time there would be a group of people. This time she wouldn't be locked in a cupboard, tasered and poisoned. She shivered at the memory and almost reconsidered her next step. Going to the meeting was a crazy idea, wasn't it?

It was probably a better plan to ring Mike and tell him what she'd done. He could send a plain-clothes Garda along in her place.

That would have been the best option. Of course, it would. But she'd have missed the first-hand experience. Experience. She refused to call it innate curiosity.

But her recent dealings with what she'd heard Mike refer to as *nefarious characters,* had, at least, taught her the wisdom of caution. Before she left home, she sent him a message to tell him where she was going. Then she switched her phone off. He'd be annoyed but she wasn't missing out this opportunity to do a little sleuthing of her own.

A little over an hour and a half later she was walking along Seafort Avenue, looking for number 22c. It was after one o'clock before she found it, tucked above a takeaway and accessed by rickety wooden stairs. There was no sign on the door at the top of the steps but standing close to it, she heard voices from within.

With a deep breath, she rapped her knuckles against the wood.

34

The voices stopped abruptly and seconds later the door creaked open.

'Hello?' A man peered around the edge, small eyes fixing Edel to the spot. 'Can I help you?'

'Hi. I'm Edel, I emailed earlier. I was told I could come to this meeting.' She waved a hand towards the road. 'Sorry I'm late, it took me a while to find it.'

A smile lit the man's colourless face. 'Oh, that's all right, come on in and join the gang.'

Gang was a slight exaggeration. There were four people sitting around a table in the centre of the room, all turning to assess the newcomer.

'Hi,' Edel said, smiling nervously. They didn't look particularly welcoming.

The man who'd let her in was obviously thinking the same. He rested a thin hand on her arm. 'You've come at a rather sensitive moment,' he explained. 'Arthur was telling us about how he felt when he heard his daughter had been killed.' He waved her to the chair he'd obviously vacated to answer the door and grabbed an empty one from a stack in the corner of the room.

'I'll introduce you to everyone later,' he said. 'Strictly first-name basis only.'

Edel wasn't sure why there was a need for such confidentiality but she muttered 'Of course' and sat.

'Please, continue, Arthur.'

For the next fifteen minutes, Edel listened to the sad tale. The beloved daughter who'd died in a car crash. Her boyfriend had taken a roundabout at speed, losing control, the car flipping over and imprisoning both. He'd escaped with minor injuries but her neck was broken on impact. They were both seventeen.

The silence when he finished telling them that he missed her every day was uncomfortable and prolonged. Edel glanced from person to person, wondering at their various stories. When the silence lasted, she glanced to her left to see tears rolling down the cheeks of the man who'd let her in. He was, she assumed, the leader of the group and she waited for him... or anyone to speak, to say something consoling, something to help Arthur move forward.

Finally, after several minutes' silence, the leader took out a large handkerchief and noisily blew his nose. 'So, so tragic,' he said. 'Thank you for sharing with us, Arthur. And you say the boyfriend lives close by?'

'Near enough that we go to the same shops, the same cafés and restaurants. Near enough that I see him getting on with his life while my darling daughter will never see another sunrise or sunset.'

Again, Edel waited for some form of guidance. Instead, the leader's expression turned solemn. 'We live in a world where the perpetrators of crimes – those people who wreck our lives – frequently go unpunished, or with a punishment that goes nowhere near meeting the crime.'

It was that moment when Edel bitterly regretted not phoning Mike. Maybe it was because she'd been thinking about

Liz Goodbody earlier, but she could hear the same hint of fanaticism in the man's voice as she'd heard in hers. Edel should have phoned Mike and passed the information on because he had been right; there was nothing coincidental about finding the leaflet in the Bennets' house and in the library. This was the connection. The Bennets, Debbie Long, and Ashley Bolger had all lost someone, the perpetrator having gone free. If Edel had told him about today's meeting, he could have sent a plain-clothes Garda and she could have stayed at home, where she belonged, writing her book.

A scrape of a chair beside her drew her attention. 'We've time to introduce ourselves now,' said the man she'd designated the leader. 'My name is Pa. This group was my brainchild. So, if you'd introduce yourself and tell us why you're here.' He looked around the room. 'And perhaps you'd all do the same for our newest recruit.'

She was there now, she might as well make the most of it and get all the information she could for Mike. Maybe it would mitigate his anger if she could provide something concrete.

'Hello everyone. My name is Edel. My husband was murdered a year ago by a drug-dealing psychopath. It was a difficult time and I'm still coming to terms with it.' The others looked at her intently. They seemed to want more, but it was all she was willing to give. 'I find it hard to talk about it.'

'I suppose they never caught the man responsible,' Pa said, his voice thick with sympathy.

She turned to look at him. His smile and his small eyes were kind. 'No, they did,' she said. 'He's serving a long prison sentence for two murders and drug dealing.'

'Good, good,' he said, each word accompanied by an emphatic nod. 'Right, okay, meet the others.' He waved a hand towards the woman on her right. 'Why don't you start, Emily.'

Emily, Arthur, Jamie and Oisin. Edel repeated the names to

herself as the introductions went on, each of them with their sad story to tell. Emily's younger sister died in a swimming accident the previous year, Jamie's father of a sudden heart attack two years before and Oisin's brother recently from a drug overdose.

'I know the bastard who sold it to him,' Oisin told her. 'The guards say there is no proof but I know it's him. I'll make him pay someday.'

Edel waited for Pa to say something positive, to steer the young man away from what sounded like a threat of revenge and was horrified when he said nothing. In fact, there was nothing positive or encouraging about the meeting. Sad stories told in sorrow. No attempt to put their pain into any context or to offer hope that their sorrow would be alleviated by time.

At two, Pa looked at his watch. 'Well, that's all for today, folks. Have a good week and I'll see you all again next Tuesday.'

Edel was first out the door, breathing the chilly air outside with relief. Had Debbie Long or her nephew, Ashley come to this meeting and talked about Cormac Furlong, the man who got away with murdering Gary Bolger? He had been dealt with; was the boyfriend of Arthur's daughter next, or the man Oisin was convinced had supplied drugs to his brother?

She crossed the road and stood watching the door, her phone in her hand as a pretext for standing there. Emily and Jamie left almost immediately, followed seconds later by Oisin, but it was several minutes before Arthur and Pa trundled down the steps side by side, deep in conversation. From where she stood, she could see their intent, grim expressions.

Edel felt a shiver run down her spine. The boyfriend of Arthur's dead daughter had better watch his step.

No, on second thoughts, he had to be warned.

35

———

West had gone straight back to Foxrock station after leaving Joanne Bennet. He saw Jarvis at his desk, the fingers of one hand flying over the keyboard while the other held a mug of coffee that he sipped as he tapped.

'Do not spill that coffee,' West warned.

Jarvis merely grinned and shook his head. 'Never going to happen.'

West took out the *Remembrance* leaflet and laid it on the desk. 'Find out everything you can about this group.'

'Will do,' Jarvis said, picking it up and turning it over. 'Pretty basic, isn't it? No details about who made it.' He held it up to the light. 'Home-made would be my guess. The edges are pretty rough.'

'Do what you can,' West said. 'It might be important.'

'Will do,' Jarvis said, putting his coffee down and getting back to work, two hands now flying over the keys.

Andrews was on the phone, West mouthed 'my office' and waited for the nod of acknowledgement before heading there and sitting behind the desk.

'You look as if the weight of the world landed on your shoulders,' Andrews said a moment later, sinking into the chair opposite.

West was still trying to make sense of the ideas his brain was spinning. 'What if–' He stopped when Andrews groaned and cupped his face in his hands.

'I hate when you start with "what if", I know this is going to be something that'll twist my head as well as my gut.'

'Well, it's twisting both of mine, and you know what they say, misery loves company!'

'Fine,' Andrews said, holding his hands up in surrender. 'Go on, hit me with your latest brainwave.'

'What if there was a group where people were encouraged to seek their own justice,' he said, trying to untangle the ideas in his head as he laid them out for Andrews.

'Like a vigilante group?'

West wagged a hand side to side. 'Not exactly, more a group of people who believed they had genuine grievances against a particular person. Say if Debbie Long went there and told some people about Cormac Furlong, for instance, and they decide to make him pay... first he gets sent to prison for allegedly raping Laetitia Summers and when he's released early, he's murdered. And say Milo Bennet goes to the same people... tells them about the death of his son and Ella Parsons' avoidance of responsibility.'

'You're linking our investigation of Furlong's murder to the graffiti on the Parsons' wall.' Andrews sounded as if he couldn't believe his ears. 'Have you lost the plot completely?'

West explained about the leaflet. 'Edel brought one home from the library and I found one in the Bennets' home.'

'Those kinds of leaflets can be found everywhere,' Andrews said, echoing what Edel had said a short while before. 'I think it's a huge stretch to see them as a link.'

'They're not affiliated to any organisation and they only have one meeting place in Sandymount so they can't be that wide-spread.' West felt a twinge of frustration. He knew he was onto something. If he could only get something solid. 'They brought Milo Bennet in last night... or rather early this morning. He was out of it, they thought it would be safer. Let's go and see if he's sobered up enough to answer a few questions. Maybe he can tell us about the leaflet.'

West picked up the leaflet as he and Andrews passed Jarvis' desk.

'I haven't found out much,' Jarvis said, his fingers freezing over the keyboard. 'I sent an email to the address on the leaflet. I haven't heard back yet.'

'Keep at it.'

Sergeant Blunt was at the front desk peering at a computer screen.

'Morning, Tom,' West said, drawing his attention. 'Has Milo Bennet sobered up enough to speak to us?'

Blunt's short, stubby index finger jabbed a key before he spoke. 'He had breakfast.' Obviously, that said it all in his opinion: a man who was able to eat breakfast was sober enough for a conversation.

'Good. Have him taken into the Big One, please.'

Five minutes later, West and Andrews sat opposite the grey-faced, pathetic figure of Milo Bennet. Andrews had read him his rights, explained the interview was being recorded and asked if he'd like a solicitor present. All the time Bennet looked at him blankly.

'You feel up to speaking to us?' West said.

Bennet slowly turned his head to look at him. 'Why not.'

'Did you paint the graffiti on the Parsons' wall?'

Bennet considered the question for a few seconds before shaking his head slowly. 'No, *I* didn't paint it.'

West caught the emphasis on the *I*. 'But you know who did. You supplied the paint and the brush.'

'I was supposed to do it.' Bennet's mouth twisted in self-disgust. 'I got there, opened the paint can... and couldn't bring myself to paint those words. Lord knows, I hate that woman for killing our son and destroying our lives but–' he heaved a sigh '– it's not who I am. I thought I could. I promised I would.' His voice faded.

'You promised who? Who did paint those words?'

Bennet wiped his mouth with a trembling hand. 'Mutually beneficial.' A tear trickled down his cheek. He didn't brush it away and it plopped onto his creased, stained shirt. He was giving every indication that he was a man falling apart.

Mutually beneficial? West looked at Andrews and raised an eyebrow. Now maybe he'd believe him. He looked back to Bennet and felt a stirring of pity. 'Can you explain what you mean?' he said gently.

'It seemed like a good idea.'

This was going to be like wading through porridge. 'What was?' West said eventually when the silence stretched too long.

'Working together to get justice.'

West had been right but his satisfaction was tempered by a deep unease. How many people were involved in this?

'For your son's death?'

A jerky nod.

'And for others?'

Bennet pressed his lips together as he looked from one to the other. His eyes looked haunted. 'I thought it was going to make things better... making them pay for what they'd done... but you know, it doesn't take the pain away... that desperate loss... that gaping hole where once there was a life full of joy and hope.'

'Who did you make pay, Mr Bennet?'

'I wanted the Parsons to move away,' Bennet said, ignoring

West's question. 'I thought if we knew they'd left Dublin completely, that there was no chance of bumping into them anywhere, that it might help. The graffiti was to be the first step in the campaign... if it didn't work, the next step would be more drastic.'

West looked at Andrews in alarm. The Parsons had no intention of moving.

'What do you mean, "drastic"?'

Bennet shrugged. 'An extra push. I'm not really sure.'

Because he isn't the one making the decisions. Frustrated, West said, 'Who is sure, Mr Bennet? Who makes these decisions?'

'Pa.'

Now they were getting somewhere. West leaned forward. 'Pa? Short for what... Patrick? Pascal?'

'I don't know, he introduced himself as Pa. We only ever used first names, for confidentiality.'

Pa? West looked at Andrews who shrugged. Neither of them knew anyone involved called Pa.

'Okay,' West said. 'Mr Bennet, can you take us through it? Who else did you make pay?'

'I was only involved with one. I was to help with that, then they'd help me with the Parsons.'

'And who was that one?' West was beginning to feel his patience fraying at the edges. He was right. He knew he was.

Bennet covered his face with his hands. 'The man in the church.' The words were almost smothered but they heard them and West looked at Andrews with a quick nod of satisfaction before turning back to Bennet. 'You're talking about Cormac Furlong, the man who was found dead in the church last week?'

'I didn't know his name.'

'But it was Pa who wanted him punished?'

To their surprise, Bennet shook his head. 'No, it was a young man in the group. He said his life had been destroyed by him and he'd never been punished enough.'

'What was his name?' West said softly, holding his breath as he waited for the reply.

'Ashley.'

Ashley Bolger.

'And you helped with this punishment?' Andrews said.

West held up his hand. 'Before you answer that, Mr Bennet, I must ask you again if you would like legal counsel.'

Bennet almost smiled. 'To save me from myself? No, I think it's too late for that. Yes, I helped with the punishment of that man.' He sat back and folded his arms in a movement that might have seemed relaxed except that his hands gripped his shirt-sleeves, tightening and loosening in a manic rhythm. 'People speak about talk being cheap, don't they? Well, that was us, with our brave plans.' His voice was suddenly devoid of emotion. 'We thought it would be easy. Ashley had told us of the man's guilt, and Pa convinced us to be judge, jury and executioner.'

Bennet held a hand over his trembling mouth for a moment. 'Do you know,' he said, 'that even though he'd used that word, *executioner*, I never... not for a moment... thought that was what we were going to do. To execute a man.'

'How did you convince Furlong to enter the confessional?'

'Ashley knew where he lived, knew that he came home on the DART every evening, and we waited for him.' Bennet sniffed. 'He was a big man, but not particularly brave. I expected him to be harder, tougher... meaner... but he came along without a whimper when Ashley held a gun to his ribs.' Bennet unfolded his arms and rested his hands flat on the table. The fingernails were dirty and chipped, he stared at them as if they belonged to someone else. 'The church was almost empty and the few people who were there paid us no attention. Cormac went into the confessional without argument. Pa was already in the priest's box. We knelt outside and waited.'

Andrews leaned forward, a puzzled frown between his eyes. 'You said you weren't expecting an execution? What did you think was happening inside the box?'

'Pa is a quiet, gentle man. I thought he was talking to Cormac, trying to persuade him to give himself up, to confess to killing Ashley's brother and serve his sentence for it.'

West saw the truth in his eyes. Bennet really hadn't known what he'd got himself into. No wonder he was falling apart. It wasn't only sorrow for the loss of his son anymore, now he was also wracked with guilt. 'So what happened?'

'Ashley and I were sitting in separate pews outside, trying not to draw attention to ourselves. After a few minutes, I heard a thud but before I could do anything, Pa came out and squeezed into the penitent's box with Cormac.' He shook his head at the memory. 'I still didn't have a clue, you know. Honestly, I would never have believed I could be so gormless.' He heaved a sigh. 'Pa came out and told me and Ashley to go into the other penitent's box to hide while the church was being locked up. I wanted to leave but he insisted we stick to the plan. He said they never checked the confessionals before locking up so we'd be safe.'

'You both went into the penitent's box?'

'Yes, it wasn't very comfortable, we had to stand. We were afraid to speak but Ashley kept getting a fit of giggles and I was half afraid he was going to give us away, half hoping he would so we could put an end to it all.'

Bennet's voice faded away and a stricken expression tightened his mouth and hardened his eyes. 'Pa had told us to stay there until he called us out. He is the kind of man who commands obedience, you know, he has a way of looking at you.

Anyway, me and Ashley were beginning to get restless then the door opened and Pa stood there grinning.'

'And then?'

'He told us to take Cormac out.' Bennet stumbled over his words. 'We still had no idea. I remember hearing Ashley gasp beside me when we opened that damn door and saw him slumped there surrounded by a puddle of blood. It was already clotting so was gloopy and slippery as we tried to manoeuvre him out. Ashley caught him under the armpits and I got him under the knees and together we carried him to where Pa pointed.'

'There was no chance that he was alive at that point?' West asked.

Bennet shook his head. 'No. His body was already getting cold.'

'What happened then?' Andrews asked.

'Pa had some black rubbish bags. He told us to strip the body and dump everything inside.' Bennet's nose screwed up. 'Death isn't pleasant. We had to use his clothes to wipe away the excrement. Pa handed us clean boxers. We put them on, then between us we got him hanging the way you found him.'

'Why in the church?' Andrews asked.

Bennet gave an age-old answer, one that hadn't pardoned others before and wouldn't excuse him. 'We did as we were told to do.'

It was an answer sufficient to dispel the lingering sympathy that was troubling West. 'And what about the Parsons? Who painted the graffiti?'

'Ashley. He had to pay back, you know, for the help I gave him with Cormac.'

'The Parsons have a baby boy, Max,' Andrews said. 'He's not even a year old. Is he at risk?'

'I wanted to stop at the graffiti,' Bennet said. 'Even if it didn't work, it was enough for me.' He clasped his hands together. 'I'm not sure Pa sees it that way though. I think once injustice is pointed out to him, he can't rest till it is righted. He's very much an eye-for-an-eye kind of person.'

West frowned. Bennet had lost his only son, the Parsons had one son. Would this Pa character go so far as to kill a baby? 'What about a son for a son?'

Bennet's eyes widened. 'No! No, he wouldn't kill a baby. Would he?'

West and Andrews, galvanised into action, rushed from the room. They stopped for a second at the front desk to explain the situation to Sergeant Blunt.

'We're heading to the Parsons' house now. Send uniformed backup. We'll need to leave a Garda unit there until we can find and pick up this Pa character. And send a car to pick up Ashley Bolger too. He's under arrest for murder.'

They used sirens to clear the traffic and pulled up outside the Parsons' home ten minutes later. They were in luck: Nick Parsons' car was parked in the driveway.

The doorbell was answered almost immediately. 'I hope you've come to tell us you've arrested the Bennets,' Nick Parsons said when he saw who it was. He didn't seem inclined to invite them in, standing with one hand on the door and another on the frame.

'May we come in?'

There must have been something in West's eyes or an unusual tightness about his mouth because Parsons immediately stood back.

'Where's your wife?' West hoped she hadn't taken their child out: he wanted them to be safe, to keep them safe.

'In the kitchen.' Parsons waved to the room behind. 'What's going on?'

West glanced at Andrews who nodded grimly. This wasn't a time for pussyfooting around. 'We have a problem. It might be better not to involve Mrs Parsons.'

Parsons opened a door behind him. 'We can talk in here. Hang on and I'll let her know it's nothing to worry about.'

Andrews and West entered the small room. A formal sitting room with the obligatory three-piece suite and large coffee table. It was a room that didn't look as if it were ever used.

'Nothing to worry about,' Andrews muttered, sitting on one of the sofas.

'Best we keep her out of it. Parsons said she went hysterical when she saw the wall, no knowing what she'd do if she heard there was some maniac looking to dole out punishment for her crime.'

Parsons returned several minutes later. He was balancing a laden tray. 'I've brought coffee,' he said, putting the tray down on the table. 'I realise I haven't been very approachable recently. Forgive me, it's not been easy.' He sat. 'Help yourselves to sugar and milk.'

'There's no need to apologise, Mr Parsons,' West said, adding milk to a mug. 'These last few months have been difficult for you.'

Parsons sipped his black coffee. 'I have the strangest feeling that you haven't come here to make it any better.'

West watched Andrews spoon sugar into his coffee. The clink of the spoon against the sides as he stirred was such a relaxing, simple sound. Sometimes he didn't like his job. Times like now. 'There's never an easy way to break bad news,' West said. 'We spoke to Mr Bennet, in fact we have him in custody.'

'Well, that sounds good!'

'Not for the graffiti, I'm afraid. He says he didn't do that but he does know who did. No, I'm afraid the charges against Mr Bennet are more serious than that.'

Despite Bennet's conviction that he hadn't realised that Furlong was going to be executed, he and Ashley Bolger had taken the man by force and led him to his death. He couldn't imagine the Director of Public Prosecutions settling for anything less than a murder charge.

West lifted his mug and swallowed some coffee, his throat suddenly dry. 'In the course of our interview with Mr Bennet, it came out that there is a group of people who are seeking justice for crimes against their families. The graffiti was supposed to scare you into leaving, Mr Parsons. According to Mr Bennet, if it didn't work the instigator would take more drastic steps.'

Parsons' jaw dropped, his mouth a perfect O of horror.

'Until we catch this person... and we will catch them... it might be best if you go and stay with friends or family. If you decide to remain here, we will provide twenty-four-hour Garda protection.'

Shock had robbed Nick Parsons of words. He slumped in his chair and looked helplessly from West to Andrews.

West put his coffee down and moved closer to him. 'We will keep you safe, Mr Parsons. A squad car is on its way. They'll stay parked in your driveway. Make sure all windows and doors are locked. You'll need to stay at home so cancel all your appointments... will that be possible?'

Parsons swallowed. 'Yes, the other dentists in the practice can cover for me. I'll ring them and let them know.'

'Do,' West said. He checked his watch. 'We'll stay until the squad car gets here.'

'What am I going to tell Ella?' Parsons said, his voice a broken whisper. 'She'll never cope with this.'

Andrews leaned forward. 'I'd simply tell her that we've assigned Garda surveillance to prevent another graffiti attack.'

'Yes, yes, that would work,' Parsons said. 'Thank you.'

There was the sound of a car crunching on the gravel of the driveway. 'That's them,' West said, turning to peer out the window behind him. He got to his feet. 'We'll have a word with them before we leave, get them to check the back of the house. If there are any developments, we'll be in touch.'

After a word with the uniformed Gardaí, West and Andrews returned to Foxrock station.

'I'll go and fill Morrison in,' West said, taking the steps two at a time. The inspector looked up as he swung into the room with the barest sound of a knuckle hitting the door. 'It's urgent.'

'So I should think.' Morrison pushed his keyboard away and looked at him expectantly. 'I hope you're going to tell me you've solved the case.'

'Not quite. It's got a bit more complicated.'

Morrison shut his eyes and groaned loudly. 'I do not need complicated. I need solved.'

'We've arrested Milo Bennet.'

'Well I suppose that's one case solved.'

'Not for the graffiti.'

Morrison's eyes narrowed. 'I can tell by the look in your eyes that you're itching to tell me so spit it out. The sooner I know the worst, the sooner I can recover.'

West took a step towards the desk and rested his hands flat on it. 'Milo Bennet and Ashley Bolger lured Furlong to the church where he was murdered. I've sent a car to pick up Bolger.'

For a moment, it looked as if Morrison was waiting for the punchline to a bad joke. When it didn't come, he did something that had never happened in the time West was in Foxrock. He stood up and moved to the corner where a pot of coffee was brewing. He poured two cups, added milk to both and handed one across to West. 'If you need sugar, you're out of luck. I don't keep any.'

'Thank you,' West said, taking a sip. It was much better coffee than they had downstairs.

'Right, you'd better explain,' Morrison said, sitting back into his chair. 'And, please, try to keep it simple.'

West sipped his coffee as he filled the inspector in. 'I'm hoping Bolger might be able to tell us who this Pa is. Meanwhile, we've put out a protection detail guarding the Parsons.' He saw Morrison's mouth twitch as he considered the implications of overtime. 'You saw the murder scene in the church: this Pa strikes me as a psychopath.'

'Sounds like a right fruitcake to me,' Morrison said. 'I agree though. Fruitcakes, psychopaths, whatever you want to call them, they tend to be unpredictable. I don't want another murder on our patch.'

Promising to keep him up to speed, West left the inspector and headed down to the general office.

'Jarvis had a reply from that *Remembrance* group,' Andrews said as he approached. 'They meet at one every Tuesday so we've missed it today, I'm afraid. But we did get an address so I have him searching for the details of ownership or rental.'

'Good,' West said. He rubbed his neck. 'Edwards and Allen are gone to pick up Ashley Bolger?'

'Yes, they left with sirens blazing, they won't be too long.'

West went into his office, Andrews trailing behind. 'Let's hope he knows who this Pa person is.' He ran a hand through his hair. 'We're so close.'

'We'll get him. Baxter is looking into the address: he'll find something for us.'

~

It was a more belligerent Ashley Bolger who arrived in the station forty minutes later.

'He wasn't keen on coming,' Edwards said. 'Even less keen when we told him he didn't have a choice and read him his rights.'

'Okay, thanks, Andrews and I will speak to him. Contact our sketch artist, Robert, and get him to work with Milo Bennet to come up with an image of this Pa guy. Tell him it's urgent.'

If Edwards were disappointed in being excluded from the interview with Ashley Bolger, he didn't say. 'Will do. If he could come immediately, we could show it to Bolger, see if he agrees and maybe Robert could make changes if necessary.'

'Good idea,' West said, getting to his feet. Out in the main office, Baxter was on the phone, frowning in concentration. When he saw West's interested gaze, he shook his head and mouthed, 'no luck.'

No luck yet. But they'd get there. He gave Baxter a thumbs up and turned to find Andrews behind him looking unusually grim. 'You ready for this?'

'We're going to get him for setting Furlong up on that rape charge too, aren't we?'

'Oh yes,' West said, leading the way to the Big One. 'Once we have his confession, we'll get the lads to pick up the lovely Laetitia Summers and she'll be charged with perverting the course of justice and anything else we can throw at her.'

Ashley Bolger was sitting with legs splayed and arms folded, his mouth tight and pinched in anger. 'You lot are going to pay for this,' he said. 'Coming into my place of work, embarrassing me. You think McD's are going to take kindly to that?'

West and Andrews sat opposite. 'I think what McD's does won't be a concern of yours for...' He looked at Andrews. 'How long do you think?'

'If he behaves, maybe twenty years.'

Bolger laughed. 'Yea, right! Listen, I've watched *Line of Duty*, I know how you lot operate. I'm saying nothing without a solicitor present.'

West picked up the file he had dropped on the table. 'Fine,' he said, getting to his feet. 'We have Milo Bennet next door, perhaps he'll be more accommodating. We'll be sure to tell the judge that you refused to co-operate to save the lives of Ella and Nick Parsons and their nine-month-old baby.' West had no idea how old the baby was, but, he guessed, neither would Ashley Bolger.

'I don't know nothing about no baby!'

'When your trick to have Cormac Furlong punished by being imprisoned for rape didn't work out to your liking...' West almost smiled at Bolger's shocked reaction. That it was still all supposition wasn't something Bolger needed to know. 'Yes, we know all about that. When it didn't work, the next step was to have Cormac killed. The graffiti didn't succeed in frightening the Parsons away so isn't it logical that the next step would also be murder? And Ella Parsons is never far from her baby.' West could see Bolger thinking this through, wondering what they knew, trying to find a way out.

'We'll leave you to wait for your solicitor while we go and speak to Mr Bennet.'

'Wait, I don't know where you heard all that stuff but it's not true.' A note of panic had crept into Bolger's voice.

'Not true that it happened... or not true that it was your idea?' West waved the file. 'Problem is, Mr Bolger, we know it happened that way.'

Bolger's eyes followed the file as West continued to wave it.

'And perhaps Mr Bennet will confirm that it was all your idea.'

'No!' The cry was automatic, pushed from him almost as if against his will. Bolger looked horrified.

West slapped the file on the desk and sat. 'So, it wasn't your idea?'

'No, it wasn't my bloody idea! It was that idiot, Pa.'

'What's Pa's surname?' West held his breath and waited for an answer. He wasn't to be lucky.

'I don't know... I swear,' Bolger insisted, perspiration bubbling on his forehead. 'He said it was to protect us all. Made it sound all very hush-hush... a bit exciting, I suppose.'

'Where did you meet him?'

Bolger slumped in the chair, all his hard-man bravado evaporating. 'I was picking Laetitia up from the library early last year and was hanging around waiting for her, reading the notice-board to pass the time. I saw a leaflet for a group called *Remembrance*. Debbie was always telling me that I should go for counselling that I had–' he crooked his index fingers in the air to make quotation marks '–unresolved issues.' Letting his hands drop to the table, he hunched forward. 'Me and Laetitia had been going out about six months at the time. I liked her a lot but she said she was tired of my mood swings so I thought maybe Debbie was right. So, I emailed the group and started to go every Tuesday.'

He went for help and ended up meeting a monster. 'Tell us what happened,' West said quietly.

Bolger sat back. 'It was what I expected at first, a lot of people talking about bad experiences. But, on my second visit, Pa took me aside. He agreed with Debbie that I had unresolved issues but whereas Debbie wanted me to forget about the past and move on, Pa told me I couldn't move on until I had dealt with it.'

Andrews frowned and held up a hand. 'How did you find out that Ian Moore was Cormac Furlong?'

There was only a faint hesitation before Bolger shrugged. 'There was an old calendar in Laetitia's bedroom, guys with their kit off hiding their bits behind cars and bikes, you know the way. It was out of date but she'd change the page now and then.' Suddenly, Bolger looked younger, more vulnerable. 'One morning I was lying there waiting for her to wake up and I saw him.' He shook his head slowly. 'I always thought I might, someday. Lots of people thought he'd topped himself but I knew he hadn't. I knew he was hiding away somewhere like the coward that he was. The coward who'd killed my brother. And there he was on my girlfriend's damn bedroom wall.'

Laetitia had told West she'd never seen the calendar. 'She helped you set Furlong up?'

This time there was no hesitation, as if Bolger wanted to unload everything. 'I lied when I said we were only going out a year, we've been together over two. I told her about him, about what he'd done. I wanted to go to the guards and tell them I'd found him but she convinced me not to. She said they hadn't believed he was responsible back then so why would they believe it now. Changing your name wasn't a crime, after all. The next time I went to the *Remembrance* meeting I told Pa about it. He told me to take charge of my own destiny.' A smile quivered and died. 'He said things like that.'

'Was it his idea to set Furlong up for raping Laetitia?'

'No, that was Laetitia's. She planned it all.' He sighed loudly. 'The night it happened, I was in the laneway when they came in. I wanted to kill him but instead I watched him and my girlfriend snogging. She kept at it until he'd shot his load into her hands. The drugs she'd slipped into his drink were starting to act and he was barely able to stand by then. We pushed him out of the lane to the main road and scarpered. My car was nearby. Laetitia got inside and wiped the gunk onto the leg of her trousers.'

'The sexual assault clinic's report spoke of extensive bruising.'

Colour flashed across Bolger's cheeks. 'Laetitia likes it rough.

That night she was like a tiger, she had me doing all kinds of stuff.'

Leaving the manipulative woman with enough bruises to help support her pack of lies. 'You didn't offer her any inducements to go along with it, did you?'

Bolger looked at West blankly. 'What?'

'Money,' Andrews explained. 'Did you offer to pay her to help you?'

'Pay her? No, of course not.'

West nodded. They'd been on the wrong track there. 'Okay, so Furlong was convicted for rape and sent to prison. Why didn't you leave it at that?'

'He only served eight months. You think that was long enough for what he did? Murdering my brother, destroying my family. Eight months!'

Revenge: it ate away at people, destroying what was left of their lives. For a second, West's thoughts drifted to another man. *Eamonn Hall.* Such a waste. As it was for this young man who might have had a chance if he hadn't hooked up with that devious, manipulative woman and Pa. They had to find Pa. 'Whose idea was it to murder Furlong?'

Bolger dragged a hand over his mouth. 'I told Pa about the rape set-up, and how justice had failed again with its miserable eight-month sentence. Pa told me to leave it to him, that he'd see Cormac got what he deserved. We had to get him to the church and into the confessional. It was easier than I'd expected. I borrowed a gun from a mate.' He held up a hand. 'Don't ask, I'm not telling. Furlong came with me and Milo, without any fuss.' Bolger's lips curled in a sneer. 'Told you he was a coward, he didn't put up the least bit of resistance.'

'You knew what Pa had planned?' Andrews asked.

There was a long silence before Bolger slowly shook his head. 'When I asked, Pa said I wasn't to worry. That everything would be all right. He told us to put him in the penitent's box of the confessional. I thought maybe he was going to make him confess to having killed Gary. If he had, he'd have gone away for a long time. It would have been right.' There was a tremor in his voice. A hand went up to rub his eyes. Or maybe wipe away tears. 'When I saw him... all the blood... I was stunned.' He talked them through carrying the body up to the altar. Pa's insistence that they clean away all evidence of blood afterward. 'He didn't want us to leave a mess,' he said.

'And you've no idea who this Pa is?'

'No, he never spoke about any personal stuff. Apart from the night he killed Furlong, I'd only ever met him in that poky room in Sandymount.'

West and Andrews spent another hour prising out every scrap of information they could before calling a halt. Leaving a very subdued Bolger to be escorted to a cell, they headed back to the office with grim faces.

'Anything?'

Baxter shook his head. 'The group leader hires the room from the takeaway below for an hour every week. Thirty euro paid in advance. Cash.' He looked at a sheet of paper on his desk. 'The takeaway owner said he believes in *don't ask don't tell.*

'Convenient. I hope you put him right.'

'I told him as owner of the premises, he has a duty of care and we'd be in contact if the Director of Public Prosecutions decided to press charges for negligence.'

West smiled. It wasn't going to happen but it might ensure the owner be a little more careful in future. The smile faded. 'Right, we need to find this Pa guy.' He looked around the room. 'Ideas, anyone?'

Blank expressions and slow headshakes. They'd hit a brick wall.

Edel walked into a silent room, all the detectives looking unusually serious. Something, she guessed, wasn't going their way. Maybe it wasn't a good time to interfere but she knew what she had to tell them was important.

'Hello,' she said, drawing all eyes immediately to her and wilting under their intensity. En masse, they were an intimidating group. When they saw it was her, there were quick smiles and shouts of greeting.

'Hi,' Mike said, walking over to meet her, a smile on his lips and in his eyes. 'Are you okay?' He always worried about her; over the last year she'd given him plenty of reason but she was hoping he'd stop seeing her as a victim. When she saw the smile in his eyes change to concern, she knew he hadn't yet. Unfortunately, what she had to tell him wasn't going to help.

'I need to talk to you,' she said, waving a hello to the rest of the room.

Mike frowned. 'I'm really busy. Can it wait until tonight?'

Edel reached into her pocket for the leaflet. 'It's about this,' she said, holding it out.

He took it from her but his eyes stayed on her face, searching. 'What about it?'

She'd never been able to hide what she was thinking from him. She saw realisation dawn, his eyes narrowing in annoyance. 'You'd better come into my office. Something tells me I'm not going to like what you're going to tell me.'

He didn't. 'You did what?' His voice was tight, anger held in by force of will.

Edel didn't think she'd ever seen him so annoyed. He shut the door of the office and glared at her, then, as suddenly as it had appeared, the anger vanished.

'I did send you a message to say where I was going... just in case.'

'It was on silent, I usually check it but...' He took out his phone and read her message. 'It would have been some consolation to get that after they found you dead.' But his voice was resigned rather than infuriated. 'Bloody hell, Edel, you'll be the death of me.' He pulled her into a quick hug, then pushed her away. 'I assume you've come here because you've found out something.'

When she murmured 'Yes,' he paced the office. 'Okay,' he said, turning to look at her. 'I haven't time to dance around here. We have two men in custody but we think the guy who runs this group is the mastermind behind the murder of Cormac Furlong. If you've found something, tell all the team. We're under pressure with this one.'

He didn't wait for her to agree, reaching behind her to open the office door and waving her out. 'Listen up,' he said, raising his voice to get the team's attention. 'We've had a bit of luck. You all know Edel, and what she's been through in the last year.'

Edel watched their reactions. How was he going to spin this one?

'Well, she decided to go for counselling and, by an amazing

coincidence–' he held up the leaflet '–she chose this place. Her first visit was today. She has agreed to share her experience with us.'

Edel looked at West in admiration. He was good. If she hadn't known better, she'd have believed his tale. The only person who raised an eyebrow in disbelief was Andrews but then he saw through everything.

She shoved her hands in her pockets and looked around the room as she spoke. 'The man who runs it calls himself Pa. I don't know what it's short for, I didn't have an opportunity to ask. He stressed the need for confidentiality without giving a reason.' There was a desk behind her and she perched on it, relaxing despite the eyes fixed on her.

'The group was small, four people all with sad tales to tell. Pa didn't have any comment to make on the relative who died of a heart attack or the sister who died from drowning but he was very interested in the other two, the man whose daughter died when her boyfriend crashed the car while speeding and the man whose brother died from an overdose. Both men spoke about wanting revenge. I waited for Pa to tell them that revenge was wrong.'

She shook her head, remembering the fanatic tone of his voice. 'Instead, he seemed to encourage them, speaking slowly, emphatically... fanatically... and said that we lived in a world where perpetrators of crimes wrecked lives and went unpunished, or with a punishment that didn't meet the crime.' She looked around the room. 'He made no attempt to counsel them or advise them that revenge was wrong.'

Edel turned to meet West's carefully-neutral gaze. 'When I left, I waited across the street pretending to be using my mobile and watched them leave. Pa and Arthur – the man whose daughter died – were last out.' There was no change in West's expression; she blinked and looked away. 'The street isn't very wide, but Pa was so engrossed in whatever he was saying and Arthur was so intent on taking it all in that they didn't notice me. Pa had a grip on Arthur's arm, he seemed to shake it as if he was making a point and Arthur... he kept nodding as if he agreed with everything that was being said.

'And that's it, I'm afraid.'

'Pity you didn't follow him,' Jarvis muttered without thinking.

'Edel doesn't work for the Garda Síochána, Jarvis, and I think she's done enough of our work for us for one day.' West's voice was sharp enough to bring a flush of colour to the young detective's face and an exchange of glances between the others.

Andrews jumped into the silence that followed. 'That's all very helpful, Edel. Could you describe this Pa for us, best as you can?'

'A slim man, a few inches taller than me, maybe five ten. Short, mousy-brown hair. Pleasant-looking, I suppose, but the kind of face you'd forget quickly. He became more animated when he spoke about justice and his eyes became a bit manic.'

'Robert is on his way in to work with Mr Bennet on getting a sketch of him,' Baxter reminded them. 'Maybe between him, Bolger and Edel we'll be able to get a good likeness.'

'I'm happy to help,' Edel agreed. At the edge of her vision, she saw West moving restlessly. He'd prefer her to be gone, she knew, but the detective in him was caught. Getting a third person's input into the sketch could only help.

'Anyone any idea what Pa could be short for?' Andrews said, breaking the sudden tension in the room. 'I was thinking Patrick or Pascal. Anyone heard it used as a diminutive for any other name?'

'Pa,' Allen repeated with a shake of his head. 'I can't think of anything.'

Edel looked at him. 'Say that again.'

Mick Allen, who'd never lost his Tipperary accent, smiled. 'Pa,' he said obligingly.

'That's it,' Edel said, turning to look at West with an excited expression. 'He didn't introduce himself as Pa, the way we've been saying it, but as *Pa*, the way Mick says it.' She looked around at them. 'Don't you see? It's *Pa*, as in father.'

38

West looked at Edel's excited face and nodded. *Pa, as in father.* Father as in priest? One of the priests from St Monica's?

Baxter was first to move. He sat in front of his computer, and after a few seconds' rapid tapping, sat back. 'Here you go, a photo of the priests of St Monica's Parish taken just a few months ago.'

West put a hand on Edel's shoulder. 'Have a look and see if you recognise him,' he said quietly and stayed close to her as she peered over Baxter's shoulder to look at the screen.

'Hang on, I'll enlarge the image,' Baxter said, tapping some more. 'There you go.'

Edel lifted a finger and pointed. 'That's him. That's Pa. Not a shred of doubt.'

'Father McComb,' Baxter said, reading the list of names underneath the image.

Andrews slapped his hand on a desk. 'Father McComb. He was moved from parish to parish because he scared people with his fire and brimstone lectures. I heard him once, he sounded a bit fanatical. Maybe there was more to it than that.'

West remembered the quiet man he'd met in the priests' house on Westminster Road. The slight, unremarkable man he'd glanced at with barely a thought. *A priest.* If they were right, this was going to be a nightmare.

'Print that photo out,' West said to Baxter, 'then see if Bennet and Bolger can pick him out.' He turned to Edel. 'Not that I'm doubting you, but it's good to have confirmation from more than one person.' There was a worried look in her eyes: he wanted to kiss it away. She'd had enough worry in the last year. Okay, she shouldn't have gone to that meeting, but if she hadn't, they'd still be floundering. Maybe it was time to accept she was intricately linked with all parts of his life.

'Why don't you sit in my office, I'll get you some coffee.' He saw her face brighten and watched with a smile as she went to sit in his office. He'd never hear the end of this. Something so simple and it took her to see it.

His smile faded quickly. 'Okay, I'm going to speak to the inspector. This is going to be his worst nightmare.'

Inspector Morrison was drinking coffee when West arrived but the story must have been written clearly on his face because the inspector put the mug down with a weary, 'Tell me.' His expression darkened as he listened. 'There's no doubt?'

'Andrews is taking the photos in for Bennet and Bolger to confirm but I don't think there's any doubt, Inspector. I'd like to bring him in for questioning. And yes,' he said, anticipating the inspector's next comment, 'I'll be as discreet as possible.'

'I'll have to ring the bishop,' Morrison said, his mouth a tight line. 'Go, do what needs to be done. I'll be waiting to hear from you.'

West left without another word and met Andrews on his way back to the main office. 'You got confirmation?'

'Neither as much as hesitated.'

West exhaled loudly. 'Right, let's go and pick this guy up.'

Andrews shoved his hands into his jacket pockets. 'This is going to be a tough one, Mike.'

There was nothing more to say. 'Give me a minute,' West said.

Edel was staring at her phone when he opened his office door. 'You okay?' he said, pulling a chair over to sit beside her.

'A priest,' she said. 'This is going to be a tough one.'

A smile flickered. 'Honestly, you and Pete, you think alike. Yes. It's going to be a difficult one but we've had them before. It's also going to be a late one. Head home, I'll send you a message later and let you know when to expect me.' He leaned forward and planted a kiss on her cheek. 'It may be an all-nighter so don't be surprised not to hear from me till morning.' He walked her to her car, Andrews tailing behind. 'Drive carefully,' he said, tapping the roof of her car before she started the engine. 'Right,' he said as her car left the car park. 'let's go and pick up Father McComb.'

There was no conversation on the short journey, each of them lost in their thoughts, mentally preparing for what was to come. They'd been there before, but it never got easier.

It was Father Dillon who answered the door. 'Detective Sergeant West, Detective Garda Andrews,' he greeted them politely. 'What can we do for you today?'

'May we come in?' West saw Father Dillon's relaxed appearance change in a couple of almost imperceptible movements; a straightening of shoulders, a lifting of his chin. He guessed that priests, like Gardaí, developed a sixth sense when trouble was brewing. Without a word, he stood back.

'We're all in the sitting room,' Father Dillon said, leading the way. 'Father Jeffreys likes to have a meeting every week so we can discuss any issues.' He opened the door into the room and waved them in.

The priests were sitting in the same seats they'd sat in the last time he'd visited, as if they'd never moved or if time had stood still. But this time, he looked at Father McComb more keenly. Such an innocuous-looking man. Such a deceptively innocent expression.

'Take a seat,' Father Dillon said.

'No, we won't, thank you,' West said. 'I'm afraid we've come with a difficult job to do.'

Father Jeffreys got to his feet. 'Don't tell me there's been another murder in the church!'

The old priest staggered a little. West put his hand out and grasped his arm. 'Sit down, please, Father. This is going to come as a bit of a shock, I'm afraid.' He saw movement from the corner of his eye and turned to see Father McComb on his feet.

'I'll go fetch his medication,' McComb said.

'Perhaps someone else could do that,' West said, holding up a hand to stop him.

He saw the knowledge in McComb's eyes, watched him assess his position, wondering if he could escape. But if he'd decided to run, it was too late. Andrews moved between him and the door.

Father Jeffreys, still on his feet, looked from West to McComb and back. 'I think you'd better tell us what is going on, Sergeant West.'

'Kevin McComb,' West said, dropping the man's title. 'You are under arrest for the murder of Cormac Furlong.' He read him his rights as the other priests got to their feet, all of them speaking at once, disbelief in every word.

'Is this true?' Father Jeffreys' voice was ragged with shock and he grasped West's arm.

'I'm sorry,' West said, covering the man's trembling hand with his own. He stepped back as Dillon and Maher moved closer to support the parish priest, each putting a hand on his shoulder in solidarity. All three priests looked stunned. 'Kevin,' Father Jeffreys said, 'I don't understand.'

'Sanctimonious fools,' McComb said, a sneer twisting his mouth. 'I've listened to you giving your all-forgiving sermons, and I've seen the penitents after you've heard their confessions bouncing with relief when they should have been bowed down with penance.'

Father Dillon pressed Father Jeffreys into a seat before turning to look at McComb as if he'd never seen him before. 'That's what the sacrament of confession is all about, Kevin. Forgiveness.'

'You would have offered that man, Cormac, forgiveness, but the soul that sins...' McComb's voice grew strident and echoed around the room. 'The soul that sins shall die. The Son of Man shall send forth his angels, and they shall gather out of his kingdom all things that offend and which do iniquity.' McComb glared at the parish priest. 'And I am such an angel, here to do the Lord's work.' He turned to West and Andrews. 'The claws of the law, too, have been removed, leaving it impotent and useless. The world needs somebody like me.'

Father Jeffreys stepped forward and stared at McComb with sorrowful eyes. 'No,' he said and his voice was heavy with sadness. 'The world doesn't, Kevin.' He turned to West. 'I'll contact the archbishop, and we'll send a solicitor to the station.' He looked as if he wanted to say more, but he turned away and yielded to the comforting embrace of his fellow priests.

'We'll wait until the solicitor arrives before questioning him,' West said, seeing Father Jeffreys nod in agreement. Both knew the wisdom of doing everything strictly by the book.

In handcuffs, McComb made a token resistance to being led away, then shrugged and walked between them and sat in the back of the car with Andrews alongside. Back in the station he was quickly processed and left sitting in a cell to await the arrival of his solicitor while West and Andrews filled in the rest of the team.

'He thinks he's an angel,' Baxter scoffed. 'Sounds to me like he's going for a *not guilty by reason of insanity* defence.'

Allen agreed. 'And he'll leave Bennet and Bolger to pay the price for Furlong's death.'

'Such cynicism.' West smiled. 'Let's see what his solicitor has to say. If McComb really thinks he's an angel doing God's work, he may be sent to Dundrum for assessment. If he is simply putting it on, they'll quickly find out.' He took a mouthful of the coffee someone had put into his hand. 'McComb has been spouting fire and brimstone for a number of years and railing against what he saw as a world full of sinners. Maybe it all became too much for him and cracked him apart.'

'Luckily, we got him before he took revenge on anyone else,' Jarvis said. 'The Parsons will be relieved.'

West's mobile phone rang. He took it out and looked at the screen. It was Edel's name. He answered it, his heart sinking when he heard the panic in her voice.

39

Edel had driven from the station with the intent of heading straight home but remembered she'd nothing taken out of the freezer for dinner and decided to divert to Dunnes Stores. The clothes there were good; she might have a relaxing afternoon shopping. She deserved it.

Having lived in Foxrock, she knew the back roads and took the turns without thought. At a T-junction she had come to a halt, waiting for a slow driver to pass, when her attention was caught by a woman on the far side of the road. She was bent almost double, her hand reaching out for the wall beside her.

A woman in trouble. Instinctively, Edel made the turn, pulled to the side of the road and stopped, getting out and hurrying to the woman's side. 'Are you all right?' When there was no reply, she bent to examine the woman's face. Her eyes were shut, her skin so pale as to be almost luminous. A very sickly woman. 'Can I help you?'

'Leave me, nobody can help me.' The voice was feeble.

Edel couldn't leave her. 'My car is here, I'll take you wherever you're going. Please, I can't simply drive away. You'll be better off at home.'

A humourless snort of laughter was the only response.

Beginning to wonder if she should ring for an ambulance, Edel tried again. 'Is there someone I can ring for you? Family? Or a friend maybe.'

'No, there's nobody.' Sad, lonely words full of pain and grief.

Edel had been there. She slipped an arm around the woman's shoulder. 'Come on,' she said gently. 'I'll take you wherever you want to go.' A gentle tug got the woman moving. Edel guided her to her car, reaching for the passenger door and pulling it open. When the woman sat inside, she pulled across the seat belt and fastened it.

Back in the driver's seat, Edel turned to look at her. 'Where to?' When there was no answer, she tried a different tack. 'Maybe I should take you to the hospital.'

'No.'

'Where then?' Edel wished she'd gone straight home. She could have stopped at a supermarket in Greystones. What was so great about Dunnes? But it was too late. She couldn't abandon this poor, wretched creature.

'Walnut Avenue.'

Edel barely heard the whispered words but she recognised the name of the road. 'Okay, let's get you home.'

It wasn't far and ten minutes later she was driving slowly down the short road. 'What number?'

'Eight.'

'Eight, right,' Edel muttered, peering from right to left, seeing a three, concentrating then on the other side of even numbers and stopping in front of the house with a brass eight dead centre of a black door. She stopped outside, got out and hurried around to open the passenger door. 'Here you are then.'

'Thank you.' The woman levered herself from the car and stood with her hand on the door, staring towards the house.

Edel took in the unkempt garden, the partially-shut curtains.

It looked abandoned, uncared for. 'Will you be okay now?' she asked. She wanted to get away from the sadness that was coming from the woman in overwhelming waves.

'You've been so kind. Please, come in and I'll make us some tea. It's the least I can do.'

Edel didn't want tea. She didn't want to go inside the desolate-looking house. 'No, I'm in a bit of a hurry, actually,' she said. She waited for the woman to move so she could shut the car door but instead, the woman stood staring, holding onto the door as if she were afraid to let go. Perhaps accepting a cup of tea was the easiest option. 'Well, maybe I've time for a quick cuppa.' Edel was relieved to see the woman nod and take unsteady steps across the path to the garden gate.

The air of neglect continued inside the house; the heating had been left on and the air was muggy and stale. Edel's nose crinkled in defence as she followed the woman into a small, untidy kitchen.

'Take off your coat, have a seat.'

Intent on getting out of the house as soon as possible, Edel kept her coat on, perched on the edge of a chair and willed the kettle to boil quickly. 'My name is Edel,' she said, more to break the uncomfortable silence than from any desire to start a conversation.

The woman turned with a smile. 'I'm Joanne. It's nice to meet you. You've been very kind.'

She looked like a woman who hadn't seen much kindness recently. Perhaps Edel wouldn't rush away after all. With relief, she saw that the mug she was handed was clean, and the milk Joanne poured straight from the carton didn't come out with an audible glug. It tasted okay too.

'Would you like a biscuit?' Joanne said, waving towards a cupboard. 'I think I have some.'

'No, thanks.'

The uncomfortable silence had returned. Joanne held her mug between her cupped hands and stared into space.

Curiosity made Edel ask, 'Do you live alone?'

'I didn't this morning but I do now.'

It wasn't the answer Edel was expecting. In fact, she'd no idea what it meant. Joanne was wearing a wedding ring. 'Did you lose your husband?'

Joanne hugged the mug to her chest, huddling around it. 'You could say that. The guards rang me earlier. He's been arrested.'

'Arrested! Why?' What on earth could the husband of this frail, inoffensive woman have done?

'He'll probably be charged with murder.'

A heavy weight of dread pushed Edel back in the chair. One of the men Mike had in custody... Baxter had mentioned their names when he spoke of the sketch artist coming... Bennet and Bolger. *Bennet!* Oh no! Of course, she remembered the case. The two boys knocked down by a speeding car. One of them had died. Milo Junior Bennet. He'd been an only child. This sad woman's only child.

'I'm so sorry.' And because she couldn't help herself, she said, 'Your husband was arrested in connection with the murder of the man in the church?' When she saw Joanne's head jerk up and down in agreement, she frowned. She should stand up and leave. How could she possibly explain to Mike that she accidentally happened upon the wife of a man he'd arrested that morning. But she couldn't. Not yet. 'I don't understand. The man, Cormac Furlong, he'd nothing to do with your son's death.'

'The perpetrators of crimes wreck lives... all lives.'

Edel had heard those words spoken only a few hours before. 'You've met Pa?'

'Milo brought him around one evening. He's very emotional.'

Very fanatical would have been Edel's conclusion. 'I still don't understand–'

Joanne held up a hand to stop her. 'It's simple. Milo helped with the man in the church, in return he would be helped with that woman.'

That woman? 'Do you mean the woman who knocked down your son?'

'Ella Parsons, yes. She refused to accept responsibility, manipulating the system to evade justice.'

Edel struggled to remember the details. It had happened a short while before she and West had gone to Clare Island. 'Wasn't there something about her being unfit to plead?'

Joanne's mouth twisted. 'Unfit to plead but fit enough to drive and kill my son.'

It was time for Edel to leave. She was well acquainted with pain and anger, but this deep wrenching sadness was beyond her. She had shuffled to the edge of the seat when she heard Joanne mutter something unintelligible. 'Sorry, I didn't catch that.'

'I said Milo wasn't able to do it.'

'Do what?' The words were out before she could stop them.

'Kill her.'

Her? Ella Parsons? Edel couldn't tell from Joanne's expression whether she was relieved or disappointed. This was a question she wasn't going to ask. 'I'd better be going,' she said, getting to her feet.

'But I sorted it myself.'

The words were barely audible. Edel wanted to pretend she hadn't heard them. She could have done, could have got up and left but one thing stopped her. She remembered that the Parsons had a young child... a baby boy... She couldn't leave without asking. 'What do you mean you sorted it yourself?'

40

'Edel, slow down, I can't understand you,' West said.

'Joanne Bennet. A gun. She wrote a letter to Nick Parsons. Told him to end it all.'

West waved to the others, put the phone down on the desk and pressed speaker. 'Edel, take a deep breath and tell us clearly what is going on.' He heard her inhale loudly and let it out in a long hiss.

'I saw Joanne Bennet,' Edel said, her voice calmer. 'She was walking along the street, struggling, so I stopped and took her home. I didn't know who she was, I swear.'

'Coincidences do happen,' West said, even as he was thinking that Edel seemed to attract trouble like a magnet.

'Yes, well I wish they wouldn't happen to me.' Edel took another deep breath. 'Joanne told me Milo had been given a gun to kill Ella Parsons but he wasn't able to do it. Joanne wrote a note and posted it with the gun through the Parsons' letterbox. That's where she was coming from when I saw her.'

Nick Parsons had struck West as a man who was out of options. Would he take this one? 'Where are you now?'

'I'm still here with Joanne.'

'Okay, stay there, I'm sending someone around.' He hung up, pointed to Jarvis and Allen and jerked his thumb towards the door. They didn't need to be told a second time.

West picked up the desk phone and rang the front desk, hoping their dependable sergeant had been less efficient that day. 'Tom, was the squad car pulled from the Parsons' house?'

Of course, it had been. West slammed the phone down on the *yes*. 'We need to get to the Parsons' house.'

They all knew the score and seconds later they were running from the station. 'Baxter, you drive,' West said and everyone veered across the car park to the red Volvo. Baxter was a good choice. He drove like a maniac.

With sirens on and Baxter driving, they pulled up outside the Parsons' house only minutes later.

Nick Parsons' car was parked in the driveway. West, Andrews, Baxter and Edwards piled out of the Volvo and looked around the typical upmarket, quiet suburban street before focusing on the house. It too looked quiet. Ordinary. They all hoped they were wrong. That it would remain ordinary and not turn into a statistic.

West rang the doorbell and the other three stood back observing, alert and ready to move.

'I've a ram bar in the boot,' Baxter said.

'Let's give it a minute before we start bashing their door in.' West leaned forward to peer through the glass panels at the side. There was nothing to be seen. But anything could be happening behind the doors. A memory flashed through his mind. Brian Dunphy lying dead on the doorstep of that house in Finglas. The woman and three children dead upstairs. He felt his throat thicken. 'Okay, Seamus, grab your ram bar. Let's get inside.'

The uPVC door yielded easily to one blow, the loud crash followed by a silence that was heavy with foreboding. Each of the men unclipped their holsters. Someone in the house had a gun; they might have need of their own.

There wasn't a sound to be heard. It didn't bode well. West took slow, careful steps towards the first door and pushed it open with one hand. The room was empty.

The next door, leading into the large open-plan kitchen and living room, was ajar and swung open at a nudge. At first, West thought the room was empty. It was Edwards who saw the figure curled up on the floor in the corner. 'Sarge, look!'

It was Nick Parsons. His eyes were shut, arms clasped around his knees. Hanging from one hand was a revolver. It was impossible to know if it had been used. There was no sign of Ella, no sight... or sound... of the baby.

'Search upstairs,' West said, nodding to Baxter and Edwards who immediately left the room. Andrews stayed where he was, never taking his attention from the man on the floor.

'Mr Parsons?' West waited a beat before saying loudly. 'Mr Parsons, can you open your eyes?'

A grunt was followed by the flicker of eyelids.

West took a step closer. 'Put the weapon on the floor.'

Parsons' forehead creased. 'What?'

'The weapon you're holding. Put it on the floor.'

Nick Parsons looked at the revolver in his hand and shook his head slowly. 'There was a note with it. It explained that this was the best way. And do you know, they were probably right.'

From the corner of his eye, West saw Andrews slowly take his SIG Sauer from his holster. He was right. It might come to that. But not if West could help it. He took a step closer to the man on the floor. 'Listen to me, Nick, it's over. The Bennets are under arrest. They're not going to cause you trouble again.' It was bending the truth a little. Milo Bennet would certainly serve time for his part in the murder of Cormac Furlong. Joanne would serve time too if Nick had used the weapon she'd supplied to kill his wife and child. There was no sound from upstairs, no shouts of horror or relief from Baxter and Edwards. But if there was death in the house, he didn't want another.

He hunkered down, meeting Parsons eye to eye. 'It's over. The Bennets won't interfere with your life again.'

Parsons shook his head. 'Ella killed that boy. It's never going to be over.' He lifted his hand and looked at the gun he held. 'I gave it a lot of thought, you know.'

West remembered Ella holding her son when they'd come to arrest her months before. Had she protected him to the end? Sadness washed through him. Her stupid and reckless act in speeding that day had caused so much sorrow, so much waste.

He thought he'd imagined the cry. Wishful thinking. But then it came again, louder, longer. A baby's hungry wail. He glanced towards Andrews, saw the relief that he was sure was echoed on his own face. The baby was alive.

'Where's Ella?'

Parsons frowned and waved the revolver, pointing it towards the ceiling. 'Upstairs.' The baby was still crying, joined now by the sound of male voices. 'Sounds like Max is awake.'

'Nick,' West said, dragging the man's focus back to him. 'Put the weapon on the floor.'

'Yes... yes, of course.' But Parsons continued to wave it about. 'It isn't that easy, is it? To shoot someone?'

West drew a breath. 'Ella is okay?'

'Asleep. Max was awake most of the night so she's catching up.' He looked at West. 'You thought I'd killed them?'

'It crossed our minds,' West admitted, getting to his feet. He took a step closer to the crouched man and held out his hand. 'I think you'd better give that to me now.'

Parsons released the revolver into West's hand and struggled to his feet. 'It might have crossed mine for a second when I read that awful letter. But despite everything, I love Ella. Plus–' he dragged up a faint smile '–I was never one for taking an easy way out. We'll struggle on and make it. That's what life is all about.'

Baxter came through the door carrying Max who was snuffling now rather than crying. 'Mrs Parsons is on her way,' he said, jiggling the baby. 'I think this boyo is hungry.'

Nick Parsons reached for his son. 'Thank you, I'll get him something.'

'We had to break your front door in,' West said. 'I apologise, but we did have just cause to be concerned.'

Nick Parsons shrugged as if having his door caved in by the Gardaí was an everyday occurrence. 'I'll get it fixed.' He buried his nose in his son's neck, making the child gurgle. 'Is it true, what you said?'

'About the Bennets? Yes, Milo Bennet will serve time for murder. I'm uncertain about Joanne Bennet but I will guarantee she won't bother you again.' West would speak to Morrison: between them they'd come up with something. The Parsons family had been through enough.

41

Back in the station it was organised chaos. Solicitors had arrived to represent Kevin McComb and Milo and Joanne Bennet, and all wanted to speak to West.

'Tell them I'll be with them shortly,' West told Sergeant Blunt with a wave as he headed up to fill the inspector in.

'What a wicked woman,' Morrison said when he heard about what Joanne Bennet had done. 'She's in custody?'

'Yes, her solicitor is waiting to see me.' West shrugged. He'd been a solicitor, he knew what the argument would be. It was one he himself would have used... Joanne Bennet was suffering from severe depression following the death of her son, it wouldn't serve any justice to have her locked up. It might come down to a trade-off.

'I assume McComb's solicitor will deem him unfit to plead,' Morrison said, his brows meeting in one hairy line.

'I have no doubt. He'll be sent to Dundrum for assessment.'

'And Bennet and Bolger will carry the can for Cormac Furlong's murder.'

West folded his arms and leaned against the wall. 'The courts may be more lenient with Bennet, but Bolger–' he shook his head '–his was a continued, calculated effort to destroy Furlong.'

'With that woman's help.'

'Laetitia Summers, yes. I'll have her picked up. She'll be prosecuted for perverting the course of justice. Hopefully, the Director of Public Prosecutions will push for jail time.'

Morrison smiled. 'You didn't like her?'

'I would have been happier if I'd been right, that she'd done it for money.'

'What was her motive? Love?'

West pushed away from the wall and shoved his hands into his pockets. 'No, I think the only person Laetitia Summers loves is herself. That's what makes my blood boil, Inspector, I think she did it for fun.'

'This has been a nasty case, Mike. Glad it's coming to a close.'

That was West's hint to leave. He made his way, slowly, back to the main office, planning what to say to whom.

As it turned out, it was easier than he'd expected. The solicitor for Kevin McComb, an officious man by the name of Malachy de Burgh, insisted his client wasn't in a fit state to be questioned.

'I've organised an ambulance to have him transferred to the Central Mental Hospital in Dundrum,' he said, as if that was the end of the conversation.

It probably was.

Milo Bennet's solicitor turned out to be an old friend of West's.

'A nasty case this,' Drew Masters said, crossing one perfectly-creased trouser leg over the other. 'My client is willing to confess to his part in the unfortunate death of Cormac Furlong but I think you and I both know he was in a very vulnerable state of mind following the death of his only child and only too open to be manipulated by someone as evil as Kevin McComb.'

'Indeed,' West said with a raised eyebrow. 'So that will be your approach.'

Masters smiled. 'I can be very convincing.'

West didn't doubt it. 'What about his wife?'

'She's broken, not bad, Mike.' The solicitor uncrossed his leg and leaned forward. 'Mrs Bennet has a sister in Cork who has been asking her to come and live with her. I can arrange for Mr Bennet to serve any time he is given by the courts in Rathmore Road.'

It would be the perfect answer. Get the Bennet family as far away from Dublin as possible. There was one slight problem. 'Isn't Rathmore Road a committal prison for Cork, Kerry and Waterford only?'

Masters waved a hand dismissively. 'Don't you worry about that. If I can persuade the DPP, will you agree?'

'It's the Director of Public Prosecutions who makes those decisions, not a mere detective Garda,' West said.

'Yes, but he'll listen to you. It's for the best, Mike.'

West wanted to remind him about the deal he'd made for Ken Blundell and how quickly that had gone wrong but truth was, Masters was right. This would be best for all concerned. 'I'll do what I can,' he said.

It was enough for Drew Masters. 'Right, I'll go and get the ball rolling. We'll have to meet some night, it's been too long since I've chatted to the lovely Edel.' With a mock salute, he was gone.

Andrews came into the office as the solicitor left. 'Bolger's solicitor is here wanting a word.'

'Has Bolger said anything else?'

'He admitted that the *friend*–' Andrews crooked his index

fingers in the air '–he got the revolver from is none other than McComb. He gave it back to him afterwards.'

'Then McComb gave it to Milo Bennet.'

'Bennet said he'd never expected his wife to do what she did,' Andrews said, sitting and rubbing a hand over his head. 'He seemed more horrified by that than the prospect of going to prison for murder.'

'Drew Masters is going to try and cut a deal. It seems Joanne Bennet has a sister in Cork.'

'And he can organise that Bennet will do his time there?'

'He says he can.'

Andrews, always the pragmatist, said, 'Sounds like the perfect solution.'

West thought of Nick Parsons, his quick anger and smouldering despair and wondered if anything, apart from turning the clock back, would be a solution for them. 'I'm not sure, but it's the best we can do.'

Andrews got to his feet and stretched with a weary yawn. 'Baxter and Edwards have taken Laetitia Summers into the Other One. She's not a happy lady. What'll she be charged with?'

'Perverting the course of justice, probably, perjury definitely. She put that poor man in prison with her lies. She'll do some time.'

'Do you think he did it?'

West didn't have to ask what Andrews was talking about. It was something he'd been wondering himself. 'I think it's highly likely that Cormac killed Gary Bolger but I'd guess it was probably a stupid, drunken accident. If he'd owned up at the time, he might have done a stretch, but it was unlikely to have been long. Instead, he gave himself a life sentence.' West got to his feet. 'I think I'll listen in to the interview.'

He met Bolger's solicitor as he left. In less than a minute he disabused him of any idea of leniency. 'Ashley Bolger set out to destroy Furlong for a crime he assumed he'd committed. When the first attempt didn't do the job sufficiently for his sense of justice, he plotted with others to murder him. If you can tell me anything in that grim tale that screams leniency, I'd be pleased to hear it.' West waited while the solicitor opened and shut his mouth. 'I thought not. The file will be sent to the DPP. Now, if you'll excuse me.'

An observation room linked the two interview rooms. Bolger had sat in the Big One. He'd been taken back to his cell and that room now stood empty. In the other, Laetitia Summers sat back with a smile that was as fake as her blonde hair and thick, dark eyelashes.

West sat to listen. It sounded as though they were nearly finished. It would soon be the end of what had turned out to be a crazy day.

'You admit to setting Cormac Furlong up to help your boyfriend?' Baxter was saying.

'There's not much point in denying it if he told you I did, is there?' There was no apology in her words, a sharp statement of fact.

'You must love him very much.'

The question amused West. Baxter, crazily in love with his beautiful fiancée would forgive anything for love. But Laetitia Summers was a different kind of woman.

She laughed. 'Give it a rest. He's okay, a fit body and all, but now he'll be banged up for years. I'm not the hanging around type. Anyway,' she shrugged, 'I wouldn't say I did it for love.'

Laetitia's solicitor, sitting quietly beside her, sensed her client was about to say something to jeopardise her position and moved to stop her talking. 'I think my client has answered all your questions.'

'No, it's okay,' Laetitia said, holding a hand up. 'I'm happy to answer.' She batted her eyelashes at Baxter. 'I've been taking acting lessons. My coach advised me to get some experience so that when I went for auditions, I would be more confident. When Ashley asked me to help him out, I sat down and wrote the script.' She leaned back, hooked one elbow over the back of the chair and clasped her hands together under her breasts. 'I think I played the part exceedingly well.'

West agreed. She'd been a great actress. He wondered if she'd use her experience in prison to get herself a good role when she came out. It wouldn't surprise him. Women like her always landed on their feet.

'She's something else, isn't she?' Andrews had come quietly into the observation room and was standing behind him. 'I'm heading home. The lads can finish up here, you coming?'

West took a final look through the window at Laetitia Summers before getting to his feet. He stretched wearily and smothered a yawn. 'It's been a long day.'

'But productive.' Andrews led the way from the observation room. 'See you tomorrow.' He took a step towards the exit, then turned back. 'You are going home, aren't you? You're not going to go back to your office and try to deal with all the paperwork tonight?'

'There was a time when I would have done,' West admitted. 'No, I'm going to check everyone is okay, then head for the hills. See you in the morning.'

Andrews was obviously happy with that, and with a wave he turned and left.

It was twenty minutes before West felt able to leave. Outside, it was dark and very cold; the snow that had been forecast floated gently around him as he walked to his car. It had been a productive day. From their point of view, the case, apart from the mountain of paperwork, was solved.

A year ago, he'd have stayed until the bulk of the paperwork was done. Now, he was happy to leave it until tomorrow.

Strangely, it wasn't thoughts of Bolger or Bennet that were running through his mind as he drove home but Baxter's simple and naïve comment to Laetitia Summers. *You must love him very much.*

Love wasn't everyone's driving force. It certainly wasn't Laetitia's. West wasn't sure it was his either.

He pulled up outside his Greystones home, the light in the hallway warmly welcoming. It was almost eleven. Edel was probably in bed asleep.

But when he opened the kitchen door, there she was, her hair bunched up in a ponytail, wearing a pair of unglamorous cotton pyjamas. She was spooning lasagne onto a plate. 'I heard your car pull up,' she said, looking up and giving him a warm smile. 'Sit, I'll have this dished up in a second.'

West saw the table set, a bottle of Guinness, a pint glass.

He looked back to Edel. Who was he trying to fool? He'd do anything for this woman.

Perhaps it should have been some romantic place, but this seemed so right. He walked over to where she was scraping pasta from the sides of the container and put a hand over hers.

'Edel, will you marry me?'

THE END

ACKNOWLEDGEMENTS

Grateful thanks to all at Bloodhound Books, especially Betsy Reavley, Tara Lyons, Heather Fitt, Clare Law, Ian Skewis, and the wonderful cover design team.

As usual, a big thank you to my brother-in-law, Detective Garda Gerry Doyle(retd) for assisting me with some of the details of the Garda Síochána – as ever, mistakes are mine alone.

Massive thanks to the writer Jenny O'Brien for helping me pull this together and for ongoing support and friendship.

To other writers in the writing community who make this such a fun job – all of my fellow Bloodhound writers, plus the writers Leslie Bratspis, Patricia Gitt, Mary Karpin, Pam Lecky, Catherine Kullmann and Jim Ody.

We writers would be lost without the wonderful support of readers, bloggers and reviewers, thanks to every one of you.

A big thanks to all my friends who help celebrate each new book.

And always left to last because you're the foundation of everything I do... my amazing, wonderful family – husband, sisters, brothers, in-laws, nieces, nephews, grand-nieces and grand-nephews, and cousins.